Shepherd's
watch

D1004962

Shepherd's watch

a SHEPHERD & WOLFE
mystery

COUNIOS & GANE

REGINA, SK

Published by Your Nickel's Worth Publishing.
March 2017

Library and Archives Canada Cataloguing in Publication

Counios, 1968-, author
    Shepherd's watch / Counios & Gane.

(A Shepherd & Wolfe mystery)
Issued in print and electronic formats.
ISBN 978-1-927756-95-9 (softcover).--ISBN 978-1-927756-96-6 (EPUB).--
ISBN 978-1-927756-97-3 (Kindle)

    I. Gane, 1973-, author II. Title.

PS8605.O8937S54 2017   C813'.6   C2017-900935-4
                                               C2017-900936-2

Printed in Canada.
21 20 19 18 17   2 3 4 5

Cover © istockphoto.com\piranka.
Book design by Heather Nickel.
Interior image © istockphoto.com\bildfokus

Production made possible with the support of Creative Saskatchewan.

www.ynwp.ca

prologue

1

Terry Butler peers through his glasses, turning the engagement ring over in his grease-stained hands.

"I don't know what the hell I'm looking at."

The jewelry store clerk leans in with a lint-free cloth and scoops it out of Terry's hands. "Diamonds are graded by many factors: their brightness and the colour of light they reflect but also their craftsmanship and size."

"What's that mean to me?"

She forces a smile. "That this ring is of exceptional value." She polishes the edges where Terry handled the band with his dirty fingers and sets it back in its spot in the display case before moving down to the end of the counter.

"Perhaps this might be more fitting?" She fetches another ring and brings it back, placing it on the soft mat on top of the glass counter.

Terry stares at it but doesn't pick it up. His eyes shift back and forth between the ring she just carried over and the one below it in the case. Maybe it's the way the light fills the display but Terry's sure that the new one doesn't shine as bright.

He doesn't know much about rings, but he knows which one his girl, Miranda, is going to like more.

He pushes a finger against the glass, leaving a dirty smudge that the clerk will need to clean later. "How much for that one?"

He probably wouldn't have spent so much time worrying about the ring if he'd known he'd be dead by nightfall.

2

Outside the jewelry store, Terry unlocks his car and gets in. He's got to get back to Huber Motors.

He knows he has the money—well, almost all the money. There's some in his savings, but it's still not enough. He might be able to set up an in-store line of credit, but that could be tricky, and payday isn't until the end of the month. He could scrape together a private advance from the safe money he holds for his side job. Then when his butthole boss, Huber, gives him his paycheque in a few days, he could replace it and no one would know he'd borrowed anything.

He drives past Donnie's Pizza and waits at the only intersection in town with a stoplight. It's Friday and Estoria is buzzing with people buying food and booze for the weekend. He checks his watch—only a few minutes left on his break—so when the light turns green, he guns it across.

At the car dealership, he scans the room for Miranda. He doesn't see her anywhere, but Huber's at his desk, signing contracts. Huber glances up at the clock on the wall, and

Terry waits for him to start something, but Huber, thank God, keeps quiet.

"Where is she?" Terry asks, blocking the doorway of his boss's office.

"What's it to you? She's got her own stuff to do."

Huber is always playing favourites with her and Terry hates it. He could be a minute late and get dragged into the office, but Miranda can go for an hour-and-a-half lunch and Huber will conveniently not be around to notice. But it's not worth getting into and Terry starts to move away.

Huber grabs an envelope off his desk and calls him back, "Hey, Butler!"

Terry walks over and takes it. He tears it open and adjusts his glasses to see the total on the cheque. "This is lower than normal!" he glares at Huber. "What gives?"

"You kept coming in late last week."

"I was helping my buddy Little Joe with his car."

"Not on my time."

"But he bought it from you!"

"Yeah, and he should have come to me to get it fixed. You don't do service calls for all my customers, do you?"

Terry shakes his head in disgust—Huber's such a dick—and is walking to the shop when he notices another cheque in the envelope.

He pulls it out. Six hundred dollars. Written on the memo line in red ink are the words DISCHARGED / LAID OFF.

Terry storms back into the office and slams the cheque on Huber's desk.

"What the hell?!"

Huber leans back in his seat, hooking his hands behind his head. "Seems Christmas came early for you."

"Cut it out! You firing me?"

"I'm downsizing."

"But the work bays are full!"

"For the guys that show up."

"I've been here since your dad ran this place!"

Huber's not having it. "In this economy, you're either making me money or costing me money. I got to cut back."

Terry's hands ball into fists. "Isn't that your new fully loaded muscle car sitting out front?"

Huber sits up in his chair. "Yeah, because I bust my ass every day."

But Terry's not done. "Oh, and that's why you're never around and it's Miranda who's running all over town doing your crap?"

Huber leans forward with a shit-eating grin. "Yeah, and what's she doing for *you*?"

Terry doesn't wait for him to finish. He's over the desk, tackling Huber to the ground. They wrestle on the floor, and Terry gets one good swing at Huber's smug mouth before a customer and a couple of service guys from the back pull him off.

"Get the hell out of here!" Huber yells as he straightens his tie and rights the chair behind his desk. "And when you see Miranda, tell her I said hi."

3

Terry fiddles with his bent glasses as he spins out of the dealership, smacking a garbage can hard and sending it skittering across the parking lot. In a last gesture of rebellion, he snatches a wrench from under the seat of his truck and pitches it at the front window of Huber Motors, but it falls short and only kicks up a little puff of dust that is whisked away in the wind.

A country song about Saturday nights and back-road parties plays while he drives across town to Miranda's. He turns the volume up, overenthusiastically tapping the steering wheel as he sings along.

Huber will likely press charges and Terry hopes they won't be too serious. Now that he thinks about it, getting the boot could be for the best—he wasn't getting what he deserved anyway. He should've quit a long time ago.

Only trouble is, this sure as shit cuts his chances at getting a line of credit at the jewelry store—and he only has about two-thirds of what he needs to buy Miranda's ring. He could likely scrounge up a little more, take the extra out of his safe money, but he'd have to pay it back without anyone noticing, and that wouldn't be easy.

And Miranda—what's she going to say about him getting fired? She'll be pissed, but maybe he could take a bit of his severance and take her out for the night. Maybe, if he got a few beers into her, they could blame Huber together.

As long as he has her, everything will work out.

4

He pulls into Miranda's driveway and walks toward the house. His hockey duffle bag is sitting on the front step, a white envelope jammed in the side pocket, but he ignores it and goes to the door. It's locked.

"Babe!" he yells, knocking. "Where are you?"

She comes to the door wearing too tight jeans, a spaghetti-strap tank top in red, and hoop earrings. Her lips are glossy, her hair in a ponytail.

"Didn't you hear me calling?"

"What do you want, Terry?"

"What do you mean, what do I want? Let me in. I'm taking you out. Supper, drinks—the works."

He tries to push the door open, but she's got her whole body wedged against it.

"Terry, stop."

"Wait, are you in one of your 'moods?'" He adds the air quotes for emphasis.

She looks past him at the duffle bag and the envelope. "Didn't you read it?"

He glances at the paper sticking out of the bag, a dull worry worming its way into the base of his skull—he's had enough envelopes for one day. "Why would I?"

"It's for you."

"What are you talking about?"

"We're over."

"Come on, enough of this," he grumbles. "Let me in."

"Take your stuff and get out of here." Miranda's face is strained. She's ready to cry.

He slides an arm through the doorway, reaching for her, trying to hold her hand. "Come on, baby, let me in. Let's talk about this."

She leans back from his grasp, keeping her weight on the door. "Terry, I'm done talking."

"Why? What happened? I thought—" He thinks about the ring and how good he had felt on the way over. "I thought we were doing good together?"

"Terry, it's just…"

"What?"

"I need something else. I need to move on."

His hand falls down to his side, and Miranda takes advantage of it to close the door on him.

The lock clicks shut.

Standing on the porch, forehead against the door, he cries out, "I love you!" but she's already gone.

5

Two hours later, Terry stumbles out of the Hillside Bar, the afternoon sun sunk low in the sky. He leans back through the door, yelling goodbye to his buddy, Bartender Chad. Only Bartender Chad seems to feel sorry for Terry and the wrongs he's suffered: Miranda's cruel words and that jerk-ass, Huber.

As he heads for his truck, Terry shifts a fresh case of beer under one arm and digs in his pocket for his keys, but all he finds are the two cheques from Huber.

He pulls them out and raises them to the sky, sneering at them. "Huber, you lazy son of a bitch." He stuffs them in his pocket and swings the beer over the tailgate into the back of his truck. "Couldn't even wait 'til the end of the month to get rid of me."

He searches again for his keys, finds them this time, and sticks the right one into the lock after three wrong tries.

"End of the month? Wait…" he mumbles to no one in particular. "If today's Friday, then—" He tries to calculate the days in his head, then on his fingers, and nearly falls over.

But the math makes sense.

"Aww, shit!"

If he's right—and he's pretty certain he is—this is the week he's supposed to do his other job. He can't figure out how he's messed up the days, but he's glad he figured it out before it's too late.

He hops into his truck with newfound energy. He's got to hurry back to Miranda's to pick up his safe money, then get to the lake.

6

He sits in his truck, scoping out Miranda's place, swiveling his head left and right. No vehicles on the road or in the driveway. No sign of her at all.

"Good," he announces, "because screw her."

He drives around to the back alley, parks the truck tight to the shed, banging his door against the siding as he tumbles out.

"Shh…"

His attempt at stealth fails, as does any pretense at sobriety. Still, he shuts the truck door gently and walks up to the rear entrance of the house with a casual air.

He peers through the window in the door, rapping on it. "Miranda? You home?"

Silence.

"Perfect."

He twists the knob, then shakes it. Locked. He checks under the welcome mat but finds nothing.

She must've moved the key.

He looks around and sees a potted plant on the patio table. He checks underneath.

"Bingo!"

He picks up the house key, waving it at an invisible Miranda. "You dummy!" He congratulates himself with a one-sided high-five, impressed by his own cleverness.

He slides the key into the lock and goes into the house, shutting the door behind him.

Inside, he forgets to remove his heavy boots and goes straight for the kitchen. There's a big bouquet of roses on the table that wasn't there the day before. He searches for a card on them but doesn't find anything; he digs in the garbage under the sink, but it's empty.

Pushing the mystery flowers out of his mind, he opens the fridge and takes out the remains of a tuna casserole. He throws the whole plastic container in the microwave. While he waits for it to heat, he stares at the bright flowers and decides to check out the bedroom.

"More than one way to find out who they're from."

He finds the computer tablet she keeps by her bedside and swipes to open it up, but it wants her passcode. He tries her birthdate, but it doesn't unlock.

"Crap."

He tries a few more combinations, using as many of her family's birthdates and phone numbers as he can remember, until it finally locks him out. He tosses it aside and searches through the bedside table, but there's nothing of interest.

Beep beep. His leftovers are ready.

He grabs his food and douses the steaming casserole in hot sauce. Spoon in hand, he goes down to the basement.

The whole space is a testament to the time and energy he put into Miranda. When they first started dating two years ago, her basement was bare concrete walls and wood joists, but now there's a small living room with ceiling tiles and a few half-framed rooms.

While he finishes the last cheesy bite of tuna, he moves to the back office and picks up the small ladder he keeps nearby. Setting the plastic container down, he climbs the rungs, reaching up to the ceiling tile behind which he hides his money. These acrobatics are too much for his inebriated brain, and he tumbles backwards into a stack of boxes of Miranda's tax receipts, scattering them across the floor.

He finds his glasses and sets them back on his face, then uprights the files and jams them back into the boxes at random. That's when he hears someone come through the front door.

"Terry? I've called the cops."

Shit, it's Miranda. Maybe, if he just doesn't move—

"I know you're in here. I saw your truck out back."

He hears her moving around the house above him, opening and closing doors. He sets the ladder up again to try and get his money, but now she's at the top of the stairs, yelling, "Terry, get the hell out of here!"

She's coming down the stairs.

He can't get the money without being seen, and she'll definitely ask questions he doesn't want to answer. He'll have to leave it and hopefully come back for it later.

He folds the ladder up and sets it against the wall, taking his tackle box and the fishing rod off a shelf before turning to go.

She's standing at the bottom of the stairs, arms folded.

"Relax," he says. "I just came back for the stuff you forgot to pack."

Miranda stares at him as he passes; she's pissed, but he doesn't care. As he goes by her on the stairs, he whispers the word "bitch" before pushing out the back door.

7

Terry drives like a maniac out of town; he's running out of time.

Every third Friday of the month for the past two years, he's headed across the lake with three coolers full of ice. One of the coolers holds a small, resealable, plastic bag full of cash that his buddy Little Joe gives him. On the far shore, he'd meet a woman named Cousin Rachel and exchange these coolers for identical ones that are zip-tied shut. Cousin Rachel isn't a member of Little Joe's family, but Terry's sure she's part of *some* family of the mob variety.

If Terry never cuts the zip ties, always keeps the coolers closed, and never asks any questions, he can keep doing the run and earn himself five hundred bucks every month. He's cool with the arrangement—ignorance is bliss—and he likes not being tossed over a bridge chained to a block of cement.

But without the cash for the coolers, he has a big problem.

He has to come up with a plan so he doesn't miss the meeting—there's no time to wait around for Miranda to leave.

Steering one-handed, he reaches into his pocket and pulls out the two cheques, adding the totals in his head. Should be close enough. Huber might be a jerk of a boss, but he does pay what he owes, so Terry sets them on the seat next to him, satisfied with his solution.

He snatches a pen from the glove box and scribbles on the memo line of one of the cheques, only to find the pen dry. He tosses it out the window, digs out a black marker from the centre console, checks to make sure it works, then signs the back of each cheque, the ink seeping through the paper. He gazes at them over the rim of his glasses, pleased that he's averted a crisis, unaware that the truck has swerved over the yellow line.

By the time he realizes, he's almost completely on the wrong side of the road and overcorrects.

The truck shoots back into the proper lane, front right tire dropping off the edge of the pavement to sink into the soft dirt of the shoulder. The wheel yanks out of his hand and the whole truck slides into the ditch. He hits the brakes, but it's not soon enough and he rams into a tree.

The jolt hits him hard—thankfully he has his seatbelt on— but he knows his truck isn't as lucky. He climbs out of the cab and surveys the damage. The bumper is crumpled, the radiator cracked, and coolant is pouring everywhere.

"Well, hell's bells," he grumbles as he jumps back in and throws the vehicle in reverse.

The metal bumper grips the splintered tree, and the whole front end squeals in protest before tearing off as he pulls away.

He aims the truck back onto the highway and guns it, not bothering to look if anyone's coming, not caring that his truck is shooting out of the ditch like a wild animal.

The temperature gauge rises immediately, but he ignores it, hoping that he'll get to the marina at the lake before it burns out his whole engine.

It just hasn't been his day.

8

At the resort area, Terry drives straight for the dock, steam hissing from the hood of his truck. His bumperless front end bonks off the wood posts that string steel cable around the parking lot, and empty beer cans and food wrappers fly off his seat onto the floor in response. He no longer cares.

He grabs a convenience store bag off the floor, jams the cheques inside, and ties it tight. He climbs out and hauls the three blue coolers from the truck box. He sticks the bag with the cheques into the bottom of one and, from the passenger side, grabs the bags of ice he bought, tearing them open, and spilling them into the coolers. As a finishing touch, he tosses a few cans of beer on top of the one with the cheques before slamming the lids shut.

"There you go, Cousin Rachel. That should keep you and yours happy 'til next month."

He can't quite reach his fishing equipment, so he climbs into the back of the truck and grabs the tackle box, rod, and a bag of bait. On the way down, he loses his footing and catches himself, but the tackle box falls to the ground, spilling hooks, floaters, and sinkers everywhere.

He shakes his head, laughing ruefully. "Nice move, Terry."

He gathers it all up as best he can, leaving several hooks on the ground in his haste. He's more interested in looking like a fisherman than actually catching a fish.

He stacks everything on top of the coolers, hoicks the lot up in his arms, and winds his way over the uneven gravel to the dock to the most beautiful thing he owns, his powerboat, *Jolene, Jolene.* All the early wages from his side job went into a down payment on this 135-horsepower, 18-foot beauty, complete with optional fishing package, bow-mounted wireless trolling motor, and casting platform—and she was worth every penny.

He scrambles from the dock to the deck and it's dicey for a second, but he pulls it off unscathed. He sets his gear down by the pedestal seat and the coolers at the foot of the portside bench. Looks like he's ready to go.

It's a five-kilometre run to the meet-up and it will likely take half an hour to get across the lake. The sun hangs over the spruce trees and he needs to get his ass in gear, but he's sure there's still time before everyone shows up.

He opens one of the coolers and pulls out a beer, cracking the can to raise it in a victory sip. "Hurray for me!"

Things seem to be finally turning around.

He turns the key and the engine thunders to life.

9

Terry glances at his watch.

"Crap."

It's almost night and the sun is hiding behind the woods, painting the sky orange, red and pink, and he can't separate the trees from the dark shadows reaching across the water toward him. He's certain he missed the cove where he's supposed to meet Cousin Rachel… or he hasn't gone far enough. He isn't positive about anything anymore and is sure-as-shit lost.

When he first started these runs, he would aim for the remains of the fire tower that stood across the lake, but the government came and knocked it down when they replaced it with computers and satellites, so now he just points *Jolene, Jolene* in the general direction and hopes for the best.

But this only works in the daytime when you can see where you're going and what the hell is in front of you. It also doesn't help that the beer has got the better of him. He grabs a handful of potato chips and jerky and stuffs them

into his mouth, hoping the carbs and salt will clear the cob-
webs from his muddy, drifting mind.

He looks back, searching for the marina, but there are no
lights on the horizon behind him and the night sky creeps
toward him with long fingers of deep indigo. He considers
pulling back to the centre of the lake, working his way back
toward where he thinks the truck is, and hoping something
will click, but that would only take more time.

He throttles the boat to half and rides parallel to the shore,
eyes darting back and forth along the shoreline, trying to
find some discernible detail, trying to recognize something—anything—that will guide him. He's never missed
an exchange, has no idea what will happen if he does—the
only thing he's confident of is that it probably won't be good.

Then he sees it—he's sure he sees it—a brief flicker of light
in the mass of darkness.

He yanks the wheel beachward, ripping a large wake behind him, and powers the engine up, not wanting to keep
Cousin Rachel waiting any longer, her or the guys with guns
who always accompany her. But he regrets it immediately.

Whump.

Terry bounces forward as the boat catches on the lake bottom. His tackle box flies off the seat, smashing everywhere.
Water and mud kicks out behind the boat and the engine's
temperature warning buzzes. He kills the throttle and pops
the engine into neutral, but he knows it's not going to be
good.

He shines a light starboard. Silt clouds the water—he can't
see anything.

He lifts the propeller out of the water and it's worse than he imagined. One prop blade is bent and he's sure he's messed up the shaft, the strut, and possibly the rudder. After flushing the engine, changing the impeller, and fixing the rest, this trip is going to cost him more than it's worth.

His gaze swivels back to the trees, hoping to finally spot his people but can't see anything anymore. No flickering light at all. At the bow, a thick, fallen tree presses low against the keel. He sighs, rubbing his head.

"Well, dammit, Terry." He cracks open a fresh can of brew, taking a long chug, and considers his options.

"Well, quitters is for shitters," he tells himself. "I've got this."

He jumps over the gunwale into the cold, dark water and is instantly sober. He moves along the hull, grabs hold of the bowline, and kicks his foot hard to move the boat out of the shallows and away from the tree. He tugs it around the rotting, gnarled roots and navigates it back to deeper waters.

Terry moves by touch and feel, placing one foot ahead of the other, tripping over slippery rocks, his legs entangled in seaweed.

The ground slips away beneath him and he sinks quickly downward, barely keeping his breath as he goes under. His clothes pull him down and he kicks wildly with inefficient strokes, grasping the bowline to pull himself back up to the surface. When he breaks the surface, he gasps for breath then splashes toward shore, dragging the boat with him until the hull catches loosely on the sand.

Giving it one last, hard tug until it's solid, Terry catches his breath before struggling back to lift out one of the coolers and haul it up the beach. He heads back one last time to

Jolene, Jolene, shivering, hands numb, to get the final container, and drags it and his sorry ass back to the beach.

He dumps it beside the other and plops down in a heap. He's freezing, exhausted, and his body aches. He really wants this night to be done.

Someone comes out of the trees.

"You won't believe the day I've had."

He turns—

Crack.

One lens of his glasses shatters and white light pops along Terry's optic nerve as he careens backward, tumbling down the beach's sandy incline. His head splashes into the water, flinging the glasses from his face.

A woman towers blurrily above him in the dark, a thick branch hanging from her hand. She moves down the shore toward him.

He touches his forehead and feels gushing blood and the tight pinch of torn, swollen skin. He'll have a hell of a goose egg tomorrow. He tries to stand, but his legs won't stay solid beneath him.

"Can you help me?" he asks, reaching out an arm, hoping she'll grab hold. "I've got a couple of beers left in the boat I can share."

She moves past him, grabbing him by the collar of his shirt as she goes, and pulls him farther out into the water.

"Wait. Help—"

The woman doesn't listen.

He's floating and can't quite get a grip.

She stops and Terry drifts past her and he's sure it's Cousin Rachel. He wants to ask her what she's doing, but she takes the stick and lays it across his chest and pushes him down beneath the lapping waves.

He tries to fight, but the cold and the beer and the crack on the head all stop his brain and body from working together.

He can see her now, up through the water, watching him, and he tries to kick himself away, to grab her arms, but his hands are tight and numb, and she pushes down too hard for him to do anything.

He yells, but all he can manage are muffled bubbles beneath the water. His vision blurs more and he can't see the woman very well at all now, but her long hair hangs above him, spreading out like feathers across the surface.

He struggles to turn, to push away, to slip from beneath her, but nothing works. He needs to inhale and tries to fight it, but the feeling is coming from deep down and he knows he can't prevent it any longer.

His body quits listening to his rational brain and inhales. Water pours down his throat and into his lungs and his whole body seizes. In a mighty effort to save itself, his body forces the water out but in its desperate attempt to breathe, it sucks in another lungful of lake water, sand, sediment, algae, and fish excrement.

Only then does Terry realize he's not going to survive this.

10

Cousin Rachel shines her flashlight down at Terry's water-logged corpse, hung up in the tangled roots of a log beached by wind and waves.

This hasn't exactly gone as planned.

She glances back at her crew, four hired muscles loaded with enough concealed pistols and knives to kill a bear, and knows they won't be pleased with what comes next. She doesn't care if they don't want to do it—this is the drug business, not summer camp.

She waves two of them over while the other two head for the van to get shovels.

"Get down there and pull him out."

She watches the two men—Amos and Daniel—go down to the shoreline and pull off their boots and socks. Amos, the heavier of the two, rolls up his loose-fitting jeans as high as he can, while Daniel strips down to his underwear.

Cousin Rachel takes a seat on a large rock, turns halfway and peers through the night toward the path. She's worked with these guys for two years now, but she never keeps her back to any of them for too long. It's hard to trust anyone in this line of work—someone somewhere is always scheming for a better position—and this cautious attitude has kept her around longer than most.

She fell into this career while working part-time at a clothing store, one of those chain outlets in a mall, with a husband who'd been recently laid-off, an adorable nine-year-old son, and ever-increasing debt. She'd kept asking for more hours but there were never enough to go around and eventually her manager, a young woman who'd work all day and party all night, pulled her aside and told her she knew ways to make extra money—as either an escort or a dealer in the clubs. Cousin Rachel was desperate but not interested; that is, until she told her husband and they found themselves considering the possibility of drug trafficking. She'd gone back the next day and agreed, and very quickly thereafter discovered she had a real knack for the business.

As she was promoted and the business got messier, she told her husband less and less. The first body she saw was an OD, and then a cleanup after a hit. Eventually, she herself had to use violence as a management tool and found that killing another human being didn't bother her as much as she thought it would. She treated each death with clinical detachment, a way to make things happen or to remove a difficulty. Now that she was in management, her bosses didn't expect her to kill anyone, but she liked to be hands-on, to leverage people's fears and remind them what she was capable of.

Gil comes over the rise, Jacob following behind, and Cousin Rachel gestures with her flashlight away from the beach.

"Go about ten yards that way. Find someplace far from these spruce roots—they'll only cause you hell—and start digging a hole."

"Like six feet?"

"Nah, two or three at the most. Just enough to keep the scavengers from digging him up."

Gil shines his light into the dark trees, uncertain.

She points her light at him. "Go on, you big baby. Not like a bear is going to jump out and eat you."

This was the essence of her job—managing the team. It was a business. She had to solve problems, run the day-to-day operations, and keep the lines of communication and product flowing to the northern part of the province.

She looks back to Amos and Daniel as they splosh back to shore, dragging the body behind them. None of their names are real—she doesn't even know the identity of the floater in the water—and she preferred it that way. She couldn't remember who had picked her moniker, only that someone had introduced her as their cousin in the early days and the nickname had stuck.

She kneels down beside the bloated body, examining him, feeling his pockets and shirt for a cell phone or wallet. She never knew the guy except for the monthly exchanges, but she knows he must've crossed somebody because he sure got what was coming to him. Sleeping on this job, making mistakes—you'd only end up getting yourself killed. Everyone has a role to play and if you fail, this is the penalty.

"No trace of the money?" Amos asks.

"Nah." She studies his face. "And he's missing his glasses."

"He wore glasses?"

Daniel pipes up, "You worked on this line for a year, you don't remember?"

"Did you?"

"Enough!" Rachel shouts, cutting Daniel short. These two can get into the stupidest fights. "Take him to Gil and Jacob and help them finish up. And no more arguments." Sometimes these guys behave worse than her kid.

The men lift the body up like they're moving a dresser and haul him into the trees, Rachel lighting the way. Once over the rise, she swings her light back over the water, sweeping the beam over the choppy, uneven surface, searching for the man's boat. The wind must've got ahold of it and pulled it out into the lake, or the currents carried it away even farther.

She sighs, pulling out her phone.

Yup, this business is all about solving problems—and she's got a hell of a big one to deal with now.

part 1

chapter 1

"Where are you going, Anthony?"

I'm halfway down the beach when my sister, Heather, calls out to me. She's lying on a blanket by our stuff, looking up from a book that's finally not something from college.

"Worried I might run off?"

She's my big sister, but I think we're way past this babysitting stage.

"No, just thinking we should go back soon."

"Give me a few more minutes."

I go down to the water. It's a beautiful summer day, but the sun beats down hot and I need to cool off.

I wade into the lake, and as expected, it's freaking cold. I hope to get used to it before my legs go numb, but either way, I intend to enjoy a quick swim before we drive back to our cabin on Dyson's Point. I dive in, the freezing water leaving me breathless, and I force a shout beneath the surface to get through the shock. Strong, fast strokes get my blood pumping before I finally surface and swim out toward the buoys.

The whole lake is buzzing with action. The beach around Heather is packed with families, teenagers, kids, old people, weekend visitors, and the lifers, like my family. Sailboats and windsurfers are out on the water, cutting over the lake where the wind funnels across its surface. Boats zip past near the buoys, water-skiers and jet skis chasing behind, and down where the lake dumps into the river, there's a bunch of boats gathered under the bridge and I figure the fishermen must have found themselves a good spot for northern pike or walleye.

I roll over onto my back and let the gentle waves carry me, staring at a single cloud drifting on its lonesome journey high above. I could lie here all day, soaking up the moment, caught between the frigid, refreshing water and the warm air and hot sun. However, my mind has other plans and a memory of my dead girlfriend, Sheri, floats to its surface. I shake it off and try not to dwell, but it lingers for a moment longer than I wish.

I pull myself up again and locate Heather on the beach; she signals that she wants to go. I take a deep breath and dive down, swimming beneath the surface, moving back toward the shore.

chapter 2

As I step out of the lake, a ball splashes nearby, spraying me with a faceful of water, and a young dad calls out, "Sorry!" I push over to it through the surf and toss it back.

"Thanks."

"No problem."

Although it's a simple interaction, I've been hyper-aware since last fall when I found myself searching for my girl-friend's killer with this guy named Charlie Wolfe. In the past, I never really thought about my actions, especially little ones like getting a kid's ball, and I'm pretty sure no one else did either. But now everything I do seems to hold weight for the people around me and they worry about what I'm up to. I second-guess most of my behaviour—it's like I have to justify myself all the time.

It's a real head game.

As I cross the hot sand, my sister calls out, "Yo, Aquaman! Your harem awaits."

I follow her gaze to a beach blanket full of tweens that could maybe be in Grade 7 or 8 if they're lucky. One waves, but it's all sorts of awkward. I'm completely embarrassed for the poor kid and I don't know what to do, so I grab a towel and cover up.

"Yeah, you better hide that before you cause an incident."

For a moment I forget everything. I wonder sometimes if Heather tries to get me out of my head on purpose.

"You have no respect for hard work, sis," I state, patting my six-pack, making sure I've turned away from my new fan club.

I hear the girls giggle.

"Could you hand me my clothes?"

"I don't know. It might devastate them."

"Please?"

She tosses me a tee-shirt. "Fine. Ruin my fun."

I pull it on, hoping the tweens will settle down. "How about we grab some ice cream on the way out?"

"Sounds good," she says with a smile, "might cool down that ego of yours after all this adoration."

"Ha ha. You know what? You can shut it."

This only makes Heather laugh more as we walk up the beach.

chapter 3

The line at the ice cream shack moves quickly and when we get to the front, Heather gets the flavour of the day, pistachio, and I order a chocolate-dipped vanilla soft serve on a sugar cone.

"Not the manliest of choices, little brother."

"I'll eat it fast. Besides, I relate to it."

She scrunches her face. "How so?"

"Because I'm—"

She realizes and cuts me off. "Nope, I won't even let you say it."

"Fine." She never appreciates my humour when it comes to our mixed heritage—Dad was born in Canada and Mom's family emigrated from Jamaica in the 1970s, making my sisters and me what I affectionately call "mocha."

I dig through my wallet to pay and Heather catches a glimpse of the photo of Sheri I still keep in there, but she doesn't say a word—another reason she's a great sister.

We take our cones and get comfortable in the shade of a tree.

As I dig in, I ask, "What happened to your boy, Isaac?"

"He's far from being 'my boy.'"

"Well, where'd he go?"

She smiles. "Let's just say he wasn't my flavour of ice cream."

It's good to be around her. Personally, I'm glad that Isaac isn't in the picture this summer because it means I get a little more brother-and-sister time before she goes back to university and I start my senior year with the busy schedule that will entail.

Heather doesn't pry about Sheri, leaving that conversational topic up to me. She's got great intuition, knowing I'll talk when the time comes.

Under the tree, out of the sun, cooling off, I listen to the breeze rustle the leaves above. Heather finishes eating, then stretches and glances at her watch.

"We should head back."

"Yeah, we should." I don't move.

"Yo, lazy ass. Jodi and Bryan leave today and we need to say goodbye."

"Fine." I gulp down the last of the vanilla ice cream, tossing the empty end of the cone to a robin digging in the grass nearby.

I stand and offer my sister a hand up. We walk down to the parking lot and as I climb into the hot car, I miss the freezing water already.

chapter 4

We pull up to the cabin.

It's small compared to the newer mansions that have been built around here recently, but it's got character and Mom and Dad will never give it up; they love being five hours away from the city. The whole area known as Dyson's Point was developed a few decades ago and my parents picked up the land for almost nothing after a big fire swept through a while back. My family built most of our place themselves. The main floor has a kitchen and living room with large windows that look out on the lake, while the bathroom, utility closet, and my folks' bedroom are in the back; the second floor has two bedrooms for Heather and me, along with a bathroom. Some small cabins feel tight and enclosed, but ours has such big windows everywhere that daylight pours in and makes the place seem larger than it really is.

The property slopes down from the ground level of the driveway to the lakeshore, and one end of the cabin is therefore built on wooden piles, which extend upward to give us a covered deck and a beautiful view over the water. It's the best spot of all. Rain or shine, we spend our time out there, reading in the hammock, barbecuing, or watching Ollie, our golden retriever, protect his territory from a couple of very bold squirrels. A set of stairs leads down to an area that is the perfect combination of manicured and wild. Oak, paper birch, and the occasional spruce tree grow along the edges of the property around a firepit and a path that leads down to the shore.

Heather and I climb out of the car and take the stairs up to the deck. I peer through the big windows but see no one. Then Mom laughs and we go around the corner to find her lying in the hammock, a glass of wine in her hand. My other sister, Jodi, sits on the deck beside her, legs hanging over the edge. They're watching Dad and Jodi's husband, Bryan, play ladder-ball in the grass below.

"I think that's one for Bryan!" Mom yells down.

Dad defends himself. "Easy now or I'll hide your favourite bottle of Merlot."

She takes another sip. "Just you try it."

I announce our arrival by jumping into the fray. "No, that's definitely Dad's point."

My brother-in-law looks up at me. "Really? You're going to stab me in the back like that?"

"Hey, you know you're never too old to be punished, Tony," Mom chimes in.

Dad offers me a fist bump, but he's too far away to make it happen so it's hilariously awkward. I can't leave him hanging, though, so I rush down the stairs to fist-bump him back—got to help the old man feel young once in awhile.

"Thank you, son." He shoots Mom a smug smile and she sticks her tongue out at both of us as I come back up the stairs.

"Hey, don't you worry, Mom. I don't play favourites. If he tries stealing anything, I know all his hiding spots."

Mom raises her glass to me while Dad nods to Bryan. "He really is the worst son, you know?"

Jodi stands, reaching her arm around me. "Little brother, the master manipulator, your treachery with our parents has earned you a spot helping me with supper."

Everyone applauds—except me.

chapter 5

Jodi and I step inside and let the screen door squeak shut.

Making supper always seems like less of a chore at the cabin than it does in the city with its day-to-day grind. However, food prep with Jodi means that she has a big sis/little brother chit-chat planned, which, considering the year I've had, might not go so good for me.

I hope to delay it as long as I can, so I pull vegetables, dressing, and bread from the fridge and hand them to her. I grab six potatoes and dump them into the sink, while Jodi sneaks in beside me to rinse some peppers. I know she's lining up a way to start into me, but a cheer from outside breaks the moment.

Out the window, I see Dad raising his hands over his head in a ridiculous victory dance. Bryan and Heather are in tears they're laughing so hard, but Mom's still heckling from the sidelines.

"God, I love those two," Jodi says as she pushes the faucet to my side of the sink.

"The old man plays to win."

She elbows me. "Can't think of anybody else like that in the family."

I wash potatoes and wrap them in foil. "What? I'm not competitive." I only partially believe my own lie.

"Oh no, not at all: rookie of the year, MVP, team captain—"

"Hey, that's not competitive. That's ambitious. They're different."

"Should we go home and look at the second shelf Dad had to build for your trophies?"

"All right, enough." I want to make a snappy comeback but draw a blank.

Jodi scoffs, "Yeah, if I were Heather, you could razz me about all my achievements, but I was the troublemaker, so you've got nothing on me."

"How *did* our parents ever survive you, Jodi?"

"You should thank me," she chuckles. "I laid the groundwork for you and Heather."

"Wait," I glance over, thinking back on all the difficult talks Mom, Dad, and I have had over a hot beverage, "tea time?"

Jodi grins. "Yup."

I shake my head, smiling. "Now I know who to blame."

"Or maybe the one to thank," she winks.

I finish the potatoes and move on to helping my sister cut the veggies.

"So, how's Mike doing?" Jodi asks. "He still have a crush on our sister?"

"Not bad. And of course."

"What's he doing for the summer?"

"He's got a job roofing with his uncle."

"Ouch, tough gig. Bryan was doing that when we first met."

"Really? Mr. Architect was a roofer?"

"He is of the firm belief that the best way to understand something is by doing it." She chops away at the carrots. "He also helped build houses for low-income families."

I'm impressed. I never thought of him as the type. "Well, Mike thinks he's all manly and will get the girls by doing it."

The door swings open and Bryan enters. "Doing what?"

Jodi leans in to give him a kiss. "Tony's buddy Mike is roofing for the summer."

He takes a cucumber from the pile. "Ugh, I don't miss those days. Hot sun, angled roofs. My calves hated me."

Jodi smirks. "Yeah, but what about your hot construction body and all the chicks you picked up?"

"Gah, I don't need to hear these things!" I groan.

"Fine," my sister says, grabbing Bryan's beer for a swig.

I watch the two of them interact, crisscrossing back and forth in sync with each other, her hand touching his waist, him giving her a peck on the cheek. I miss having someone like that and quickly force the thought away. "So, Bryan, you had enough of the World Ladder-ball Event?"

"Man, that was epic. Your dad plays for keeps."

Jodi grins at me, but Bryan leans into her. "Reminds me of someone—"

"What?"

"Ms. Scrabble Queen? The destroyer of Monopoly? The killer of—"

She cuts him off, "Okay, fine. Our whole damn family is competitive."

I chuckle. "Roasted."

Bryan stares out the window. "Ah, but look at them."

Jodi and I watch. Dad's telling an animated story, and Mom and Heather are completely entertained, smiling hard and laughing loudly. Mom leans in and kisses Dad. It's awesome. Even during this last year, the two of them have stayed solid.

"Ben's got it figured out," Bryan says as he gives Jodi a friendly hip-check, "I need to learn his secrets."

Jodi pulls out a stack of marinating chicken from the fridge and hands it to him. "Secret number one: go light the barbecue, get the meat on."

"And secret number two?"

"Bring your wife another beer from the outdoor fridge."

"Barbecue, meat, beer. Got it." He pauses at the door. "Tony, want one?"

"Yes, please."

"I don't think so," Jodi pipes up. "You aren't even a senior yet."

"I will be in less than two months. Besides, it's not like I've never had one." I glance at Bryan, hoping to negotiate.

"Don't look at me. I regret even offering."

I turn to Jodi, awaiting her final decision.

"Leave it until supper. See if the old people offer you one," she suggests.

It's a fair strategy and I don't argue.

He goes outside and Jodi pulls down the oil and spices for the salad dressing before asking, "How's Charlie?"

There it is—the question she's been biding her time and building toward. She wasn't around when everything happened, so all she has to go on are stories from the rest of the family.

"I'm not sure." I'm not trying to avoid the question; the trouble is that I really don't know.

"Aren't you two friends?"

"Yes," I pause. "I think so."

"But you don't know what he's up to?"

"Nope." I haven't got an answer and it bothers me.

"You two don't hang out?"

"Well, we did. Sort of." This is getting messy.

"Doesn't he text?"

"Not so much. He's private."

"How so?"

"It's hard to explain. He's just a different kind of guy, Jodi. He's not the same as someone like Mike."

Jodi finishes up the dressing and sets it on the counter beside the salad and veggies. She quietly assesses what's been done and what we still need to do—but she isn't done with me.

"When's the last time you heard from him?"

I ponder the question. "Couple of months."

She looks out at our laughing parents. Mom grabs Dad to give him a big smooch on the lips. "Mom and Dad seem to like him."

"Sometimes I wonder if Mom and Dad felt sorry for him." I'm surprised to hear myself say it.

"I don't think they'd do that. I think they care about him, but it's different, you know?"

I nod. She's right. We aren't about pity and Charlie isn't either.

She hands me her beer and I take a sip. It's delicious and I like that she's offered—but I know it comes with a price.

"So, he's not around much anymore?" she asks.

"No, not really." I take one more swallow, trying not to push my luck.

She glances out at Mom and Dad, then back at me. "Good, because if you ever pull the kind of crap that you did in the fall again, you're going to have to deal with me."

"Jodi—?"

"No, Tony. I might've driven them a little crazy back in the day, but if something bad happens—"

"Nothing bad is going to happen to them."

She stops, shaking her head at me. "No, you idiot. I'm not talking about them. I'm talking about *you*. The only reason you're still alive is dumb luck. If something happened to you, it would destroy them, you know that? And you and Charlie chasing after a serial killer? That's about as stupid as it gets."

She takes her beer back. "If you do something to yourself, then you do something to this family. And if that happens, you and I are going to have a moment far worse than any tea time with Mom."

I know not to take her warning lightly.

She gulps the last of the beer, dumping it into the collection of empties. She's at the door before she looks my way. "You coming?"

My mind spins. "Sure… right behind you."

chapter 6

We sit back in our chairs with our bellies full, the remnants of a delicious summer meal growing cold on the table.

Bryan puts his hand on Jodi's back and gently rubs it. "Well, boss, should we get packed and on the road?"

She leans into him. "As long as you drive while I sleep, sure."

I smile, remembering the long road trips we'd take as kids when Jodi would claim big-sister status, sprawling out across the back seat of the minivan, sticking her younger siblings together in the middle row.

Dad tosses up his arms. "But who's going to clean up?"

I roll my eyes because I know he's hoping I'll do it, but Mom intervenes. "You are, old man."

Heather and Jodi smile and nod, pointing at him as well.

"And why is that? I'm the Ladder-ball King."

"Yes, exactly. And it got you out of making this meal," Mom adds.

He groans. "The servants of Alexander the Great wouldn't get away with this mutiny. Or Hannibal!"

"Or Tutankhamun. Yes, we get it." She picks up plates, stacking them on her arm. "But at least you have your Cleopatra to help."

"I think I'm being taken advantage of here because I'm the oldest. Or is it the best looking?"

Mom kisses him on the cheek. "How about all of the above?"

"Fine. But this is the last time," Dad grumbles before pushing away from the table and going into the cabin to work. "And it was Mark Antony and Cleopatra, not Tutankhamun."

As the screen door plunks shut, Jodi eyes Mom. "You knew that, didn't you?"

"It's always good to know how to get something out of your spouse." Mom winks at her as she follows Dad inside.

Bryan eyes Jodi. "You don't do that, do you?"

"No, of course not," she says, taking his hand in hers, but I'm sure she's not being entirely honest. Jodi pulls him out of his chair and they go in to finish packing.

I gather up some glasses and carry them to the kitchen.

"Anthony," Mom calls, "you're off dishes duty. Take Ollie for a walk."

"What about Jodi and Bryan?"

"You'll be back before they leave."

Ollie is beside me in an instant. He's brought over his leash, which he's somehow pulled down from its hook. It appears that I have no choice.

chapter 7

Ollie drags me down the path to the lake. He loves the water and if I didn't keep him on his leash, he'd be in up to his shoulders. Usually, I'd let him have his fun, but if I take him back with stinky, wet fur this late in the day, Mom will make me clean him up.

"Sorry, buddy. You'll have to leave those ducks for another time. I don't want to spend half an hour drying you off."

The wind kicks up big waves and shakes the leaves in the trees, completely obliterating any chance of hearing whatever conversation might be going on in the cabin. I'm sure they're talking about me—lately, everyone checks in with everyone else to see how I'm doing. I could be defensive about it, but I'm not—those five people up in that cabin care more about me than anyone I know and they're simply trying to navigate the events of the last year the best they can. Unfortunately, none of them really knows how I'm doing because I never shared much with anyone. I pushed it deep inside.

Except that strategy didn't work entirely. Before Charlie and I stopped the psycho who killed Sheri, he murdered several other girls too, and Charlie and I witnessed some pretty horrific stuff. Memories of Sheri keep surfacing and I can't ever quite get past the pain of them; it lingers like a hard knot in my chest, tighter some days than others, but always there. At some point after it all happened, I began waking in the middle of the night, soaked in sweat from bad dreams. Ollie must have known something was wrong because he started sleeping in my room with me, snoring away on his back, reassuring me the world was safe.

People were talking and rumours circulated around the school. Occasionally, some drunk at a party would ask about what happened, but I'd just shake my head and change the subject or walk away. Others who knew a bit more about it thought maybe I was in the detective business and they'd come to me, hoping I'd find a lost iPhone or a missing bike. I'd shut them down too—or tell them off, depending on what I thought of them.

To cope with all the memories, nightmares, questions, and the head games I played on myself, I stuck to a routine of exercise, school, and visiting with friends. I threw myself into basketball training, working harder and longer than the other guys on the team, until my brain and body were exhausted and I was unable to overthink anything. I stayed focused in class and got probably the best marks I've earned since Grade 6. On the weekends when I couldn't train or do any more homework, I'd hang out with Mike or my other teammates and avoid being by myself. Instead of running away from my memories, I visited Sheri's grave on the last Wednesday of every month.

It all seems to have helped. I reversed the failing grades I'd had during the fall and even ended up on the honour roll. I found a real rhythm with the team and we started kicking ass in our games. Best of all, I'm stronger and more filled out than ever before because of all the extra training I've been doing.

Ollie gives his leash a tug and it brings me out of my thoughts. He nips at the waves as they roll in and we walk slowly to the point where the fish rise and gobble up the water bugs skimming across the calm surface.

After everything happened, they gave us civic medals of honour—well, only me, because Charlie never showed up—but the ceremony was quiet and small. The city kept most of it hushed and out of the papers, not wanting to celebrate vigilante justice. All the cops said was that we chased a guy down at the university who threatened a girl and he turned out to be more than we realized.

But no matter how much Charlie and I had tried to help, we only made it more difficult for Detective Gekas, the officer in charge, to get the charges to stick. When I saw her at the ceremony, she didn't come talk to me and I thought she was done with us for good, until she showed up on my doorstep one snowy Saturday morning to tell me the trial date was set—and for me to stay as far away from the proceedings as possible.

And Charlie?

He was the only one who really got what had happened last fall. If anyone was able to help me through all of it, I'd say it would be him.

Except he's disappeared.

We hung out together for about a month after Sheri was found, but without a mystery to solve, something to bind us together, we really didn't seem to have much in common. He seemed happiest on his own, moving between spaces and people, and we eventually drifted apart.

I don't blame him—it was as much my fault as his—but it was nice to have someone I didn't have to explain everything to, someone who knew what I was feeling but could leave all the emotion and anguish of Sheri's death unspoken. It was a comfort.

A warm wind blows across the lake and Ollie comes over. I give him a good scratch behind the ears. The conversation back at the cabin must have moved on by now, so I stand and give him the signal and the two of us walk back.

chapter 8

Mom, Dad, and Heather are standing beside Jodi and Bryan's car when Ollie and I come up the path.

"Hey, slowpoke," Jodi greets me, "time to say goodbye."

I let Ollie off the leash and he rushes over for his requisite belly rub.

Jodi embraces Mom and Dad. "Thanks for everything."

Bryan shakes Dad's hand and hugs Mom and Heather. "It was a good long weekend."

Jodi comes over and gives me a big squeeze. "Take care of yourself, little brother."

"I try."

"I know you do. Just be careful."

"I will."

"Because if you don't," Bryan chimes in, "Big Sis is coming after you."

I laugh. I go to shake his hand, but he pulls me in for a half-bro hug. He's a cool enough guy—Jodi made a good choice.

They hop in their car and back out of the cabin's short drive leading to the cabin. We give a final wave as they pull away.

Dad turns to me. "Ladder-ball?"

"Okay, old man, but you're about to be put in your place."

Mom turns to Heather. "Well, I've had enough testosterone for one day. How about we leave them to it and go down to the waterfront?"

I smile as another peaceful evening sets in.

chapter 9

Sunday morning and I sleep almost until noon before a mosquito buzzing around my face wakes me. I shoo him away, but I'm unsuccessful and finally open my eyes to stare at the empty bunk above. After Jodi and Bryan left, Heather immediately took over their room, leaving me on my own.

The smell of bacon, eggs, and coffee wafts in and I drag myself out of bed.

"I'm heading out for supplies," Heather announces as I come down the stairs from my room.

"Well, good morning," Dad says to me, eyeing his watch, "or should I say afternoon?"

I ignore him in favour of the coffee and pour myself a cup. I give it a sniff, certain it's way past its prime but take a sip anyway. "Ugh."

"Well, then make yourself some fresh stuff."

I shrug and grab some cream and sugar to muzzle the taste and make for the couch.

Dad stands at the stove. "You want a couple of eggs?"

I nod.

"If you want anything from town, now's the time to tell me," Heather calls out, "I don't want to hear any complaints about what I didn't pick up after the fact."

Looking at Mom, Dad can't resist a jibe. "Kids these days just don't understand."

"I know," Mom says, pointing at Dad's old-school landline phone on the wall. "We have these devices that allow our voices to travel through wires."

"And I believe you have a similar device that uses satellites—"

"Okay, enough," Heather cries out, "I'm leaving. You deal with them, Tony."

I salute her. "Aye, aye, Captain."

Dad brings over a heaping plate of spinach, tomatoes, peppers, and onions, topped with eggs and bacon.

"What is this?"

"Your daily serving of vegetables."

"Looks like last night's salad."

"Eggs-actly!"

I sigh. "Too early for Dad jokes."

"Fine. Eat up and don't complain when people feed you."

Mom changes the subject. "Your dad and I are going out for a walk, Anthony."

This feels like an invitation, but I need alone time as much as Mom and Dad do. "Have fun."

I get the nervous glance from her that I've grown used to.

"Don't worry. I'm going to read…" I grab an old paperback from the bookshelf beside me at random. "*The Stand.*

It seems…" I turn over the gigantic book in my hand and try to force a smile, "thick."

"Very good." Dad replies and in a flash I'm alone in the cabin with the last of my breakfast and a fat, dog-eared novel.

chapter 10

By mid-afternoon, I'm deep into the book. It took a little while to get going, but now I'm excited to turn every page. I go read outside for a while, lounging in the hammock, enjoying the sun, before coming back in to grab a ginger ale and sprawl on the retro orange couch by the big bay window. The living room is bright, but the sun has shifted to the other side of the sky and soft shadows fill the room.

Knock knock knock.

I jump, staring at the front door. A silhouette rocks back and forth. Likely a neighbour from down the road who needs something.

I open it, and there stands Charlie Wolfe.

"Hey." He cracks a smile, the kind that makes me think he's happy to see me.

I'm not sure how *I* feel, so I don't say a word.

I study him, taking in as many details as I can. He looks the same, except he's gotten some sun. He wears a hoodie, a pair of old jeans, and is carrying nothing but his name, which is strange for a journey all the way up here.

He raises an eyebrow and shrugs as if to cue me to speak.

Still, I say nothing, but I'm thinking about everything. Where've you been for the past few months? Where did you go as soon as school was out? Why didn't you return any of my texts? And the big one: How the hell did you find our cabin?

"Uh, hey?" he repeats.

I want to say so much more, but all that comes out is "Hi."

His smile grows. He walks right past me inside.

"Come on in," I say. I can't help the sarcasm.

He stops in the space between the kitchen and the living room and gazes around. I pull the door shut to keep any more mosquitoes from getting in.

"Now this… is exactly what I expected."

I'm not sure if this is a dig or a compliment, but Charlie isn't a dick like that with me, so I believe he's being sincere.

"It's all right," I say, feeling a little self-conscious.

"All right? Beats my place hands down." He eyeballs the interior slowly. "And that's my actual house, not my summer home."

I stand there, silent.

He notices where I've been sitting on the couch. He glances at the ginger ale, then picks up *The Stand*. He looks at the page I'm on. "Big book for you, Shepherd."

"I started this morning."

He nods. "You'll like it. A pop culture classic," he says, smiling again, "a battle between good and evil." He puts it down carefully, making sure not to lose my page.

"Why are you here?"

He ignores the question and checks the coffee pot, recoiling slightly at this morning's remains. He goes to the kitchen cupboards and finds a bag of coffee, checking the label. "Ethiopia. Hmm. Very nice. I love dark roasts."

He opens another and pulls out the coffee filters. I can't figure out how he knows his way around our kitchen; it's like he's done it before.

I move over by the sink and fold my arms across my chest. "How did you find this place?"

He smiles smugly. "Did you know that dark beans have less caffeine than the regular ones? They lose it in the roasting process. Interesting, right? Because Joe Public thinks darker coffee equals stronger coffee and that must mean more caffeine. Not the case. It's actually less."

He opens a drawer and digs through it before pulling out a measuring spoon. He scoops out a portion of the coffee grounds and puts it into the coffee maker.

"Charlie," I try again, "how did you—a guy who doesn't even have a car—get here?"

"Shepherd, relax. I'm here. I found you. Now, do you mind?"

I shrug, giving up, and step out of his way. He takes my place at the sink with the coffee pot.

"Whoa," I caution, "non-potable." I point to a water cooler in the corner.

"Got ya!" He proceeds to fill the coffee pot from the cooler but then pours the water into a clean saucepan he finds on the stove. He lights the gas and I take a seat, resigning myself to the fact that he's going to do whatever the hell he wants.

"How long have you had this place?"

"A while."

He cracks open a plastic container to find some blueberry hemp seed muffins. He takes one and bites into it. "Delicious." He swallows. "Your dad make these?"

"No, my sister, Heather."

He thinks for a moment. "The middle one?"

"Yes."

Going to the fridge, he takes a block of cheese out of a drawer. He unwraps it carefully but then breaks off a large piece with his fingers. I grab a small plate from the cupboard and slide it his way, hoping he'll take the hint. He ignores it and chomps away at the chunk of cheddar.

I wonder if he even ate on his journey here... from wherever he came.

"Man, I really like cheese." He rewraps the rest of the block and puts it back.

The water steams in the saucepan but doesn't boil and he pulls it off. He fiddles with the coffee maker, leaving the basket hanging open and sliding the coffee pot beneath. He plugs the bottom with his finger, pours the hot water over the grounds, and stirs it with a spoon. I figure it must be hot, but he seems not to care. After a minute or so, he releases his finger and it starts streaming into the pot and he pours more hot water over the beans. It immediately smells delicious.

He pours in the last of the water from the saucepan, and while it trickles through the coffee filter, he moves over to a cupboard and finds the coffee mugs. Again, I'm amazed by his accuracy. He offers me one, but I decline, so he pours himself a single cup once it's finished dripping. He slides the pot back onto the hot plate.

"I hate letting a fine cup of coffee overcook, but one has to improvise in the wilderness."

He stares at the magnets and pictures on the fridge and I recall his theory that they reveal a lot about a family. He nods but says nothing, until his attention is caught by a black and white photo of a man on the shoreline with a fishing rod and a decent-sized fish. "Who's that?" he points.

"My granddad. Mom's side."

"He's like you. Only browner."

I laugh, realizing how much I've missed his bluntness. But it's true—everyone says I resemble my mother's father. I've got my dad's height, but I can't argue my striking resemblance to Granddad.

"What did he do for a living?"

"He was a labourer. Worked in a wood mill."

"Where?"

"Ontario."

He nods, then goes to scope out the rest of the cabin. "Where's the family, Shepherd?"

"Mom, Dad, and Ollie went for a walk and Heather went to town."

"Cool. It'll be good to see them."

Charlie sinks into the couch and I cross the room to a chair beside him. I see his relief as he takes a load off. He's tired—must be—had to have been a hell of a lot of work getting here without a car. He leans back, settling into the soft cushion, and inspects me.

"You're taller than the last time I saw you. And you've filled out. Not so scrawny."

I take a deep breath. "Charlie, what are you doing here?"

He shrugs again. "Thought I'd come see you."

"Just like that? You thought you'd head north five hours to an unknown, remote location just to say hi?"

He smirks. "Sure. Why not? Don't us poor kids deserve a holiday too?"

He's testing me, seeing what reaction he'll get, but I'm not in the mood. He waits a moment more, but when I don't bite, he moves on. "How long are you staying out here?"

I don't know the exact answer. "I think most of the summer, on and off."

"Yup, I've heard good things about these northern lakes."

He's up to something. "Like what?"

"Things happen here all the time. Did you know there are barely any alien sightings in this entire province, but there's been nearly a half-dozen right in this area?"

"You believe in aliens now?"

"They say they follow ley lines."

"What lines?"

"Spiritual pathways that criss-cross the earth."

"Really?"

"And an old-timer told me on the way here that the bridge over the river has a mysterious hitchhiker haunting it. You pick him up and before you finish crossing the bridge, he's disappeared."

"I've heard that one. There's also a graveyard just down the road that has ghost lights floating in it."

"People wander out into these woods, see weird shit, and get lost. Just south of here, some farmer went out to mow his field—"

"Mow?"

"Plow, mow, whatever... he disappeared into thin air. Or the two hunters that got separated and one of them was never found."

"Yeah? Maybe he was abducted by your aliens."

"Or there was this kid in the '90s who went into the woods and never came back—"

"Charlie, stop. Really, what's this all about?"

"Stuff happens to people all the time. Like there could be a geocaching murderer who leaves GPS coordinates to someplace online, and then someone comes searching, and *hyah*! They murder you with an axe."

"No—"

"Or someone kills people from all the towns around here and dumps their bodies in the middle of the lake, but the town names spell out a secret message to someone else, like 'Love Elbow Dildo.'"

I laugh despite myself. "Dildo's in Newfoundland."

"Whatever. There's got to be something weird we can investigate—"

"Stop."

"Come on, Shepherd. Don't you miss solving mysteries, stopping bad guys. You know, the good ol' days?"

My smile fades. "The good ol' days? Like when we were searching for my dead girlfriend?"

"I didn't mean it that way."

"Or when two other girls got murdered?'

"Shepherd—"

"Or maybe we should ask Robbie if he liked losing his leg to his knee and walking with a cane?"

"Okay, enough."

But I'm mad now. "No, not enough. What happened to you?"

"What do you mean?"

"Where did you go?"

"Away."

"But *why*? What was so important that you had to run away from everything?"

"Because…" He's awkward and uncomfortable, standing up, trying to move away.

"Because why?"

He stares at the bookshelf full of games gathered from garage sales and handed down as gifts through the years. He finally relents, turning to meet my eyes. "Because maybe you're not the only one who lost someone."

Wait, what? My glare softens and I feel like we just cut each other to the bone. "Charlie…?"

He shifts away, shaking his head. "Shepherd, don't. Don't give me that shitty sympathy face."

"But—"

"Nope. Not having it." He pauses, head tilting to the side, studying the shelf, "Wait. Shit, is that a cribbage board? I haven't played that in forever!"

He's moved on. His guard is up again, and I have to accept it.

"You want to have a game?"

"Hells yeah!"

chapter 11

Two games later, we're tied, with him winning the first and me skunking him bad in the second. Now we've gotten serious, studying our choice of discards carefully. It's his deal, so I start.

"Four."

"Seven."

"Ten." I take my points.

"Fifteen." Charlie smiles, moving his peg two spaces.

"Twenty-five."

Charlie's face crumples. "Go."

I take my point, enjoying the moment. I barely hear the door squeak before Ollie rushes Charlie.

"Hey, boy!" he exclaims, breaking from the game to greet the dog with a fur-ruffling back scratch. Ollie twists around, plopping down on Charlie's feet to claim him.

Mom and Dad are right behind and they seem happy to see our new guest.

"Charles! What a surprise!" Mom moves in as if to hug him but has a moment of hesitation and steps back. "How've you been?"

"All right," he says.

With Mom beside him, I notice that he's grown as well.

"Charlie." Dad steps forward and offers his hand to Charlie, who shakes it firmly. "Good to see you."

"Are you hungry?" Mom wants to know.

"No, Mrs. Shepherd. I found myself one of those delicious muffins and a piece of cheese."

Mom scrutinizes me like I should have offered.

Charlie notices. "Don't blame your son. I helped myself."

"Well, I'm glad you did."

"He didn't really offer me much of a chance," I interject.

Charlie catches my eye and winks.

"What is that gorgeous smell?" says Dad, going to the coffee maker.

Charlie beats him to it, grabbing a mug to pour him a cup. "That's nice."

I smile. "Your beans, prepared by a master barista."

"Oh, that reminds me." Charlie goes outside and comes back lugging a big backpack that has years and miles on it. He digs down into it and pulls out a one-pound bag of coffee beans.

"I got this for you, Mr. Shepherd. Something to drink while reading."

Dad glances at the bag. "Seattle? Very nice." He nods in approval.

"And this is for you." Charlie hands Mom a small package fastened with a twine bow. She unwraps it to find a tiny pinecone on a chain.

"There's an artist in the British Columbia Interior who makes these cool original pieces of jewelry out of things she finds in nature."

"It's beautiful," Mom exclaims, admiring it.

I notice Charlie's not dragging anything else out of his pack. "Where's my gift?"

"Uh, your opportunity to bask in my presence?'

"Nice," I say, rolling my eyes, "do you have a gift receipt so I can return it?"

"Watch your manners, Anthony," Mom scolds.

I don't need to see Charlie to know he loves it.

Dad takes a seat, coveting his warm cup of brew. "So, you've been travelling out West?"

"A bit."

"And what brought you this way to our place?" Mom's tone is caring but inquisitive.

Charlie shrugs—his standard answer for everything. "Hadn't seen you all in a while and I thought I'd come by."

"Are you staying at the campground?" Dad and Mom are bouncing the questions back and forth; it's a friendly version of good cop, bad cop.

"Actually, I was wondering if you would mind me pitching my tent down by your firepit."

"Nonsense. Anthony has space in his room."

This comes as a surprise. "Wait, what?" Bunking with Charlie is the last thing I want.

"Are you sure? I never want to overstay my welcome." He sounds like a grown-up, scheming his way in. I'm certain this was his plan all along.

"Nonsense," Mom says again. "You're welcome here as long as you like."

Well played, Charlie Wolfe, well played.

chapter 12

Now that Charlie's sticking around, Mom asks us to go pick up some tinfoil to help make supper.

"Sure…" I agree. "Where's the keys?"

"Slow down, Steve McQueen—" Mom says.

"Who?"

I hear Dad groan from the living room.

"You're not going to town," she says. "You can get it at the store down by the dock."

"But it's expensive."

"And convenient, and doesn't involve sending you two off in a car. Supper won't be long and Heather's already on her way back from town."

Charlie pipes up, "The docks? C'mon, Shepherd, that's got to be only a five-minute walk."

With Charlie siding with my folks, I give in. "All right. Let's go."

chapter 13

As we walk, Charlie takes his phone out. He seems disappointed. "What's with the Wi-Fi around here?" he asks, waving his phone in the air, trying to get a signal.

"There isn't any."

"Yeah… what's that about?"

"Some places don't have any."

"But why?"

I glance at him. "Because there are no towers."

"I don't get it. Why wouldn't they put any up?"

"There's one on the other side of the lake. You can sometimes catch a signal down by the water."

"That's dumb."

"It's about enjoying the peace."

"Peace isn't a place, Shepherd."

"Okay, Obi Wan."

"Don't you care if you can't get in touch with people while you're here?"

"It's about leaving the city behind. Getting close to nature." That's what my parents say all the time, anyway.

"Sure. I get the nature thing, but no Wi-Fi at all? It's isolating."

"That's the point."

"I just think that it's weird to be out here and have no way of making contact. It's uncivilized. Primitive."

"You don't leave the city very often, do you?"

"I do." He seems offended by the suggestion.

"Oh, yeah, like your trip out West."

He stares at me, smiling, not saying anything.

Guess I'm going to have to ask. "So what were you doing out there?"

"Never thought you'd ask, Shepherd, but there you go, being a big boy. I've trained you well."

"You didn't answer the question, Charlie."

"No. No, I didn't," he says, and stays quiet for the rest of the trip to the store.

chapter 14

The local resort store is only open in high season and is filled to the rafters with the weirdest collection of stuff the summer campers and cabin people might need. It resembles a small log cabin with a screened window walk-up where you can order ice cream. Inside, tall shelves hold every necessary camping, fishing, hiking, boating, and grocery item anyone could ask for. A sign hanging behind the counter announces that they have fishing licenses for sale.

Freddy Bears, the guy who owns the shop, enters through a door at the back that leads to his sleeping quarters. Bears isn't his real last name—no one will tell me why people call him that, but he's had it for as long as I've known him. He plops down on the stool by the register. He's a big guy, always ready to talk Dad's ear off with some story, but he's always seemed a little unfriendly towards me. I'm not quite sure if it's a racist thing, a kid thing, or a little of both.

"Hey, Mr. Bears."

"Uh, yeah."

Charlie's scanning the aisles and I immediately worry he's going to rip something off, so I beeline straight for the tinfoil and take it to the till.

"That it?"

"Yup."

I look for Charlie to make sure he's still on the up-and-up, but he's right beside me, dumping a handful of items on the counter.

"These too."

I stare down at what he's brought over. "What is this?"

He points. "That's a road flare, that's a bear banger to scare them away, and that is Tannerite, which is an explosive."

"An explosive?"

"Well, a binary explosive. You mix it and it's safe, but if you hit it with something like a bullet—" he makes a gesture with his hands that implies a big bang.

"That legal?"

Charlie gets a devilish grin. "Oh, yeah."

Freddy runs it through the till. "That'll be $95."

I shoot Charlie a look, but he's already pulling out his wallet. "Allow me."

chapter 15

Outside the store, Charlie takes his phone out of his pocket, taps away at it a couple of times and shoves it back in his pocket, frustrated. "Can we please search for a signal?"

"Is it really that bad?"

"C'mon, man. I need to stay connected."

"With who? Who do you need to talk to?"

"I got my peeps."

"I can't imagine you with peeps."

"You know: blogs, comments, forums, subs...?"

"Honestly, I don't know—at all."

"And that, ladies and gentlemen, is why you can live in this godforsaken forest."

Charlie and I walk down the hill toward the waterfront, but I regret it immediately. An RCMP patrol boat is waiting at the docks while a couple of officers load supplies. A marked 4x4 truck and trailer pulls over to a grassy area that serves as a parking lot.

Charlie grins. "You know what? I take it all back. Things just got interesting."

Seeing Charlie and the police in the same vicinity worries me. "Let's leave them alone and check for a signal down by our dock."

"Come on, Shepherd, aren't you the least bit curious?"

"No not at all."

Charlie ignores me and walks over to the officer who's just climbing out of the truck.

I keep my distance, leaving him to his conversation. Charlie's nodding a lot and the cop hands him a sheet of paper, which he studies before folding and sliding it into his back pocket. When he's done, he comes back to where I'm standing.

"Country cops are so much nicer."

That he has an opinion on it astounds me. "I've never had the opportunity."

"Oh, yeah. If I were to walk up to one in the city, they'd immediately be suspicious."

"Well, look at you."

He ignores me. "Of course, I still don't trust any of them, but they sure act nicer here."

"What'd he have to tell you?"

"The cop in the city?"

He's just messing with me now. "What was on the paper? A coupon for doughnuts?"

"That's a terrible stereotype, man, but I have to admit, a doughnut sure sounds good right about now."

We walk away from the store back toward the cabin.

"Come on, Charlie. What did he say?"

"They said they were searching for a man in his late thirties named Terry." He grabs the paper from his back pocket and hands it to me. "Do you recognize him?"

I unfold a missing poster for some dude, Terry Butler, who wears glasses, a baseball cap, and a little facial scruff—basically like every other guy in this area.

"Maybe he just took off for the weekend."

"He's been missing for over a week. Friday was the last time anyone saw him. They found his boat out by the bridge, but he wasn't in it."

I think back to yesterday when I was swimming and saw the crowd of boats out there. "Wait. Is *that* why you're here?"

Charlie turns to me, shocked by the suggestion. "No!"

"Really? You didn't know anything about him?"

"No, Shepherd, what do you take me for?"

"So you're not here for some big adventure in the woods?"

"Of course not. I came to see you and your folks."

I hope that Charlie's being honest, that he's not searching for anything other than a decent cell signal. I'm hoping the rest is coincidence.

I hand back the poster as we approach the cabin.

"But you know," he says, "it *is* interesting that this guy ends up missing—"

"No," I say.

"When you've got two master sleuths together again—"

"No."

"Think about it," Charlie urges, "another thrilling escapade for Shepherd and Wolfe!"

A chill runs down the back of my neck when he says that. "No."

"Aww, c'mon," he whacks my shoulder with his fist. "We might be this guy's last hope—"

I turn on him. "Nope, and that's final."

"Jeez, Shepherd. You need to gear down."

"Listen. We're going to take Mom's tinfoil into the cabin and we're not going to talk about this guy anymore. Got it?"

"Sure, Shepherd, sure."

As we turn down the driveway, Charlie pulls out his phone and checks for a signal again.

"Ha! One bar."

Whatever, I think.

When we're at the door, Charlie exclaims, "Two. No, three! The power of the future is now." He looks at me, "I bet poor Terry wishes he had a phone with such great service right now, since there won't be any crime-fighting duo to come save him anytime soon." Then he snatches the tinfoil out of my hand and pushes through the doorway ahead of me.

I hear Mom say, "Thanks, boys, for helping."

"Always a pleasure, Mrs. Shepherd. It's what we do."

chapter 16

Charlie stares out the window at the water. "Can we chop wood?"

I glance at him, trying to figure out if he's joking.

He looks at me. "You have a firepit, right? Let's get it ready for tonight."

I'm immediately suspicious that he wants to get me alone to convince me to do something about this missing guy, Terry, but by the time I'm out the door, he's already down the stairs, axe in hand, shirt yanked off. He's not lean but built solid, and I'd like to know his magic formula for transforming doughnuts into muscle. There's a tattoo of a compass on his left pectoral.

"Where's your shirt, Chuck?"

"It's hot. I only have two shirts and I prefer not doing laundry. And it's Charlie. Or Mr. Wolfe. Or Major Tom."

I'm sure if I check my phone, he's already changed his name in my contacts to match.

He walks over to the woodpile and grabs a log, being selective, like he's choosing fruit at the grocery store. He hauls a piece of firewood up, puts it down, pulls another, then puts the first one back.

"Are you going to—"

"Give me a minute."

I step away, raising my hands in surrender. He still hasn't mentioned the missing guy, but it's not like him to leave something alone.

Finally, he picks up a piece of wood and stands it vertically on the ground. It tips over. He stands it up again, slowly taking his hand away before clutching at it again as it starts to teeter.

"If you just—"

He gives me a glare as he finally gets it to stand.

"Okay, never mind."

He takes a step back, gears up, and swings down hard at the log.

Whap.

The axe head misses, but the log catches the handle, jarring his whole hand. I can see it hurts like hell, but he shakes off the pain.

"You okay?"

"Fine."

He swings again. This time, the axe bites, but the results are less than stellar and the axe is now jammed. He lifts the whole thing up, slamming axe and wood together against the ground, hoping it'll split, but it only digs a hole in the dirt. He strikes it again and again, slowly worming the axe through the wood until it separates, all except for a long strip of grain that holds the two pieces together. He tears them apart, seeming satisfied but breathing hard.

He takes another piece of wood. This time he makes his selection more quickly. He sets the log up and goes through the same process, working hard to split it in two.

He swings and misses completely.

"Easy, man," I wince. "I know we've been through a lot, but I really don't want to sew on a toe."

"Relax," he pants, as he swings again and again, until it finally splits, the pieces shooting sideways. "There." He's sweaty and exhausted.

"For someone who is so skilled in the world of technology, you know very little about the basics of chopping wood, Mr. Wolfe."

He glares at me, but he's too tired to argue.

I hold out my hand. "May I?"

He doesn't say a word, just hands me the axe. I take it from him and toss it on the ground. "Now, I feel a little safer."

I take a log from the pile and lean one end across the far side of the big log that lies beside the woodpile.

"Okay, now, you interested in learning something you don't know?"

He says nothing, but he's watching intently. I pick up the axe, pull it back and swing in a smooth, strong stroke.

Whump.

The head hits and the log splits—safely and easily, despite my non-traditional method.

"My grandpa showed me when I was a kid. The wood doesn't move and if you miss, the axe sticks in the cross-piece before it ever hits your leg. It also takes way less energy."

I toss the two pieces to the side and grab a larger log.

Whump.

Again, it splits easily in two. I lay them side by side on the cross log, splitting them into four pieces. I toss them out of the way.

"It's about surface area, balance, and impact." I lay another log down. "Want to try?"

I offer the axe back to Charlie and he takes my place. I set a piece of wood for him and step back. He swings and it splits in two.

"Easy, huh?"

"Maybe," he mumbles, but his face shows surprise at the little effort it took.

I put another block of wood down. He hits it with the axe. Two pieces go flying.

"Well, how about that, Shepherd. You know stuff." He grabs his own piece and carries on.

"I can help, you know."

"It's okay. I need the practice."

"Well, practice makes perfect," I joke.

"Hey, nothing's perfect. Only better."

He keeps chopping and soon builds a satisfactory pile of firewood ready for the evening.

"That's lots. Mom and Dad should be happy."

"Cool." He seems content with his progress, his face sweaty, his hands dirty and red from the work. "I'm going to see if I can get a cell signal." He sets the axe by the woodpile and grabs his shirt, heading down the path to the dock.

It's only after he leaves that I realize he never brought up the missing guy once.

chapter 17

By the time Charlie's back from the lake, Heather's returned from town.

"Hey," she smiles at him. "You're a bit off the path."

"Yes, I am."

Without missing a beat she carries on, "You like cinnamon buns in the morning?"

"I do."

"Well, then, we've got you covered. These are the best in the province."

Charlie plunks himself down beside her. "The best? Even better than that place on 14th?"

She nods.

He eyes her. "I'm skeptical because I barely know you, but since your Shepherd's sister, I'll give you the benefit of the doubt."

"Well, that's nice of you."

Mom calls us to the table and we find our seats.

Charlie takes a place beside Dad and admires the food. "This looks good."

We fill our plates and Charlie is modest in what he takes, but I'm guessing he'll be ready for seconds before the rest of us. And possibly thirds.

"Hey, City Boy. Pass the salt," Heather calls out.

Mom and Dad laugh. Charlie gets a big smile on his face and hands over the shaker.

Even though he's been to our house in the city a couple of times, he's never been so warm and social. Watching him with my family now, it feels like he's always belonged at this table.

He polishes off his first plate and reaches for a second helping of pasta salad. "This is really delicious. Who made it?"

"Ben," Mom answers.

"Excellent work, Mr. Shepherd," he says, shovelling more into his mouth.

"Charles, please don't speak with your mouth full," Mom cautions.

I swear he's taken aback by it, but he chews and swallows before replying, "Sorry, Mrs. Shepherd."

Dad leans forward to top up his wine. "So how was it out West?" he asks.

Charlie waits a moment, but he's only finishing what's in his mouth before he answers. "Seattle was a good scene to explore, but no point in staying anywhere too long."

"Mom said you were in British Columbia," Heather says.

"Yeah, I was picked up by a couple driving a huge boat of a car outside of Everett. They had their air conditioning cranked so high, I was freezing, but I didn't want to be rude

and ask for a blanket. And even though they were only taking a ferry out of Burlington, they took me all the way to the
border so I could walk across."

Dad, reliving his own youth, says, "I hitchhiked across
Europe after high school and I used to love strolling into
countries."

Charlie nods but doesn't seem to have any aspirations for
such an adventure.

"What were you in BC for?" Mom asks.

This time he doesn't have food in his mouth, but he still
pauses a little before responding, "Dealing with some family
stuff."

"Someone out there you know?"

Charlie nods. "Yeah. My dad."

Last time we talked about it, he'd said he never knew his father, so this comes as a surprise, but he doesn't add anything
else about the man and no one in my family chooses to pry.

There's a bit of an awkward moment before Charlie changes the subject. "Anyway, by the time I was ready to make my
way back, I was out of money, so I ended up working as a
farmhand."

I drop my spoon for dramatic effect.

"Yeah, yeah, Shepherd. And I was about as good as you'd
expect. Do you realize how bad cows smell?"

"You *are* a city boy!" I tease.

He shoots me a look but continues, "I did some work,
hauling fruit from orchards to the stands for a week, and
that got me a bus ticket back to Calgary. But I was stuck next
to a guy who smelled like cheese, and although I really like

cheese," he says, gesturing at me as if I'll back him up on this point, "this wasn't good cheese."

I sit back and watch him entertain Mom, Dad, and Heather. It's interesting to witness. The frustration and surprise I felt when he reappeared at my door has melted away, and I've remembered that feeling of connection I had with him through all the troubles last fall, and how I knew by the end of it that I could trust him with my life.

chapter 18

By the end of the evening, almost every plate is empty and we are all full. Charlie stands to clear the table. "Anthony and I can clean up."

I'm not quite sure what I think about him volunteering me, but I rise and help out.

Mom, Dad, and Heather meander outside as we get to work. He fills the sink with water. "So how's basketball, All Star?" he asks.

"It took a while to get back into it, but it's good to be back on the court."

"Yeah, I saw some of your games."

Really? "Which ones?"

"I don't know. That one at that school near that place. Oh, and that other one."

I catch him grinning and know he's just messing with me.

"But hey, you're good out there. You've got what it takes. Well, except for the passion."

I glare at him. "What's that supposed to mean?"

"Hey man, you have a lot of drive, but you need something else."

"Like what?"

"I don't know, I'm not your coach. I wouldn't worry though. You'll find it. You're that kind of guy."

This is classic Charlie—giving you a compliment while simultaneously punching you in the face.

He's not done, though. "So what was it like going back to school after stopping a serial killer?"

"I don't know," I say, defensive, thinking about Sheri, the bad dreams, the head games, the whispering in the hallways, and now Jodi's threat of going all Big Sis on me. "What was it like for you?"

He passes me a handful of cutlery to dry. "Can't tell you. I didn't stay around much after a few weeks."

"Why not?"

"Well, they thought I was weird to begin with. Once word got around about what we did, they'd gossip every time I walked by. I couldn't handle it."

"So you went to visit your dad?"

"Eventually."

"You never mentioned him—"

He sets down the plate he's scrubbing and shakes the suds off his hands. "Shepherd, I don't want to talk about this stuff. It's not fun and it's not interesting. So let's stop, okay?"

I nod. "Is that why I quit hearing from you?"

"Come on, really? You sound like an ex-girlfriend. 'You never talk to me anymore, you don't text—*wah, wah, wah…*' You and I have nothing in common really, except being good at stopping bad guys."

I set the glasses I've dried into the cupboard. "One bad guy."

"So what. We did it, didn't we? No one else did. Certainly not Gekas."

"And we made such a mess of things that he almost walked."

He ignores me. "Whatever, but if all you want to do is go to school, play basketball, and hang out with your buddies, that's fine. Just don't expect me to wait around."

"Why not? You're the only who understands what I went through."

"Oh, so this is just about you?"

"That's not what I meant."

"I get that it was hard on you, but holding onto the past isn't my thing."

"What about you telling me never to forget?"

When we'd first started searching for Sheri, he'd told me to never let her memory die. His intensity had seemed to come from someplace secret.

"Remembering her and whining about the past are two very different things," he tells me now. "One is about using it to do something and making a change in this world. The other is the complete opposite of that."

I fold the wet towel and hang it over the oven handle to dry, "What about the dreams? The bad memories I just can't shake?" I glance over at him. His back is turned as he pulls the plug to drain the water.

"You know, when I was working in the orchard, there was this dog that kept hanging around, wanting to be my friend. I hated it because it had the same colour fur as that one from the basement."

I shudder at the thought of the dead dog the killer had left for us to find.

"Every time I thought about it," Charlie adds. "I'd remember that smell of rotting flesh and wanted to gag." He watches me. "So you know what I did?"

I wonder if I should let him finish this story.

"I went out and used a day's wages to buy the best piece of steak I could. Then I cooked it, sat down, and shared it with that dumb mutt in the orchard."

I stare at him, confused.

"Sometimes our monsters make sense and are right in front of us. But sometimes, we don't want to see them because they're obvious and that scares us, and that's when we need to lean into the fear, because it's never, ever going away."

"What are you talking about?"

He wipes the counter clean and hangs the cloth over the tap. He examines the kitchen, admiring his work. "Should we join the others?"

"Charlie?"

He beams from ear to ear. "Aww, Shepherd, you know what I'm saying. I'm going to go searching for that missing guy, Terry, and sooner or later, you're going to help me."

chapter 19

Charlie heads outside to join my family by the fire and I rush to catch up to him, to argue with him, but he's too fast and is sitting down beside them before I can say anything. He finds a spot between Mom and Heather, so I sit across from him beside Dad.

Heather roasts a marshmallow and hands it to Mom, who squishes it between two halves of a sandwich cookie.

Heather offers the stick to Charlie. "You want to try?"

"No, thanks, I'm still full from supper. Besides, I don't want your brother having to worry about me burning down the forest."

I'm too flustered to deliver a comeback and can only force a grin.

"Well, then, you're definitely not allowed," Dad, who may have had one too many glasses of wine at supper, pronounces "or I'd have to punish you... after you cut all my wood and did all my dishes—"

Mom chimes in, "And made you coffee. You'd feel so guilty, it would ruin you."

Charlie smiles, enjoying the kidding and the compliments.

The fire is warm and meditative, and we all stare quietly into the flames. I glance at Charlie occasionally, but he's ignoring me. He'll keep nagging me to find this missing guy until I agree to help, and I'd like to keep saying no, but I'm certain he'll break me eventually. When he gets something into his head, it's hard to derail him—he's like a dog with a bone.

"Well, old man, ready for bed?" Mom asks, and I see Dad doing the slow blink, trying to fight the sleep that's beginning to overtake him. He nods and the two of them go up the stairs into the cabin.

Heather sits beside Charlie. I want her to go up to bed as well, but I'm not sure what I'll say to him when she does.

"It's late enough," Heather says, peering into the fire "but I've been quiet for too long." She turns to Charlie. "You know that shit you two pulled last year?"

I look at her, slightly shocked. She's never spoken about those days to me. Ever.

Charlie nods, keeping his guard down. "Yup."

"That was the stupidest thing anyone has ever dragged my brother into. And you deserve every ounce of hate I hold for you."

Charlie nods again, smiling.

"But you stopped that—" she changes her tone and continues, "you stopped him. And you saved those two girls. And you definitely protected the ones he never got to, the ones we'll never know about." She glances over at me. "I only wish that you two had stopped him sooner."

Charlie watches in the firelight and I think he's gotten off easy, but she's not done. "But I don't know you and I don't know why you're here and I don't trust you. If you do anything that hurts my brother, you can bet your ass I will hurt you back."

She gazes into the flames for a moment longer before finally pushing herself out of her chair. "Well, I think that's enough for tonight. Make sure you pour water on the fire before you go to bed."

Charlie watches as she ascends the steps, disappearing into the darkness beyond the firelight. He picks up a stick and stirs the coals.

"Why'd you come to me, Shepherd? Why'd you ask me to help you when Sheri disappeared?"

"I don't know. You seemed like the kind of guy who knew how to solve problems."

"Why not wait for the cops?"

"It seemed like they were going too slow and Sheri would be…"

"She *was* dead, Shepherd. Even before we started."

I study him, watching the orange flickering pull him out of the darkness.

"You knew that from the beginning, didn't you?"

"Yes."

"So why'd you help?"

"Because we needed to find her, no matter what."

I move over, sit beside him, taking the stick he's stirring the coals with from him. "If we go searching for this guy, Terry, he's probably dead too, right?"

"Yes."

"And we may never find him?"

"Yes."

"Then why bother? If it's too late?"

"Because we're here. And doing nothing is more harmful than us trying."

"See that's the thing. I don't get that. You like this stuff and you're good at it. Why do you need me?"

"Well, since your folks were nice enough to give me a place to stay and food in my belly, having you with me as I come and go looking for answers would sure make things run more smoothly."

"And that's it?"

Charlie winces, like he's in pain. "You're not really going to make me say this, are you?"

"What?"

"You—" he sighs dramatically, gesticulating with his arms. "We… You… Help… Complete… Make whole…"

I enjoy watching him struggle to come up with an honest compliment while also acknowledging his failings.

"Listen, we work well together. You make up for my short-comings. We make a good team." He sees me smiling. "Okay, just cut it out."

I lean back in my chair, taking it in. I remember Jodi's warning and turn to Charlie. "He probably drowned, right?"

"Yup."

"And we're just looking for the body."

"Yes."

"But if he didn't, if this becomes something bigger—"

"It won't."

"But if it does, we stop immediately, okay?"

"Deal."

I hope he keeps that promise if the time comes.

chapter 20

On Sunday night, Cousin Rachel goes for her evening run. Main Street Estoria is quieter than a graveyard and only three cars pass her during her workout. She does a lap around the main drag, probably the only person ever to do it in running shoes, before pressing on toward the hill.

It's been three days since she got here and things are moving slowly. After burying the body, she sent half her team, Amos and Gil, home and booked Daniel, Jacob, and herself into two rooms at the motel. They are on cleanup duty now, until all the loose threads are tied up or time runs out and they can't do any more.

This guy Terry had made a real mess of his life before getting killed. His girlfriend had kicked him out and his boss had fired him. He had no home to his name and it wasn't until his boat washed up yesterday by the bridge that anyone noticed he'd been missing. It's sad when even the drug dealers you supply don't care enough to notice that you're no longer around.

Unfortunately, this ambiguity made her job tough—not knowing about the people you work with is great when someone gets caught, but it creates real problems when you need to clean up their mess. She still doesn't know where or who he made his deliveries to, so it was going to require a bit more time and work.

Thankfully no one had found his body yet and she hadn't heard about anything unusual like a big stack of cash being found after it washed up on shore, so they still had time.

She reaches the top of the hill when her phone rings. It's her husband. She slows to a walk and answers it.

"Hi, there."

"You still working?"

Although she didn't share as much as she once had, they had developed a code for the trickier parts of her career. "Yeah, the client is hesitating."

"Jonathan's swim team competes next Thursday. Will you be home?"

Dammit! She hates missing her son's matches. It was his second year on the team and he'd really developed. "I hope to wrap things up here by then."

"He wants you to promise."

She hates when her son puts her on the spot. "I'll do my best."

"All right, I'll let him know." She knows her husband understands that it might be a hard promise to keep. "You're making sure to eat your veggies?" he asks, his way of checking that she was staying safe and watching her ass.

"Yup, as always."

"Okay, miss you. Love you."

"Love you too."

She hangs up and tucks the phone back inside her pocket. Regaining the speed of her run, she passes the turn toward the golf course and continues toward the school.

The night before, she'd left her team behind and visited the girlfriend's house on her own. The boys were good at grunt work, but they're like a pair of rampaging rhinos when it comes to things that need to be handled carefully. When she got there, no one was around. Whatever relationship the woman had with Terry, she wasn't so busted up over his disappearance that she was spending her nights crying at home. Cousin Rachel saw that the woman hadn't let him get too close—there wasn't a trace of his stuff anywhere inside the place, including anything that might tie Terry to Cousin Rachel. She didn't turn the house upside down, but she felt confident this guy hadn't left any evidence lying around. Which was good.

Earlier that afternoon, she had sent Daniel and Jacob to follow up on a lead at a local pizza place, but they didn't find the guy—someone named Little Joe—they were looking for. As she races along the curve past a nursing home and a hospital, she regrets not going to the restaurant herself; she can be more persuasive than either Daniel or Jacob.

She has a lot to do over the next few days—more people to visit, more messes to clean up before they lead back to her bosses. Of course, if anyone tries to block her progress, she has no qualms about removing them—her job is about solving problems—even if it means spilling blood.

And now, she has even more incentive. She's made a promise to her son and she intends to keep it.

part 2

chapter 21

The morning light of Monday wakes me. I'm not sure what time it is, but it feels early. The cabin is quiet and I haul myself out of the lower bunk, careful not to wake Charlie. I'm not sure if he's a light sleeper, but he was absolutely bagged when he went to bed last night.

I'm not much better, and though I'm making my way to the bathroom, I feel absolutely zonked. I tossed and turned last night, thinking about our conversation.

I agreed to see if we could find this Terry guy partially out a sense of duty to my friend and partially because I believed what he said, that we could make a difference. I mean, I'm sure Charlie will do whatever he wants, and I know I don't have to do this, but I'm becoming aware of another feeling, one that I didn't expect or even want—excitement!

When I go downstairs, my eye is caught by a note from Mom on the kitchen counter: *Gone to the resort for breakfast with Dad and Heather. Then the beach. Taking Ollie with us. Be back at lunch. Enjoy your morning.*

It's 7:30. A little early but if I get ready quickly, I can take advantage of the quiet and enjoy my book in the hammock before Charlie gets up.

There's still a little coffee in the pot so I grab a mug. I take a sip, staring out the window at the still, blue lake through the lush forest. It's going to be a beautiful day. That's when I notice the distinctive taste of my cup of java. This isn't Dad's heavy-duty brew and can only be—

Charlie walks by the window, dressed like he's been up for hours. What the hell?

I open the door. "Charlie!" I whisper.

He's distracted and doesn't hear me.

I raise my voice, nearly yelling, "Charlie!"

He stops dead on the stairs and turns his head. "Hey, good morning."

He's quite the sight in baggy jeans, superhero tee-shirt, sneakers, and his trademark shaggy hair.

He drops whatever mission he's on and trots back up to me. He reminds me of Ollie, tail wagging, happy to see me. I wonder if I should offer Charlie a treat?

"What's for breakfast, Sleeping Beauty?" he asks.

He's always hungry—maybe he really is a dog. "I don't know. Let's find something."

We go back inside.

"What time did you wake up?"

He ponders. "Five."

"In the morning?"

"Obviously."

I snort with disbelief. "And Mom and Dad?"

"Maybe an hour later. Your dad got up when he smelled my coffee. And your mom shortly afterwards. Oh, there's a note from them—"

"I got it."

"Cool." Again, he manoeuvres around the kitchen as if he's been here a dozen times before, making a fresh pot of coffee and pulling out stuff for breakfast. We work together and cook up a huge stack of pancakes in no time.

"You think that's enough?" I say sarcastically.

"Hopefully, but if not, we can always find some leftovers."

I think he's serious.

We dig in.

Charlie makes sure to swallow before saying, "Do you know the old lady down the road—Diane, I think? She likes the reefer."

"Sorry, what?"

He pours more syrup on his pancakes. "Diane smokes pot. She's got to be what, ninety?"

"She's not ninety."

"So you know her?"

"Of course. I think she's been out here even longer than us."

Charlie scarfs down his first pancake and flops another onto his plate. If I don't start soon, he might eat mine too. Quickly, I spear a couple of mouthfuls.

"Then you knew she smokes pot?

I shake my head. "How do *you* know?"

"She told me."

I almost cough up a pancake.

"Whoa, careful." He pounds me on the back

"Thanks." I take a gulp of juice. "She *told* you?"

"Yeah. I was walking by and she smiled and said 'Hello,'" Charlie says, adding an English accent even though I know Diane doesn't have one, "and I say 'Hi' back, the way people in small towns are supposed to. Then we start talking and she assumes I might have some stuff because well…" He gestures at his overall appearance, then shrugs and keeps eating.

"She asked that straight up?"

"Yeah, but I told her I didn't have any and she was disappointed because she had run out and it was going to be awhile before she'd be able to buy some."

"Thank God."

"Dude, she has arthritis and it helps her feel better and sleep better and it makes her happy. She seems really nice."

"How about that." I lean back in my chair, thinking about this new knowledge. "Diane is a pothead."

"No. She's got arthritis and is self-medicating, Shepherd. It's different."

"Okay, then."

Our stack of pancakes is shrinking.

Charlie continues, "You know what else?"

"The old man down the street makes meth?"

"No. Really?" He catches me watching him but seems to take the notion seriously, "that hadn't occurred to me, but I'll check him out later."

I wonder if he actually will.

"Anyhoo," Charlie goes on, "the people in the red log cabin down the street? They vacated the premises but left a window open on their second floor."

"You didn't go inside?"

"Well, yeah, because it's the neighbourly thing to do."

"Holy crap, Charlie!"

"Relax. I just closed it for them and left."

"And that's it?"

He doesn't answer immediately, then he laughs, "Of course, Shepherd. What kind of delinquent do you take me for?"

"Exactly..."

"Also the house just before the turn? That couple's going to break up. They were screaming at each other and it's way too early in the morning for that shit."

I take a sip of coffee. "Did you case this whole lake?"

"It's called gathering intel and it's good to be prepared."

"For what? We're in the middle of nowhere?"

"Do I need to remind you about our man, Terry?" He unfolds the missing poster the cop gave him and lays it out between us.

"Don't remind me. What did you find out?"

"Not much. We need to get on the ground and do some serious recon."

"Okay, how?"

"It's time for you to take me to town."

chapter 22

Charlie waits on the deck while I get dressed.

Mom and Dad come through the door as I'm lacing my shoes and she immediately wants to know where we're off to.

"I was thinking of taking Charlie into town, showing him around?"

"Really? That's thirty minutes away and a lot of gas."

I'm not surprised—trouble tends to follow us—so I scramble for a new excuse. "He was hoping for some Wi-Fi and a coffee."

"We have coffee. He brought some."

Crap. Darn you, Charlie, for being generous. "He said that's for Dad, not for him."

"I think you guys can stay home. Maybe take the canoe out—"

Charlie enters with the tank from the barbecue in his hand. "I've got the propane, Shepherd." He stops as if Mom and Dad's presence surprises him.

"Oh, sorry, Mr. and Mrs. S. I should know better than to bring something like this into the cabin." He quickly ducks out and sets it on the deck, then steps back inside. "I was thinking about making supper for you all tonight as a way to say thanks, but then I saw the tank was nearly empty, so I thought we could go to town, pick up groceries, and get some propane."

Charlie's generosity startles Mom and I can already see her defenses melting.

"Unless that's a problem," he says. "I don't want to cause any trouble or anything."

"No…" she hesitates, wisely sensing there's maybe more to this than she knows, "but maybe—"

"You know," Dad interjects, "if Charlie's cooking is as good as his coffee, I'm all in."

Mom sighs, any further argument now cut short. "Fine," she says, handing me the keys from the cupboard, "but no speeding—you're not familiar with driving on gravel roads. And back by five."

"Deal."

As we leave, Charlie attempts assurance, "Don't worry, Mr. and Mrs. S. I'll keep him on the straight and narrow."

I'm positive I hear them both crack up as the door shuts behind us.

chapter 23

Charlie puts the tank in the trunk, tosses his backpack in the front by his feet, and in minutes, we're heading to town. Right away, he's adjusting his seat, moving it forward, pushing it back, flipping the visor, positioning the air vents, and rolling down his window.

I've got to know. "So, how much propane did you let out of that tank?"

"Shepherd, I'm shocked you'd think I'd pull such a stunt!" He leans over and turns on the radio. A staticky country song from the '70s warbles through the speakers. "What in the hell is that?"

"It's called AM radio."

"Oh, I've heard about this. Always thought it was a myth." He spins the dial, trying to find another station. Another country song pops up followed by a farm report on wheat futures, whatever that is.

"Sorry, man," I say. There's only a couple of stations and the clearest one plays religious country music.

Charlie goes to turn on the CD player. "Here's hoping your dad doesn't let me down."

Opera blares.

"Ack!" he cries, ejecting the CD to read the label aloud. "'The Flower Duet' by Leo Delibes from *Lakme*? It sounds like something from an airline commercial."

"I'm sure that's Mom's. The things you do for love."

He rifles through the glove box, finding a few CDs. "Jack Johnson, Etta James… nice."

"You like Etta James? Isn't she just for old people?"

I get the glance, of course, but he decides not to comment in favour of assessing the next album. "Cool and the Gang? What the—?" He tosses the CD out the window.

"What are you doing?" I yell, slowing down.

"He won't miss it," he says, grinning.

In the rearview mirror, a swirl of dust unravels behind us. Emboldened by Charlie's presence, I decide I've got better things to do than search for an old CD. I step on the gas.

"Now, *here* we go." Charlie smiles. "*Greatest Hits, CCR.*"

I'm not sure if I'm into it, but it's better than the garbage on the radio.

He slides it in. "Bad Moon Rising" starts up and so does Charlie.

It's not my style of music, but because of Dad I've been listening to it all my life and know every word. It's fun, bouncy, and I sing along about earthquakes and lightnin' too.

Charlie shows his approval and adds air drums. "Shepherd, you're full of surprises."

"It's my parents' fault."

"Nope," he disagrees, "it's to your parents' credit. Thank them."

Embracing the moment, I blast down the road and onto the main highway, cracking into the chorus with Charlie by my side.

chapter 24

By the time we pull onto Main Street, "Down on the Corner" is blasting and we're in a great mood. The sun is out and it's an excellent summer day.

"I'll take you to a coffee shop where you can Wi-Fi your brains out. Sound good?"

"Perfect!"

I pull up to Cup of Joan's and the place is filled. It's 10:30 when we get there, so all the townspeople have settled into coffee row to gossip about the day's events.

Inside and the smell of fresh baking hits us. Charlie grabs a seat in a window booth, dumping his backpack beside him, pulls out his phone and starts tapping away. I slide in across from him.

He nods at the woman behind the counter. "That Joan?"

"That's Laurie. Her mom was Joan."

"She took it over?"

"Her mom passed away three years ago."

He nods. "Sucks." He watches Laurie for a moment. "She's cute."

"Back when I was younger, I'd make my parents let me order dessert just to get her over to my table."

"Aww, Shepherd, was she your crushie-crush?"

I laugh. "Yeah, you could say that."

He glances back at her. "What is she? Thirty?"

"What is *with* you and your bad judgment of people's ages?" I do some rapid math. "She's gotta be twenty-four."

He winks. "Nice. Into the older women!"

I glare at him as Laurie comes over with a pot of coffee.

"Hi, Tony. Long time, no see." She turns over my cup and fills it.

"Hey," I say. I can't help but notice how pretty she is.

"Who's your friend?" she asks.

"Laurie, this is Charlie."

Charlie stops whatever he's doing on his phone. "Thanks for the gift of your internet."

It's probably the best he can manage as far as social graces go.

She flashes a smile and her dimples show. "You're welcome. Being out here without a signal can be a scary thing."

He takes a sip of coffee. "Wow, now *that* has some bite."

"If it's muddy hot water you want, we have one of those down the street—"

"Oh, no. Don't get me wrong. I approve wholeheartedly."

"Well, I believe you should start with good beans and proper brewing if you're going to open a coffee shop."

Charlie raises his cup in respect.

Laurie's intrigued. "Tony, where did you dig up this connoisseur of good coffee? Same school?"

Charlie and I exchange a glance. I recall the day I first saw him digging in the dirt in front of Sheri's school. My stomach tightens automatically.

Charlie plunges in. "I guess you could say we met at school. But we also work together sometimes."

I exhale; none of that is a lie. I also can't help but notice how willing he is to answer her.

Laurie smiles at me. "Awesome. Anything else I can get you besides the coffee?"

"Yes, two of your best doughnuts, please."

"Strawberry-orange and apple cinnamon?"

I smile. "You know me well."

Charlie is back on his phone, head down, focused. "And two for me."

I scowl. "Pay attention. I just ordered."

"Yeah, for yourself, right?" He looks up and I know he's not kidding.

I gaze at Laurie, sighing. "We'll have three doughnuts. Give him the first two and then *one* for me. Your choice on the last one."

"Sounds good." She smiles, touching me on the shoulder, and walks away.

I study him. "I'm impressed. All her questions didn't bother you?"

"I like people who ask questions—it illustrates who they are, what they care about, and what they want to know. But it takes the right kind of person for *me* to care enough to answer."

"And she's the right type?"

He nods. "Yeah. There's something honest about her."

It's fascinating how he thinks about people, as if we're all one big, never-ending collection of data that he uses to understand humanity.

Charlie smirks but doesn't bother to meet my eye when he adds, "Besides, she wants you."

I can't say I haven't noticed that Laurie's shown more interest in me lately, but I let it go.

"What wrong, Shepherd? Why not get her number?"

I don't answer and Charlie puts his phone down for the first time since we got here. "All right, story time—"

"About what?"

"Just shut up and listen, Shepherd. One time, maybe two years ago, I was at lunch and there were these three girls, a grade or two older than me. They were a part of the student council, athletics—you know, exemplars of the student body."

I wonder where he's going, if he's trying to take a dig at me, but I let him continue.

"There were also these other kids that came to our school—ones with messed-up lives, most of which they couldn't control. And these three girls start talking about them—not about how screwed up they are, but how they're raunchy and gross, all of which was bullshit."

His phone *bings*, but he ignores it.

"So I sat there and just listened to it all go down. Not because I wasn't pissed off—I was—but because I thought it wasn't my problem. Then Sheri—your Sheri—walks over, because, you know, these girls are her friends and I think she's going to hang out with them, but instead she totally lays into them, defending these poor kids whose troubles are bigger than themselves. And I thought to myself, well there goes a Class A human being."

He picks up his phone again but keeps talking. "Sheri was pretty cool, Shepherd. I get that. But she wouldn't want you to stop living for her. In fact, I'm hoping she'd be pissed off if you did." He nods toward Laurie, who's on her way back to our table with a plate of doughnuts. "It doesn't have to happen now, but at some point you need to fully come back into this world."

When Laurie arrives, Charlie glances at me and loudly announces, "I'm going to take a whizz, so don't touch my doughnuts." And with that, he gets up, leaving me with a surprised Laurie, dirty glares from my fellow patrons, and my head spinning.

chapter 25

I wait for Charlie to return, staring out the window, watching the cars drive by, and thinking about what he said. I'm not interested in a new relationship or asking anyone out; I'm not ready to move on. I don't think I'm holding onto memories of Sheri too tightly, but I still haven't met anyone who makes me feel the same way. Laurie is pretty and I think I'd have a lot of fun on a date with her, but I also know there's something missing.

Charlie plops down beside me. "Except for the Wi-Fi, this place is like a time machine: classic diner counter, old farmers drinking coffee and eating pie, posters on the window for hired hands. What's next? Soft drinks in bottles?"

I point to a kid wearing neon colours who could have been pulled out of the '80s at the counter, sucking at the straw in his bottle of root beer.

"Unbelievable."

Charlie pulls the plate of doughnuts over to his side, and leans in close, taking a deep whiff. "These smell amazing."

He picks one up, takes a bite and nods his approval before pushing the plate over to me. I chomp down on one and it's truly the freshest and most delicious sugary treat I've tasted in forever.

He notices my mug is empty. "Want some more coffee?" he asks, but before I can answer he takes off with both cups to the counter.

He stands beside a couple of older men wearing baseball caps that I'm guessing have the names of farm dealerships embroidered on the front and I can't help but think that he belongs here. This is one of his skills, blending in so well that no one can see him while he observes everything.

Laurie's busy in the kitchen—I can see her through the serving window—and she signals to Charlie that she'll be a minute more. He acknowledges her with a nod and comes back to the table.

"Well, that was productive," he declares, plunking himself down.

"How so?"

"Small town people like their scuttlebutt, Shepherd."

"What did you hear?"

He doesn't say anything until Laurie comes over to refill our cups, then poses a question, "Do you think it's weird that this Terry guy got fired and went missing around the same time?"

I stare at him. "Huh, what are you talking about?"

Charlie leans over to me. "Terry was a mechanic at the local car dealership—"

"Huber's," Laurie interjects.

I know the place. It's been around forever.

She glances at Charlie. "Do you know Terry?"

He shakes his head. "No. But word gets out."

"That it does." I add, looking up at Laurie. "We saw some cops and Charlie asked what was up. They said they're searching for him."

Laurie looks from Charlie to me, then sits down beside me. Her perfume is nice.

"What's worse," she tells us, "is that he got dumped at pretty much the same time."

"Well, there's a shitty day." Charlie gives me a look that says *Laurie thinks something's up*. "How do you know he got dumped?"

"Most things don't stay quiet too long around here. But his ex, Miranda? She also worked at Huber's as a 'receptionist.'" She uses air quotes.

"Do you know her?" Charlie asks.

"Went to school with her. She always told us how she was going to be an actress or something. After graduation, she went away for a year or so, then came back. Something happened, wherever she went."

"Like what?"

She shakes her head. "Don't know. Some say she couldn't handle living in the big city…"

Charlie watches Laurie's finger run along the handle of the carafe, then says, more of a statement than a question, "But you think it was something else."

Laurie smiles. "Spreading rumours isn't good for business."

I don't envy her being the focus of Charlie's questions and I'm not entirely sure what they have to do with the missing man. "Charlie…?"

I try to hold his gaze, hoping he'll move on, but it's Laurie who changes the subject. "Anyway, Miranda's just a secretary now, answering phones and getting coffee. She always thought she was better than everyone else, but here she is, stuck right back here with the rest of us."

Sounds like Laurie isn't only talking about Miranda.

"And Terry wasn't the worst guy she could've been with," Laurie adds. "The woman from the jewelry store said he was planning to propose."

I'm intrigued. "So why do you think she dumped him?"

"My guess? She was messing around. Not sure who with, but as a woman living in a small town... trust me, it's definitely possible. Sometimes we'll do anything for excitement."

Laurie's staring at me and I catch myself staring back.

Charlie interrupts, "Thanks, Laurie."

She looks over at him and the moment is broken. "You're welcome." She stands up and moves to the next table to offer them a refill too.

chapter 26

When Laurie's out of earshot, I lean in and ask Charlie, "When were you going to tell me?"

"Tell you what?"

"That Terry was fired—"

"And had a girlfriend!"

"Charlie!"

"What?" He realizes I'm upset. "Okay, fine, I'm sorry."

"Remember how we talked about communication—" It feels like we've covered this ground too many times before.

"Yeah, yeah, don't start whining."

"You're the one who asked me to help this time, not the other way around. So you share or I'm out."

Charlie waves off my concern. "I know, I know." Then he smiles, "But listen: Terry got fired *and* he had a girlfriend *and* she dumped him."

"Are you... *happy* about this?"

"No, no," he says. "It's just—he's no longer simply a missing guy. Shit happened to him, *then* he went missing."

I can see the wheels turning in his deviant brain and feel a slight rush of anticipation rising in my belly before a pang of worry pushes it all back down.

Charlie taps his phone on the tabletop before slipping it into his pocket. "We should get going."

"Why? You've satisfied your addiction?"

He nods, but I know that's not it. "Charlie…?"

He ignores me and goes to the counter.

Laurie meets us at the register. "Your bill?"

Charlie smiles. "Yes, please. But can I also get two honey-dipped to go?"

I can't believe it. "You just ate two."

He's offended. "Hey, I was going to share!"

Laurie smiles as she bags up his treats. "How long are you staying, Charlie?"

Charlie looks over at me then back at Laurie with a grin. "Francis Bacon says, 'Friends are thieves of time.' I guess I'm going to stay until the vault is empty or the cops show up."

Laurie stares at him and I cringe. A second later, I lean over to her and say, "I don't like letting him out of his kennel much, but if I don't, he wets himself."

She giggles.

Charlie shoots me a dirty look. "Really? You went for a pee joke?"

I shrug.

"Fine, but that was worse than your dad's puns."

Laurie hands Charlie his bag of doughnuts and I pay. We go out the door and back into the sunshine. He's already into the bag, grabbing his doughnut.

"Want yours?" he offers.

I shake my head, glancing at my watch. We don't need to get the propane and groceries quite yet and I can tell Charlie's got more on the agenda. "Let me guess. You want to check out Huber's?"

"Thought you'd never ask."

chapter 27

We pull into Huber's, an all-in-one dealership, repair shop, and gas station on a corner of Main Street.

We give it the once-over. "Seems like Huber's doing well," I say.

"You've been here before?" Charlie asks, chewing his doughnut thoughtfully.

"Dad used to occasionally fill up here."

"Not anymore?"

"He always said they charged too much for gas."

Charlie notes the price on the sign. "Yup, about two cents more."

His eye for details is impressive. "Is there anything you don't notice?"

He brushes off the compliment, but I think I see him smile as he climbs out of the car.

I follow.

"Place is in better shape than I remember. Less run down."

"And see that?" he says, pointing. "Propane."

Sure enough, a tank swap station sits along the far end of the building near the service doors.

"I'll go get us a fresh tank while you go inside."

"And do what?" I ask

"Look, listen, and learn, Shepherd."

Charlie always makes it sound easy.

He sighs. "We're teenagers, picking up stuff for the folks, right? Act natural and no one will ask." He jams the last bite of doughnut into his mouth.

Makes sense. Most people wouldn't mix reconnaissance missions and teenagers—but Charlie's not most people.

chapter 28

I walk in and scope out the interior of Huber's. It feels like a failed attempt at an upscale dealership. Red cement floors show the wear and tear of years and the faint smell of gasoline and oil slips through the back door that leads to the garage area. Fake plants and a display of winter tires stand near the tall picture windows that let in too much sun. The whole space is roasting, except for a small spot by the counter where a tiny air conditioner grinds away. Opposite the windows are shelves of oil, washer fluid, and spare parts, along with a wall rack filled with magazines, gum, and chocolate bars that have likely melted in this heat.

Beyond the counter, the office area is separated from the front by more windows. A woman works at a desk behind the glass, thumbing through grease-stained folders and tapping things into the computer with abnormally long, painted nails.

I'm not sure, but I'm guessing this is Miranda.

A man in a golf shirt comes in behind her and a faint flicker of memory tells me that this might be Huber's son. He sets a coffee down beside her—nice of the boss to offer—and leans over to see what she's up to on the computer. She points and talks without making eye contact, but from this angle, it seems like he's got the perfect pervert's view down the front of the tight-fitting dress she's poured herself into.

Something else doesn't feel right about what I'm seeing, though, and when she stands and turns to talk to him, she taps his stomach with her fingertips and another memory of Sheri flashes across my mind's eye—laughing, poking, grinding my gears to start something silly, staring at my lips when she wanted a kiss, the smell of her skin, close to me and yet so far away—

Wait, this is too intimate. Shit, what a cliché. Miranda's doing her boss.

I recall the horrible feeling I had when Sheri wasn't texting back, when I hadn't heard from her in days. It was a sick feeling, thick and black in the pit of my stomach. I didn't feel like laughing or flirting. I just wanted to find her or hear from her or distract myself from that heavy, awful feeling. Now, as I watch Miranda, I'm angry.

"What's this about? I've never understood." Charlie has snuck in behind me, standing at the rack, contemplating a porno magazine wrapped in plastic with stickers over the naughty bits. "So they're naked and doing it. Big deal." He dismisses the idea. "Whatever. I guess some people are into it."

Between what I've gathered about Miranda and my anger over her infidelity, Charlie's sudden appearance and his apparent disgust with sex magazines leaves me a bit speech-less. I would've thought all of this was right up his alley.

He gently knocks a set of fuzzy dice, making them swing. "Now, forget magnets on fridges. *These* say something about a person." He takes a car magazine off the rack and flips the pages.

"Charlie," I whisper, "I found the boyfriend."

He whistles, staring at the magazine sideways like a center-fold. "Check out the torque specs on that!"

"Charlie," I repeat, a bit louder, "I found the boyfriend."

"Her boss, Huber."

I stare at him. "You knew?"

"Of course. Well, I had a strong suspicion anyway."

"Look." I point and Charlie puts the magazine back on the rack and leans around me so he can see what I'm seeing. Miranda has quit touching Huber, but now his hand is on her waist and she's not moving it.

"Sure doesn't seem like a girl who's sad about her missing boyfriend," Charlie says, keeping his voice low.

"Nope."

"But we know that's her for sure?" he asks.

"Not really."

"I think we need to get her alone to find out. And maybe ask some questions."

Charlie goes to the window and stares at a big red muscle car with low-profile tires parked out front. It's a pathetic mid-life crisis vehicle with way too much detailing, ground effects, and accessories. It's so excessive, it's ridiculous.

"How much you want to bet that's Boss Man's? Can I get your keys, please?"

I hand them to him and he runs out to Dad's car to grab his backpack from the front seat. But before coming back in, he studies the muscle car's license plate.

"Even has his name on the vanity plate," Charlie chuckles under his breath to me as he digs through his backpack. Finally, he pulls out what appears to be an old cell phone.

"Um. What's that?" I ask.

He shows it to me. "A couple of classmates are amateur car thieves—they built it as a rolling jam between the signal from a key fob and a car. You flip it on and it blocks you from locking your car."

"You're going to steal his car?"

Charlie's eyebrows shoot up. "'Course not," he says, all defensive. He slides the switch. Immediately, the alarm on Huber's car starts blaring, as do a couple more cars across the street.

"My guys never could get it working right," Charlie says with a grin.

Huber looks up instantly and snatches at his keys. He points the key fob past Charlie and me, but the car alarm continues whooping. Frustrated, he steps out from the counter, trying again.

Zip, zilch, nada.

"What the—" He forces a smile at us as he pushes past and outside. He tries again with no success, then attempts to open the car door. Now he's pissed, struggling between pushing buttons on his key fob and tugging on the door handle. Finally, he calms down enough to unlock the car manually.

"What did you do?" I ask, but Charlie can't hear me over the deafening sound.

He shakes his head, laughing as Huber eventually gives up and starts the car. The over-powered engine rumbles to life before he drives around to the garage side of the building.

We can still hear the horn blasting away in the back bays, though it's a bit quieter now.

"Was it supposed to do that?"

"For car thieves? No. You sort of want stealth in that line of work." He smiles broadly. "But for me? Worked perfectly."

chapter 29

We watch the woman we think is Miranda going about her work behind the big office window, seemingly oblivious to what's going on around her.

"Not real good at customer interaction, is she?" Charlie sighs.

"How do we get her out here?"

Charlie walks up to the front desk and takes a business card from the stack in the clear card holder next to the phone. He takes out his phone and dials the number.

Seconds later, the phone on the front desk rings several times, but no one comes to answer it. Miranda doesn't even look up. Eventually, it goes to voicemail.

"This woman needs a new career." He hangs up his phone and calls again.

At the repeated ringing, she sighs visibly and takes a sip of her coffee. Finally, she pushes away from the computer and walks out to the front desk.

Charlie hangs up and slips the phone into his pocket.

The woman grabs the receiver and says, "Hello, Huber Motors." She waits a second, listening to the silence, before trying again. "Hello?" She shakes her head.

"Did they just hang up?" Charlie asks goes over to her. "That's just rude. You'd think with caller ID the days of prank calls would be over."

"You'd think that, wouldn't you," she agrees.

"Some people will always be wiseasses, I guess," Charlie adds.

Miranda glances from him to me. The sight of two teenagers in her shop only seems to annoy her more. Still, can't neglect a potential paying customer. "Can I help you?"

Well, if this is Miranda, I can see what Laurie was talking about. She definitely thinks she's better than us and I feel Charlie's ire rising.

"Do you need to have your car checked out?"

Charlie nods to the tank beside our car. "Nope, just some propane."

She peers outside and sees Dad's high-end vehicle. She's impressed.

"Also, I'd like to purchase this map." He tosses a coiled book on the counter. "Oh, and this fuzzy peach air freshener." He digs a little plastic-wrapped paper tree out of his pocket and sets it on the map book.

She picks it all up and walks over to the register.

Charlie watches her, assessing. "We're not from here," he continues. He steps away from the counter and nods at me. "Go on, money man. Pay the good woman."

I feel like he's casting his line and I'm the hook. Guess it's time to put my interpersonal skills to work.

I step to the counter. "You don't give me the impression of being from here either," I say.

"What do you mean by that?" she asks defensively.

"You're too—I don't know—city?"

The tight crease between her eyebrows disappears as she, curious, lowers her guard.

"I just imagine a small town admin assistant being different." I throw in a smile, turning on the charm.

And she softens. "That's nice of you to notice. Most people around here call me a secretary. They don't realize I'm more than that."

I lean on the counter, making eye contact. "No one minds their own business, do they?"

"Small town gossip is a killer," she agrees.

"No privacy?"

"Yeah. One of the reasons I liked the city better, I guess."

"The city? Where are you from?" I ask.

"I lived out east for a while," she tells us.

"Then you moved here." We're on a roll now. Maybe I can get what we need.

"I'm from here originally." She grimaces as if she's unhappy to admit this fact.

"You miss it? The city?"

"Yeah," she says.

"I bet it's hard to even get a decent cup of coffee in this place."

"Seriously," she rolls her eyes. "What I wouldn't do for an expresso."

Behind me, Charlie coughs at her mispronunciation. We ignore him and he wanders back to the magazine rack—though I'm sure he's eavesdropping

"I know what you mean." I'm trying to get to the info we want, but I'm starting to feel sorry for this woman. "Is that coffee shop down the road any good?"

She snorts. "No. The service is shit, the coffee is bad. I wouldn't go there."

Nope, Laurie and Miranda are *definitely* not friends.

"So why stay here, then? You'd be great in the city."

She winces. "Well, it didn't work out." She searches for the right words. "You end up being so anonymous there…"

She's pretty for small town and probably had talent, but when she got to the city, she was a little fish in a great big pond, and was probably ignored in a way she wasn't used to. It's kind of sad, no matter how rude she is to potential customers.

"It's nice here, though," I say. "And a woman like you? You must have lots of guys chasing after you around here."

"Well…" she giggles, "yes." Her friendliness seems genuine.

"Ah, I can tell there's someone special."

She blushes. "There is now."

"Only now? There wasn't someone before?"

Her grin fades. "Yeah, but he was going nowhere."

Now we're getting to the truth. "That's too bad."

"He didn't care about nice things. Things were always just good enough for him."

"It's tough to be with someone who isn't on the same page."

Charlie wanders away to look out the front window—his apparent boredom makes our conversation seem even more natural. Somewhere in the near distance, the blaring horn of Huber's muscle car finally stops.

"It's true," Miranda says into the sudden silence, eager to complain about Terry. "He'd come to work. Go home. Drink beer. That's it."

"He must've taken you out for supper or something?"

She laughs. "I'd be so lucky. He'd rather be on the lake with his buddy Pete than go out."

This is interesting. "The lake?"

"Yeah, their monthly fishing trip. I'm sure it was just an excuse to get wasted."

"But you never went?"

Miranda eyes drop to her fingers as they pluck the metal coils of the map binding. "He'd take me out other times, but his trip with Pete was sacred."

"He'd choose hanging out with someone else over you?"

She nods. "Third Friday of every month and no girls allowed."

"Huh. Just like clockwork, hey?"

"Yeah, I'm pretty sure he'd've pissed on schedule if someone told him to."

"Doesn't sound too exciting, I've got to say."

I must've hit on something because she gets animated and leans in too. "Right? A girl wants passion."

"And the new guy? He's all about the romance?"

Her dimples appear and they make her kind of cute. "Yeah. He's great."

As if on cue, Huber comes in from the back. "What's going on?"

Miranda pulls back. "Nothing."

I can see it in his eyes—some black teenager he's never seen before, talking to his girl, and a shaggy haired kid lurking around his store. He's instantly suspicious.

"They were—" she pauses and it doesn't help the situation, "just asking me about when I lived in the city."

I feel I should help. "Also, buying some propane."

Then Charlie's at the counter. "And this map and fine fuzzy peach air freshener."

"Really?" Huber's tone is condescending.

Charlie nods and I stand there smiling like the guiltiest fool around. I'm sure Charlie will give me crap about it later.

Miranda speaks up, "Honest, Brent—"

Huber glares at Miranda and I figure he's going to scream at her once we leave. He's only been here for thirty seconds and already it feels too long.

"Well, then. Is there anything else, *boys*?" Huber says, making it clear who he thinks is in charge.

"Nope, just the propane… and this." I push Charlie's stuff closer to the till.

"Miranda, help these kids out so they can be on their way." He says her name with bite; his instructions sound more like an order.

Miranda rings in the air freshener and map book, and I notice her fingers trembling.

Everything I've done to get Miranda talking melts in Huber's presence.

"That'll be $32.07," she says.

I pull out my wallet and take out a couple of bills. Charlie scoops up his stuff as soon as her hands are on the cash.

With Huber being such a dick, I feel sorry for her. "It was really nice talking with you, Miranda. I hope you make it back to the city."

She forces a sad smile as we walk out.

chapter 30

We're almost to the car when I realize Huber has followed us out. Charlie immediately gets into a defensive position while I distance myself behind Dad's vehicle.

"Who the hell are you kids?"

Charlie channels his glorious inner punk-ass, opens the air freshener, and gives it a deep whiff. He savours it for a second before releasing a big, contented sigh. "Just a couple of customers."

"Don't bullshit me. What do you want?"

He takes a step toward Huber. "We were just wondering if Terry knew about you and Miranda in there?"

Huber looks like he wants to grab Charlie and rough him up, but there's enough people driving past on Main Street that causing a scene would be bad for business.

"What are you? Some little drugheads thinking you can roll on in here and bust my ass?"

"Nope," Charlie says. "It's just that you don't seem too broken up that Terry's gone missing."

Huber pushes Charlie against the car. "You suggesting I had something to do with that?"

I can see Charlie's pissed as he pulls himself off the hood and straightens his shirt, but he doesn't let it rattle him. "No. But I'm sure the police have some questions for you."

Huber smiles, shaking a finger at him. "See, kid, that's where you're full of crap. You came down here to threaten me and you've got nothing."

Charlie is unfazed and stares angrily at him. He's waiting. This guy is enough of a loud mouth that he just might fall into Charlie's trap and tell us exactly what we want to hear.

"I don't know who you are or what you want, but the cops? We're old buddies around here, and they know all about me and Miranda. When he kept breaking into her house, *I* was the one who called them. So don't try your empty threats on me or I'll be sure to talk to them about *you*." He pokes Charlie in the chest. "Now you and the black kid can get off my property. Make sure to never come back. Got it?"

I swing the propane tank into the back of the vehicle and am more than ready to leave, but Charlie stands his ground a moment longer. He sniffs the air freshener again.

"You know, this is kind of stale. Can I get a refund?"

chapter 31

I drag Charlie off Huber's lot before it comes to blows. It's a good thing Dad doesn't go there anymore—he'd for sure get terrible service if he ever took the car there again.

We drive down Main Street and I'm thinking we've had enough excitement for the day. Time to get the groceries.

"Expresso?" Charlie exclaims, out of nowhere.

"Seriously?" Now it's my turn to exclaim. "That's what got you riled up?"

He waves a dismissive hand. "She sounded like a hillbilly."

I stare at him and he's actually offended by her misuse of the word. I know he likes his high quality coffee, but seriously? "Um, hello? You almost got in a fist-fight with a dude in the middle of Main Street."

"So? It's *es*presso! *Ess.* Not *Ex*!"

I erupt into laughter so sudden and hard I almost can't breathe. I always think I know how far he'll go and then he surprises me again.

Charlie sighs. "But you, Shepherd. Colour me impressed. She played right into your tall, dark, and handsome charms."

"Not as much as Huber played into yours."

Charlie gleams at the thought. "Yeah, that was almost too easy."

"He's definitely a suspect."

Charlie glances over at me. "Still just a missing person case, Shepherd."

"I know. But he's not doing himself any favours."

"No," Charlie agrees. Then adds, "Did you see his fingernails? Really well kept. I think he even waxes the hair on his hands. The guy doesn't like getting dirty. Weird for someone who owns a garage."

"So he's not really a tough guy?"

Charlie considers it. "Possibly. I was pushing him pretty hard back there, and he should've taken a swing but didn't."

"Maybe he thought it would look bad?'

But Charlie's already shaking his head. "He could have gotten away with it. Two kids come in, causing trouble. And like he said, he knows the cops."

"So you were pretty sure he wasn't going to clobber you?"

"Well, not at first, but the more I pushed, the less likely I thought he would. He had all kinds of opportunity but didn't take it."

"Meaning, he has nothing to do with Terry's disappearance."

"Meaning, he's a pussy and would never do it himself."

"He could've hired someone to kill him."

Charlie slugs my arm. "Remember, Shepherd, Terry's not officially dead."

"Yeah, fine," I say sarcastically, "so you think Huber hired someone to politely show Terry the way out of town?"

Charlie takes it seriously, though, talking it through. "Huber dresses pseudo-rich with those logo golf shirts. He probably picked them up at some outlet mall so he didn't have to spend big money. He's either cheap or seriously in debt, so hiring someone to get rid of his girlfriend's ex would be the last thing he'd do."

I'm confused. "Then, what? Is he a suspect or not?"

"I don't know, Shepherd. This is just the way my brain processes things."

"And what about Miranda?"

"The secretary?

"Admin assistant," I snicker, but Charlie ignores me.

"She seemed pretty upset." Charlie's tone is thoughtful.

"And scared of Huber when he caught her talking to us," I add.

He nods his agreement. "But we shouldn't rule her out just yet. When you start snooping into these things, it's often the least suspicious person who's to blame."

Charlie pulls out his phone and taps away at it. "Turn left up ahead."

"Why?" We were almost at the grocery store. "Where are we going?"

"Miranda's. I think we need to do more than just scratch the surface, dig a little deeper."

I sigh, knowing whatever he has planned, it probably won't be legal.

chapter 32

We drive east from Main Street down a picturesque street. Tall pine and spruce trees border the yards. We pass the town's water tower and Charlie whistles at it.

"You could totally throw somebody off that if you needed to."

I stare at him.

"What?" he says. "I'm just saying it would be easy to fake a suicide."

"Is murder all you think about?"

"Hey, that's how we keep one step ahead of all the crazies."

"And you wonder why people shy away from you."

"Yeah, yeah." Charlie checks his phone. "Take a right on the boulevard after the hill."

Ah, information in the digital age! Everyone's private information at your fingertips, if you know where to look.

We crest a small rise and leave the rest of the town behind us in the valley. I turn south and the trees come to an end. The road opens into a double lane thoroughfare. Newer neighbourhoods comprised of long rows of similar-looking homes appear, their ornamental shutters and ornate house numbering are the only things that distinguish one from another.

"Man, even in small towns they go for this homogeneous esthetic." Charlie points. "Slow down... there."

I take another left until we get to the end of a long street. Miranda's house is at the end, a simple bungalow with an attached garage. Although the yard is well manicured, the only splash of character is the three giant garden butterflies fastened to the white vinyl siding. Tall lilac bushes separate her yard from a small alley that borders the farmer's field spreading out to the left of her property.

"Your mom likes those, doesn't she?" he comments now, pointing at the bushes.

I shake my head. "What you notice is freaky sometimes."

He shrugs. "Personally, I prefer the impatiens that border the sidewalk and driveway."

I gaze at the little white and pink flowers and laugh. "You done talking horticulture?" I ask, parking a few houses down from Miranda's.

Charlie studies the view. A neighbour mows his lawn, while a few kids play in a sprinkler in the front yard of another house. In the rearview mirror, two women talk at the end of a driveway and a teenager details his pseudo sports car with a chamois.

"There's an alley past the lilac bushes. Turn right there."

I follow his instructions and drive past the house and behind it.

"Go to the next street."

As we roll past, I see a young couple out walking and a little girl playing hopscotch on the sidewalk.

"One more."

I continue on and he assesses the next street.

"No nosey neighbours. Perfect."

I pull over and slip the car into park. "Okay. Now what, detective?"

"Follow my lead." He grabs his backpack and climbs out of the car. By the time I join him, he's fiddling with a piece of paper and studying the house numbers.

"What are you doing?" I ask.

"Faking we're lost."

We backtrack down the small lane by the field, pretending to search for a house in case anyone's looking out their kitchen window.

"How are we getting inside? This isn't a construction site or a house in the suburbs. People pay attention in small towns."

"I know."

I think he's excited by the challenge. "So what's the plan?"

"We go through the back."

"Just like that."

"Hey, last time we did this, we saved someone's life."

"Yeah. And all we had to do was deal with a psychopath." It's hard not to be sarcastic with Charlie.

"And wasn't it worth it?"

"Sure, but Terry's not likely to be jammed up in Miranda's attic, is he?"

Charlie tilts his head like Ollie when he thinks I have a treat.

"You don't really think Terry's in there, do you?" I ask.

Charlie shrugs. "Only way to know is go inside and case the joint. Look, Shepherd, the back door's probably not even locked. The rule of small towns is that they trust everyone."

We walk down the alley until we arrive at Miranda's lilacs.

The backyard is like the front: well maintained but lacking personality. The old fence running around the perimeter is held together by a few recently replaced boards and could use a paint job. We slip through its gate, behind the shed and into the yard. An open cement pad juts from the back door. She's got a barbecue and a patio table with two faded plastic chairs, but a potted geranium is the only thing adding any colour to the white exterior of the house or the grey concrete slab.

Charlie saunters up to the back door and points to the welcome mat. "See, she's inviting us in."

"You owe me a doughnut," I say, unhappy about the crime we're about to commit.

"Fair enough," answers Charlie.

He tries to twist the doorknob. Locked. He kneels down to study it. "Lock's pretty new. See, no scuffs or scratches."

"She must have changed them after she kicked Terry out."

He steps back and pulls up the welcome mat. Nothing. He drops it back in place.

"You can see where the key used to be under the mat," he says, "but she's moved it."

He crosses to the potted plant, lifting it. Nothing there either.

He studies the back of the house. "She really didn't want Terry back. If there was any hope of them getting back together, she'd've left the locks a little longer."

He kneels down and opens his backpack, pulling out a little zippered kit. Inside is a series of thin metal strips only a centimetre or two wide.

"What're those?"

"Lock picks. I made some in shop," he says.

"What happened to your bump key?"

"See that lock? Really high end. It's unbumpable."

"I thought it could get you in anywhere?"

"Too many unsavoury people were using them and lock manufacturers stepped things up."

I think about this. "But that kind of lock in a town like this…"

"Overkill, yeah."

"Do you think she felt unsafe?"

Charlie concedes to the idea. "Douchebag Huber did say Terry tried to break in a few times."

I'm getting anxious. "Can you hurry up? The neighbour's going to be done his lawn soon."

It takes him only a second and the lock pops open. He catches my glance. "It's called practice, Shepherd. Geez."

"Still weird."

He gestures to the open door. "Ladies first."

chapter 33

Here I am, uninvited in another stranger's house. I'm still not comfortable with it—which I'm thankful for. I hope it never starts to feel right.

"What are we looking for?"

"Any sign of involvement in Terry's disappearance."

"Like what?"

"I don't know. Does anything look out of place? Or too much in place? What's missing in this picture?"

"Could you be any more vague?"

"Use your instincts, Shepherd. You'll know it when you see it."

I shake my head and go to the front of the house while Charlie goes to the garage.

The whole place is very feminine. The interior decor is pastel shades and there's that cheap, mass-produced, designer art on the walls that everyone buys. I peer out of the small window in the front door and see the neighbours across the street. I can hear the guy with the lawnmower next door. I open the front closet to find nothing unusual, but, taking Charlie's words to heart, I note there's only women's stuff hanging in it, no men's shoes or coats.

If Miranda's dating her boss, he's not staying here.

Several framed photos of Miranda are scattered about, but there are none of anyone else, including Terry. A vase of flowers wilts on the dining room table, and in the kitchen, a couple of bills in her name lie on the counter, along with junk mail from a boat store. Beside this is an electronic tablet. I press the button and it's password protected, so I leave it, knowing I'll never crack it.

The stairs to the cellar are off the kitchen, and although my previous experience in a stranger's basement didn't end well for me, I move cautiously down them.

The whole space is a dusty-smelling, half-finished mess. There's a kind of secondary living room with ugly, dated furniture and shelves stuffed with boxes along the far wall. Light from the small basement windows spills inside.

There are a couple of framed-in rooms with half-finished ceiling tiles. One contains a washer and dryer, the other has a salmon pink toilet, sink, and shower.

At the back is what appears to be an office, filing cabinet and desk piled high with file boxes. A cheap treadmill covered by a stack of plastic bags filled with old clothes sits in the corner.

I can hear Charlie tromping around on the main floor, opening and closing doors and drawers. As I go back upstairs, I hear the toilet flush.

Seriously?

"Don't judge me. I had to go," Charlie calls out. How does he always know what I'm thinking? "Besides," he adds, "I was checking the bathroom."

We stand at the intersection of the hallway between the front hall, living room, and kitchen. Nothing seems out of place, too precise or in any way out of the ordinary. There's not much going on here. If a house reflects a person, Miranda has an almost empty personality. It's not cozy or comfortable. It just is.

"You see anything?" I ask.

"Nobody in the garage, if that's what you're getting at."

"Nothing up here or in the basement."

"No. It's pretty clean. Sort of—"

"Boring."

"She isn't interesting enough to be a killer," Charlie agrees.

"If Terry's even dead," I remind him. He smiles at me catching him on this.

We go back into the kitchen. There's a handful of magnets on the fridge, one advertising Huber Motors, and three little daisies that hold up a grocery list.

Charlie opens the fridge and grabs some sort generic diet cola.

It hisses and pops as he opens it, taking a gulp. "Delicious." He lets out a quiet burp.

He sees me staring. "You want one?" he gestures.

I decline.

"Not much here, Shepherd. If she was planning to dump him, it was in the works long ago. Nobody clears out that quickly, not even weekend guests." He takes another sip and his eyes fall on the tablet on the counter.

"Well, now, *that's* useful." Charlie smiles and sets his drink on the counter.

"Let me guess. You think you can figure out her password?"

He raises an eyebrow at me, accepting the challenge, and grabs his backpack. "This one? You don't even need to guess."

He pulls out a baggie and shakes out a small memory card and a paperclip. Popping open a little door on the side of the device with the paperclip, he slides the card in, then starts pressing buttons until the tablet restarts and text pops up on the screen. He taps and flicks his way through a couple of screens, confident in what he's doing. He yawns—I think he's actually bored—as he restarts the tablet again, and the next thing I know he's flipping through Miranda's photos.

"Emails are always good to read, but for my money, photos are the window to a person's soul."

But Miranda's albums are almost all food porn and selfies.

"There's nothing there," I say.

Charlie looks at me. "You'd think that, wouldn't you."

He scrolls to the bottom of her photo albums and opens the trash folder. "Everyone thinks deleting your photos after downloading them just whisks them away, but most photos require a double delete. Now, let's see what you've been hiding, Ms. *Ex*presso."

He stops at a photo of Miranda in underwear and high heels—at least, I think it's her. It's this kitchen, but the head is cropped.

"More like Ms. Sexpresso, am I right?" Charlie's got a big goofy grin, but when I don't bite, he finishes his stolen drink and continues zipping through the pics.

"Wait," I whisper.

"Yup, I saw it too." He stops and scrolls back up to a photo of her and Huber holding hands by a brightly lit water fountain in front of a large hotel.

"That's the douchebag, isn't it?" Charlie asks.

"Yup. And that place is in Las Vegas."

Charlie scrolls down some more until he finds a photo of the couple in an airport. "See the date stamp?"

Friday, the day Terry went missing.

"Timing doesn't work," Charlie concludes matter-of-factly.

"They're innocent," I say.

There goes the most obvious theory about Terry's sudden disappearance.

Charlie shuts the tablet off and ejects his memory card, putting it and the paperclip back in the baggie and into his backpack. He rinses out the drink can and finds a recycling bin under the sink.

"Really?"

"Hey, Shepherd, we all need to work together to save this planet. You ready to go?"

"Absolutely."

chapter 34

As I drive us back to the cabin, Charlie opens the map book he bought from Huber's.

"What is with you and maps?"

"What do you mean?"

"You can hack into computers and find out the most trivial details with a search engine, but here you are kicking it old school with paper."

He runs his hand over the page, studying every detail. "I don't know. I like seeing the lay of the land before me. Screens are always too small to get a good view. But here"— he scrutinizes his surroundings—"here, I can see how all the places in-between are connected." He leans in close, running a finger over the paper, then peers out the window across a field. "Like here, the road bends because past those trees, there's an inlet on the lake." He flips the page, continuing his journey on the map.

The pavement turns to gravel and a long poof of dust trails behind us. Trees and bushes grow to the edge of the road and I love how civilization suddenly feels so much further away.

"Do bears ever attack people out here?" Charlie inquires.

"Not that I've ever heard of. Why? You think Terry got eaten by a bear?"

"Maybe. Nature is the only thing that doesn't make sense. I don't trust it."

I don't know if he's serious, but Charlie goes quiet again. When I turn at the road to Dyson's Point, Charlie asks, "Do you mind if we stop by Diane's before we go home?"

"Um, okay?"

We pull up in front of her property. Lawn ornaments and wind chimes decorate her front yard. A carved sign says THIS BEACH LIFE and a four-wheel ATV sits in her driveway.

Charlie opens the glove box and takes out a scrap of paper and a pen. "I'll be right back."

As he walks to her front door, he scrawls something on the sheet. He doesn't knock but instead jams his note between the screen door and the frame. Then he goes over to a statue of a raccoon and slips something under it.

He gets back in the car.

"What was that?"

"Just a little medicinal aid."

"What?" I'm hoping it's not what I think it is.

"She's a nice lady, so I thought I'd leave her something."

"You've been carrying drugs around?"

"Relax, Shepherd. I just bought it."

"From where?"

"The dude who filled our propane."

"From Huber's?"

He nods.

"Who—? How—?"

"Don't blow a gasket. It's amazing what people share when you ask the right questions."

"Like what? 'Do you have drugs?'"

"Yeah. It's all about being direct. Anyhow, it's just a quarter and Diane could use it."

"And what? You left a note saying, 'Hey, it's Charlie. Here's some pot. Have fun lighting up.'"

He glares at me. "No, it's anonymous."

"So?"

"She's in pain. You know you're desperate when you're asking a perfect stranger for help."

I think about what he's saying.

"Not to mention lonely," he adds. "Who hangs out with her? Checks up on her? You?"

I don't say anything.

"I didn't think so."

Who would've thought: Charlie Wolfe is a humanitarian.

chapter 35

We pull up to the cabin and carry the bags of groceries into the house. Dad grabs them and unpacks the steaks.

"Wow, those are some nice cuts. We have you to thank, Charlie?"

"Nope, it's all Shepherd."

Dad glances at me.

"It wasn't me. I was given strict instructions of what to search for."

"Now, you'll have to excuse us, Mr. S.," Charlie says, pulling out the vegetables, "we have to get to work."

Dad picks up the eggplant, smelling it. "Nonsense. You got all this. Let me make it."

Charlie folds up the bags. "No way. A deal's a deal."

Dad leans in. "Charlie, every time we come out here the rules change and they never let me cook. Give me this one meal."

I can't believe I'm watching Dad almost begging Charlie.

"Fine," Charlie concedes. "But only because I have complete faith in you."

Dad reaches for a knife, but Charlie stops him. "You have to promise me though that you keep Mrs. S. and Heather's hands off it."

"Deal."

chapter 36

Dad asks me to set up the propane tank before I wander off, so I grab it from the trunk. After I screw it in, I see Charlie down by the shoreline and I grab a couple of drinks out of the fridge before going down there myself.

He's sitting on the dock, feet dangling in the water. He looks relaxed.

"Thirsty?"

"Thanks." He takes the can from my hand. "You don't seem like a pop-drinking family."

"Oh? What *do* we seem like?" I'm always curious to know how Charlie interprets us.

He shrugs. "More like some froufrou bottled carbonated water."

"Maybe with a hint of lemon?"

He nods as he cracks his can. He takes a swig and makes a face. "What is this?"

I'm already smiling. "Generic brand carbonated water."

"With lemon?"

"Lime," I laugh.

"Well, at least it's not soy milk."

We clink cans. "Amen."

A couple of pelicans soar by and we watch them swing behind some trees.

"So this whole lake is a part of a river system."

"Yup. Used to be a lot lower until they built dams further down."

Charlie contemplates the spot where his toes dip in the water. "So this was a whole bunch of land before?"

"That's why you see all those trees floating around." I nod to the tangled root system sticking up out in the middle of the water. "They flooded the place and all of that eventually got uprooted."

Charlie scrutinizes the lake. "You're saying that big old tree out there could be half a century old."

I shrug. "Don't know. Maybe less. Maybe more."

"And where do they go? Do they end up on shore?"

"Some do. Many follow the currents all the way down the river."

"So if Terry ended up in the lake, he'd be carried wherever the water took him?"

"Maybe. Or gotten tangled up in some underwater tree branches." It hits me how low our chances of finding this guy are.

Charlie perks up. "Well, if he's stuck down there, his body will start to decay, create gas, and float to the top like a balloon."

"You know too much about this stuff."

"It's about being informed," he says. "Trouble is, this water is freakin' cold and that'll slow the process. Then there's how far he sinks, what he was wearing, what the currents are underneath—"

Charlie screams and jumps up.

"Dude! What the hell?" I say, startled.

He flails desperately. "There's a thing on my foot!"

"Stop moving."

He holds up his foot and I lean over to study it. On the top of his index toe is a fat, juicy, black worm.

"That's a leech," I say matter-of-factly, "and a big one at that."

"Well, get it off!" he shouts.

I love this—I mean I *really* love it. I touch the leech with my finger, and it coils a little but stays attached.

"Frick! Don't play with it!"

Heather wanders down from the cabin. "What's all the hollering about?"

"Charlie's got a leech."

"Oh, this'll be good!"

I smile at her. "Heather, maybe we should be nice."

Charlie stares at us, his face filled with anxiety.

"Hey, remember that one leech of yours?" Heather asks.

"I was, what, six?"

She nods, enjoying tormenting the poor guy. "And you held my hand while you cried like a baby." She offers a hand to him. "Charlie, it's okay if you want someone for support."

"You guys!" he gasps. "Just get rid of it already!" He doesn't seem impressed by our humour.

"Come on, Heather," I prompt. "Give him a little dignity."

"Fair enough."

He cries out, "What do we do?"

Mom's coming down the path toward us.

"Charlie's got a leech!" Heather calls to her.

"I figured."

"Are you guys for real right now? It's feeding on my blood!"

Mom kneels beside him and takes his foot, studying it. "Charles, take a breath. You know, doctors sometimes use leeches in minor surgeries and even in plastic surgery. They secrete peptides and proteins that work to prevent blood clots. Who knows, this little guy could be used to help some-one with diabetes who might otherwise lose a limb."

"Please, Mrs. S., take it off," Charlie pleads, eyes wide with anguished hope.

Mom pulls a shaker of salt from her sweater pocket and sprinkles it over the little beast. Immediately, it releases and rolls off. "There."

I pick it up and toss it back in the water.

"Gross! And you swim out there?" Charlie shudders.

"There aren't that many. Seriously," I say. "And you saw how easy they are to remove."

Charlie rushes off the dock, several feet from the water. Mom, Heather, and I can't help but laugh.

Funny how a guy who can take a punch—or give a punch, for that matter—who isn't afraid to rummage through the carcass of a dead dog, or tangle with a serial killer, can freak out over something so small.

I guess we all have our limits.

chapter 37

Charlie insists on setting the table. He argues that he needs to make up for not cooking and embraces the whole process, not letting any of us help. I think he's enjoying it, which makes me wonder what supper at his house is like.

Dad doesn't fail Charlie. The steak is on point and the salad he made is insane. Charlie expresses his gratitude and fills his plate. Heather's eyes widen and she nods to his overflowing dish, but I wink back, knowing that Dad couldn't be more pleased by this unfettered appreciation of his culinary skills.

That my sister and I can communicate without speaking is one of the great perks of our relationship.

"Mr. S., what did you do with this lettuce? I've never tasted anything like it!"

"Three rules I always follow when making salad. First, a solid base layer of greens. Second, choose your flavours carefully. In this, I have ricotta, cherry vinegar, and warmed spices—"

"Warmed?"

"—at this hour, you want something that raises the body temperature for the evening. Cinnamon, cloves, ginger, mustard seed. Not too heavy. Just enough."

"And the third?"

"Drink plenty of wine and quit following dumb rules," Dad says, smiling.

Charlie smiles too, enjoying the banter. "Of course, in my case," and here he raises his glass and tips it toward Dad in a mock toast, "carbonated grapefruit water."

"Until you're of age, yes. Unfortunately, results may vary," Mom says jokingly as she pours herself some more wine.

"Right you are, sweet wife," Dad says, clinking his own glass with Mom's.

Ring ring ring.

Mom stares at the landline on the wall. It rarely makes a noise.

Heather rises and answers. "Hello?" She turns toward Charlie. "Yes... yes... two seconds..." She sets the phone down, scrutinizing Charlie. "It's for you."

He gets up from the table and picks up the receiver. "Hello?" He steps around the corner, the spiral cord stretching to its max, but we can still hear him from down the hallway. "Yes, this is Charlie Wolfe." He pauses as he listens to the person on the other end speak before replying. "Really? Oh that's good to hear." There's another long pause. "Yes. Okay, thank you."

He hangs up and sits back down, digging into his food. We all stare at him, wondering if we should ask.

"Charlie, what's going on?" I finally inquire.

"Oh, it seems I lost my wallet when we were picking up groceries. Some nice old lady turned it in."

"Really?"

"Yeah. Which is good since it has my ID and bank cards and few other sentimental photos and stuff."

Mom is concerned. "And how did they know to call here?"

"Not sure." He pauses, milking the moment, before snapping his fingers and saying, "You know, I did find the cabin number before I headed up here—in case I got lost."

Heather frowns. "Interesting, since the number's unlisted."

Charlie just shakes his head and grins as if Heather should know better before turning to Mom and Dad. "I don't suppose Shepherd could take me into town tomorrow to retrieve it?"

They know he's put them in a corner.

"If it's about gas money," he hurries to say, "I'll be happy to fill up the tank. I'd just really like to get my wallet back."

"Don't worry, Charles. You guys can drive in tomorrow," Dad responds. I can tell Mom wishes otherwise.

"Thank you, Mr. and Mrs. S."

We silently enjoy our food until Heather asks, "So, Charlie, how long are you staying?"

I'm a little shocked by her candidness. Whatever leniency she has for me is not allowed to Charlie.

"We said as long as he likes," Mom says firmly.

I think she totally gets Charlie's gig, and sees cases more unfortunate than his at her clinic. She might not know the details, but she understands where he's coming from, probably literally.

"'True friends visit us in prosperity only when invited, but in adversity, they come without hesitation,'" Dad quotes.

I roll my eyes.

"Theophrastus," Charlie replies, and Dad's impressed.

I feel a sliver of jealousy, but Heather pushes her point. "But you weren't invited."

Charlie flashes a smile. "Ah, but if I play my cards right, I may be someday."

"So we never did hear what adversity brought you here?" Sometimes my sister is very perceptive, but I can see her question has left him speechless.

Mom's fork clinks as she sets it down.

"Leeches, Heather," I interject, breaking the mood. "Clearly, he's here to protect us from the leeches."

"Oh, no, Shepherd. They're all yours," Charlie remarks.

I'm thankful when everyone laughs, even Heather. But I don't think she's done with him yet.

chapter 38

Evening takes us to the fire and a bag of marshmallows, and I watch as Charlie sets his first two on fire. I can't figure out how a guy with so many problem-solving skills can suck so bad at anything to do with nature or camping. By the third marshmallow, he gets the hang of it and I teach him how to pull off the toasted outside and eat the crisp gooeyness.

Eventually the night gets the better of my parents and they leave. Heather follows shortly thereafter and then it's just Charlie and me.

"Wow, your sister was totally cross-examining me at supper."

"Yeah, sorry about that."

"No, it's cool." He's animated.

"Yeah?"

"Totally. I'd hate to face off against her in court, though. She's scary."

I take the marshmallow stick from Charlie and set it just above some coals on the edge of the fire. "So, a nice old lady found your wallet?"

"Isn't that the darndest?"

"I don't suppose it was by the suppositories."

"You know, I'm not really sure. You fine with going in to-morrow?"

"So long as you don't wake me at the crack of dawn. I'm supposed to be on vacation."

"Whatever you say, princess."

"I'm guessing you don't only need a Wi-Fi fix?"

"Well, doughnuts, coffee, then Wi-Fi…"

"And then?"

"I'd like to know why Huber thought I was on drugs."

"Um. Dude. You *did* buy some pot from one of his employ-ees. Maybe he saw something or maybe they told him."

"Yeah, but why would he think I'd care enough to give him a hard time?"

"What are you talking about?"

"He called me a drughead and said something about us going there to bust his ass."

"Why would someone on drugs care about *him*?"

"Exactly. But that's not the only thing. Supplies are drying up in town."

"What do you mean? Like drugs?"

He nods. "That quarter ounce I bought? The guy said it was all he had and it was way too over-priced."

"So? Maybe he took you for a city boy and scammed you."

"He's not the only one."

I stare at him. "Diane?"

"Somebody was delivering to her and I want to know who."

"Does any of this connect with Terry?"

"It's about picking at threads, Shepherd. Sooner or later, I'm hoping something will unravel."

chapter 39

Cousin Rachel sits in Cup of Joan's, sipping her coffee and watching the pretty little thing who runs the place. The young woman works her way back and forth between the tables, taking orders, prepping, serving, and clearing the dishes away. Cousin Rachel remembers her own days working in the service industry—and hating every minute of it. Dealing with customers and all their needs and complaints. She'd come home grouchy and miserable, always needing time to decompress before spending time with her son and husband.

It takes a certain kind of person, she thinks.

Despite this Terry business becoming a hell of a thing to deal with, it hasn't fazed her. One man's stupid actions had burnt this whole town and there'd be no coming back here for a long time. But her bosses could move on to another place and set up shop and recover. They'd have to rebuild the infrastructure, forge new relationships, and find the right people to deliver. It would take lots of time, money, and patience, but there was always a demand for what they were selling.

Best of all, Cousin Rachel and her bosses dictated the terms, which made customer complaints a thing of the past. You can't pay up? Oh, well. Don't like how we treat you? Deal with it. Don't like our prices? Don't matter. Feel like we don't care about you? You're absolutely right.

She'd become a happier person after getting into this business. Despite the occasional layovers in towns like this one, she was generally able to arrive home relaxed, with enough energy to spend more time with her family, and be present in the moment with them.

She goes back to her to-do list. Although the restaurant around her is busy, she's not worried. If one of its nosey patrons does get curious about what this stranger is doing in town, they'd understand nothing if they glimpsed at her notes: a collection of code, initials, and chicken-scratch numbers that's difficult to decipher.

But Rachel understands all of it.

The writing at the top refers to a guy named Goat Friesen. When he wasn't hanging out at the Hillside Bar, he was pushing amphetamines and coke on the workers from the nearby potash mine who used his cocktail of drugs to get through their long shifts. The little symbol beside his name means that Cousin Rachel has dealt with him, sending him down a narrow, bottomless hole that he won't be getting out of again anytime soon.

She raises a hand and the waitress quickly comes over.

"Busy day for you," Cousin Rachel says.

"Yeah, but I can't complain. 'Busy is better than bankrupt,' my mother always said."

"Smart lady."

"Yes, she was. Want a top-up?"

"Yes, please. And the bill."

As the server walks away, Cousin Rachel can't help but admire her attitude. She could never have maintained one like it.

She goes back to her list. The series of coded letters below "Goat" spells out "Jeannie," aka Genie's House, who sold LSD, PCP, and ketamine out of her fashionable, upscale home on the hill. There's also a little symbol beside her name that indicates Cousin Rachel took her on a one-way road trip.

Unfortunately, Cousin Rachel's list of notations is incomplete. Little Joe, the one who had set her up with the dead guy, has been picked up by the cops. She doesn't like having him in jail; he might open his big, fat mouth if they try to intimidate him. She doesn't have enough resources or the appropriate contacts to deal with him on the inside, but as soon as she has a chance, she'll take care of him too.

The waitress brings over her bill and Cousin Rachel opens her purse. She tips well, not so extravagantly as to draw attention, but definitely far better than the locals, who probably don't respect the work this woman does for them on a daily basis.

She checks her schedule one more time. It's Monday. Little Joe will be released soon. The police won't hold him for too long because he kept his hands clean in public and was smart enough to distribute his stuff through a gang of young punks. Her plan was to greet him at his home, then take him out to a nice spot behind his salvage yard where she would slit his throat. She'd figured she could still make it to her son's competition on time.

She stands, gathering up her notebook and phone and slipping them into her bag. She gives her bill and money to the woman behind the counter dealing with a crotchety old hag who's upset that her meal hasn't yet arrived. As Cousin Rachel reaches the door, she can't help but think that, yes indeed, it takes a certain kind of person to deal with people like that.

chapter 40

When morning comes, I keep my eyes closed, listening to the birds chirp, not wanting to get up. Finally, I drag myself out of bed, only to find Charlie in the chair beside me.

"You've got to stop being so creepy," I mumble.

"You told me to let you sleep in, so I did."

I didn't expect him to keep his promise.

"It's not normal, you know, sitting beside someone and staring at them."

"I wasn't staring at you."

Right. "How long have you been there?"

"Not that long."

"Still, super weird. Hand me my shirt, would you?"

Charlie hands it to me and I put it on.

"Why didn't you go hang out with Diane?" I joke.

"She wasn't around."

"Really? You've checked already?"

"Of course. We going to chit-chat all day, Shepherd, or are we going to get going?"

"What about coffee? Or breakfast? Maybe a morning swim?"

"Coffee is made. And need I remind you that we will be having doughnuts for breakfast. And swim? With those gross bottom-feeders around? Not a chance."

I laugh and make my way to the kitchen. "I'll get you into the lake yet."

chapter 41

As soon as we get to town, we go to the grocery store and pick up Charlie's wallet. He isn't inside long and when he hops back in the car, he asks me to take him to Cup of Joan's.

Laurie's at the counter. "What can I get you two on this fine Tuesday morning?"

"Your tallest cup of coffee," Charlie says immediately before scanning the doughnuts. "What do you suggest for a breakfast of champions, Laurie? What's your favourite?"

"Can't beat the honey bourbons or the marshmallow bananas—"

"How about a classic, like a chocolate dip? Do you like something like that?" He gives me a sideways peek and I shake my head. Guy has a sugar addiction. Also, he doesn't give up.

She says, "Hey, you can never go wrong with them. They're always tasty."

"Then I'll take two"—he works it out—"actually, *three* chocolate dips to go."

I'm pretty certain I'll eventually get one of them, but I'm not entirely positive.

As she steps away to get the coffee, he turns to me. "You get that? She likes chocolate *dips*."

"Yeah, yeah," I say, laughing. "But you don't get to go there."

"Why?" he asks, grinning. "You offended?"

"No. But it's not your joke to make. And if Heather won't let me joke about it, why should I let you get away with it?"

"Got it," Charlie smiles. "I'm too vanilla for ya!"

I shake my head and am glad when Laurie returns with the doughnuts and coffee.

Opening his wallet to pay, he asks her, "So, where do all the cool kids hang out?"

She takes his money. "How cool are we talking?"

"Me cool."

She eyes him up and down. "I'd say Donnie's Pizza." She hands him his change, but he leaves it on the counter for her. "Behave yourselves in there," she adds.

I wonder what she means, but the bell on the door jingles. Charlie's already outside and I have to rush to catch up.

chapter 42

Charlie's chewing the last of his doughnut as we step into Donnie's.

I've been here a couple of times to pick up food when the fridge at the cabin was empty at the beginning of the season, but I've never come here in the middle of summer. The place is dark and grungy, nothing like Cup of Joan's. The space is small: five booths along one wall, two tables in the middle, and a long table across the far end.

A young couple, maybe my age, sits in one booth, while an older woman eats alone near the window on a mismatched chair with a cracked vinyl seat. In the kitchen, a guy in his thirties—likely a former dishwasher who now runs the place—drops a basket of fries into the fryer. Smoke and the hiss of steam fill the kitchen.

"Hungry?" I ask.

"Nope, still enjoying my doughnuts, thanks." He rubs his stomach.

I observe the empty seats. "Where is everyone?"

Charlie tracks down a door at the back, which leads down a hall and past the washrooms. Another door takes us to the top of a stairwell and the faint sounds of binging bells and music rise up from below.

"Arcade," Charlie announces.

As we descend, I keep my hands off the railing—who knows what's been on there? The walls are painted black, pockmarked with white dings in the plaster. The stairway opens to a larger space lit by black lights that reflect off scribbles of neon paint. The periphery is lined with pinball machines, old and new, and a pool table and foosball table grace the middle of the flashing, noisy room. Still, the place is jam-packed; there's someone at every game, playing or just hanging out and watching the points rack up. I follow Charlie into the mix, seeing kids who've barely hit puberty next to a couple of people who I'm sure graduated from high school several years ago.

When I see a pinball machine in the corner called *Dr. Dude and His Excellent Ray*, I feel it pretty much sums up the out-of-body experience I'm having. Its synthetic sitar music and tie-dyed, robe-wearing main character makes me feel like a traveller from the future. Everyone's clothing is a year or two behind, the music is from the '80s and '90s—power ballads and Europop—and I'm positive I'm likely the third or fourth, if not the first, black kid they've ever seen in their lives.

"This place be trippin', huh?" I chuckle over my shoulder to Charlie.

Nothing. He's gone.

I flip into search mode and am moving rapidly along the one side of the arcade looking for him when the trap music kicks in and strobes light up the room like psychotic paparazzi. If I was stoned, this might be enjoyable, but right now, trying to spot Charlie, it's downright annoying, like a trippy *Where's Waldo*.

A big guy about my age, probably on a hockey team judging by the haircut, is coming my way. I have a sneaking suspicion that he's not on his way over to help.

"You lost?" he asks.

"Nope. Just looking for a friend."

"I don't think he's here."

I glance at him. "Why not?"

"I'm pretty sure I'd recognize one of *your* friends around here."

I try to ignore this asshole and keep an eye open for any mid-height, shaggy-haired teens wearing a backpack, but he keeps trying to get in my face.

"Yo, buddy, I'm right here!" he says.

The music fades to a dull roar in my ears and I get ready for a fight. I might be able to land a punch or two at least, but he's solid and will likely take me out pretty quick. I'd feel a little better if I knew Charlie was nearby before continuing this conversation.

"Matt!" a blond girl yells, coming over to grab his hand. "What are you doing?"

"Just having a talk with my new friend here."

She stares me down and I can tell she's got the same winning character traits as her boyfriend. But apparently I'm not worth it. "What are you messing with him for?" she says dismissing me. "I got what I needed. Let's go."

Matt glares at me, unwilling to back down, so he leans in close. His stinking aftershave makes me want to puke. "You come in here again looking the way you do... I will personally drag you up the stairs and kick you into the street."

He tacks on a smile and I want nothing more than to give him a quick uppercut and bust a few teeth. But I hold back. He walks away and he and his girlfriend disappear up the stairs.

Someone calls me from behind, "Tony!"

I turn to see Ali, a girl I used to hang out with as a kid. Every summer we took swimming lessons together at the local pool and would go to a movie or the fair when it was in town. But as we got older, she wanted more from me than friendship and we grew apart, seeing less of each other every year until I quit hanging out with her altogether.

"Hey, Ali," I say, feigning excitement at the sight of her. I know it's a dick move to put on an act like this, but my blood is still boiling from my encounter with that asshole. In fact, right now Ali's actually a good distraction.

"When did you get here?"

"The pizza place or the cabin?"

"The cabin, silly. I know when you got to Donnie's. Your friend Charlie told me."

"You met Charlie? Here?"

"Where else, ya goofball?" She slaps my arm—hard.

Now I remember why she's never really been a dating option. "Where is he?"

She points to a motorcycle racing game, and there's Charlie. He's with two other guys, watching someone else get a high score. There's a paper cup with a straw sticking out of it in his hand.

I'm angry and relieved all at once. God! Is this how parents feel when they lose a kid? I want to punch him—but I won't.

I walk over to him and he keeps staring straight ahead. "Trey's up for high score," he says.

"Great."

He realizes it's me. "Oh, hey, I thought you were Ali!"

On second thought, maybe I will punch him.

"Where's *my* drink, dickhead?" I ask, pissed off.

"Ask Ali. She bought it for me." He's as casual as can be, and all of a sudden my brain pops like a pressure cooker.

I pull him aside. "Why would Ali buy you a drink?"

"She was just being nice. Besides, I told her she was cute. Girls like doing stuff like that." He sucks on his drink and then winks like the player he is not.

"Where the hell did you go?"

"Well, I went to check things out, learn a thing or two. I did tell you I was going and that I'd be right back, but you weren't listening. I came back to get you and you were gone! So the real question is where were *you*?"

"Dealing with some racist asshole!"

"Oh, yeah, I saw that. Pretty intense."

"You saw me? Why didn't you come help me out?"

"Did you *see* that dude? I didn't want to get in a fight with him. He seemed big."

I get in his face, anger burning a hole in my gut. I truly want to punch him but know how easily he can take me down. "What the hell are we doing here?"

He smiles. "Watching Trey."

"And who the hell is Trey?"

"Trey is… wait for it…" The group of kids cheers, throwing up their hands, high-fiving the guy on the motorbike video game. "Trey is the new champion!" Charlie rushes over to give Trey a fist bump.

"Good for Trey," I say flatly.

Charlie comes back to me. "So Trey is the champion. He lives nearby with his dad, who's a farmer and an MLA."

"An MLA," I repeat. *Where* is this going?

"Member of Parliament for his RM."

He can tell I have no clue what he's talking about. "Come on, Shepherd, keep up. His dad was elected to government for this area. His mom's in rehab and I think this is as badass as he gets." Charlie does a quick scan around the room before saying, "Now the guy next to Trey in the button-down shirt with the man bun? *He* deals."

"What?!"

"Don't worry. Soft stuff."

"You didn't buy any more, did you?"

"I didn't even buy my drink, dude. But your buddy, Matt—"

"*Not* my buddy."

"Yeah, yeah, Shepherd. Anyway, his girlfriend, the blond, she bought something off Man Bun over here."

"You learn anything else?"

"There's a couple hundred-dollar misdemeanors like public intoxication and tagging around here, but nothing too serious."

"Good to know," I say. Like I said, it's tough not to be sarcastic around Charlie.

"Oh, and that girl, Ali? She's made out with him and him and, oh, her." He points to three random people scattered around the place.

"Huh? How do you do it?"

"What?" he asks.

"Get elbows deep within minutes? I've been coming to this town for years and I don't know a sixteenth of this stuff."

"Because you don't go looking for it. I guess that's the difference." He finishes off whatever it is he's drinking—by this point I don't even care. "I'm done. Ready to go?"

He sets his cup down on a pinball game and heads up the stairs.

All I can do is follow.

chapter 43

"We need to go back to Miranda's," Charlie says as we get into the car.

"What? Why?"

"Because the circumstances around our missing person just got a lot more interesting."

Charlie must see that I don't quite follow because he explains, "Donnie's is where teens go for all their recreational drug needs. There was a lot going down in that arcade."

"It's a drug front?"

"Nah," he shakes his head. "That's where the cops have it all wrong."

"What do you mean?"

"Donnie's is the place to go, but they think Pete Johnson, the guy in the kitchen with the french fries, is trafficking."

"Isn't that the Pete that Miranda said Terry went out fishing with?"

"The same. But I don't know how legit any of her story is."

"You mean, they're not buddies?"

"Well, they might be, but people say Pete's always around during the week. Doesn't sound like he's the type to take a workday off to go fishing."

"So is he dealing out of Donnie's, or what?"

"Nope. He just turns a blind eye to it all. But the cops keep shaking the place down."

"So they know *some*thing's going on, they just don't know who's doing it."

Charlie nods. "Then on Saturday, the cops searched everyone: pockets, purses, backpacks, pat-downs—all pretty intense. They didn't find much of anything, but a guy named Little Joe got picked up and tossed in jail."

"And since Terry went missing around the same time—"

"Why would they spend a whole Saturday looking for drugs instead of for him."

"Unless they suspect Terry's involved," I add.

"Exactly," Charlie agrees. "Rumour also has it that Terry and Little Joe are buddies."

"Better buddies than he is with Pete?"

"Way better. They hang out, get drunk together, work on each other's cars… whatever it is that guys do."

I stare at him. "You really don't know, do you?"

He shrugs. "But it gets even more interesting. Yesterday, some tough guys showed up asking about him; they roughed up a few guys when they didn't get answers."

It sounds like something from the movies. "What? Like undercover cops?"

"Seriously, Shepherd? In this town? I don't think they'd go to such lengths."

"Then who were they?"

Charlie shrugs. "I don't know, but they don't sound friend-ly."

"So why back to Miranda's? There was nothing there."

Charlie doesn't answer right away. He seems to be ponder-ing something, then says, "Huber said Terry tried breaking into the house. Why?"

"Because she dumped him. He wanted things to return to normal."

"You saw the place. There was barely anything of him in it. That wasn't his world."

"Maybe she cleaned house, got rid of all the memories."

"When? Before or after her weekend trip to Vegas? Before or after she found out he was missing and the cops were hanging around? Whatever she may have tossed wasn't a lot. The place had such a woman's touch; he barely existed in it." He points at me like a teacher wanting the right answer. "So, what's so important that he needs to sneak back inside?"

"He wanted something."

"And we need to figure out what it was."

chapter 44

We turn and drive down the long street that ends at Miranda's house. I can't shake my nervousness. Breaking in once was bad enough—twice seems really dicey, like we're pushing our luck.

Charlie reads my mind. "I know you think it's a bad idea going back in there, but we'll be more efficient this time."

"You mean because we've been there before."

"No, because we know what we're searching for."

We do? "And what the hell is that?"

Charlie scratches at his shaggy hair. "Something Terry wants to hide."

"Are you serious?"

"What?"

Unbelievable. He really *does* think this is a perfectly sensible plan.

"Is this how you always work?" I say, "with only the vaguest of ideas of what you're doing?"

He nods happily. "Pretty much. The unknown is where the secret lies, and no one usually bothers to search there."

Right. "Why don't we just tell the police?" I ask. "They're already suspicious of him."

"Because they won't know what they're searching for."

"But neither do we!"

"No." He smirks. "But we *do* know how to think like a criminal!"

Guess he's got a point there.

As we approach, we see a police car parked across the street from Miranda's house.

"Seems like maybe someone needs a little extra protection," I observe.

"Yeah, maybe. Or maybe the cops want a second look too," Charlie replies.

I can't see a way to avoid them. "Now what? We tap on the window and say 'Excuse me, Constable, would you like to rock-paper-scissors to see who gets to go in first?'"

"Cheeky, Shepherd," Charlie snickers. Then he points, "Turn left."

I turn, driving away from Miranda's street and the police car.

"Pull over," Charlie says a few seconds later. "We can walk."

We climb out and double back, casually strolling into the alley behind the houses across from Miranda's.

Stucco garages and old fences with peeling paint border the lane and there aren't many sightlines into people's backyards. As we walk past a shed, a dog rushes up to the wood fence and barks loudly through a gap. I flinch at the sudden sound, but Charlie is unfazed.

"He's serious about protecting his territory," I say, hoping my dread isn't as obvious as it feels when the dog lunges again at the seven-foot fence and his head pops over the top.

"You go on ahead. I'll be there in a second," Charlie says over the barking as he unslings his backpack.

This isn't reassuring. "You're not going to do anything to the dog, are you?"

"Are you nuts? No!"

I don't know why I asked, but with Charlie, I'm never quite sure what to expect.

"Go on," he says again, waving me away. "I'll be right behind you."

I make some distance between Charlie, the dog, and me. The beast continues barking and I think Charlie must still be back there, when he suddenly appears beside me.

"What were you doing? Taking a piss?"

"Necessary actions."

I don't like the sound of that, but he doesn't let me ask anything else. "Keep moving to the end of the alley, then turn right."

"Toward Miranda's?"

He nods.

"And the cops."

"Yup."

I follow his instructions but keep having to slow down for him. He's ambling along, apparently without a care in the world. At one point, he even stops and picks a blade of grass and offers it to me; when I refuse, he cups his hands around it to make a whistle. It's like he's bored, waiting for something to happen.

I have to know. "Charlie, we're not going to try and get in there with that police car out front, are we?"

"Just wait, Shepherd," he advises.

We come to Miranda's street and Charlie moves down the slope of the road towards the field,

I'm nervous when I see the cops in the car. "I think they're watching us," I say.

Charlie doesn't seem to care; he's scrounging around at the edge of the field. "Hey! I haven't seen one of these in forever!" He brings over an old, brown beer bottle with a short neck. "They called them stubbies."

"I don't care," I tell him. "What are we doing?"

He shrugs. "Relaxing?"

Just then, the cop's lights flare on and the siren whoops as the car accelerates toward us.

"Shit!" I exclaim.

But Charlie just waves at the officer as the car turns down the alley in the direction we just came from.

"Where's he going?" Then I see it, a column rising up behind one of the houses down the block. "Is that smoke?"

But Charlie's all business now. "What are you waiting for, Shepherd? Time for us to move."

chapter 45

Charlie gets to Miranda's back door and is inside in record time. I rush in behind him.

"Did you start a *fire*?"

"Just a shed."

"Dude!"

"Let's say it was necessary. Now, shut up so we can think."

Who can think? My brain can't process much right now so I just watch as Charlie moves swiftly down the hallway into Miranda's bedroom. The window faces the street and through the sheer curtain I can see a crowd of neighbours gathering. Moments later, fire trucks show up.

Charlie barks at me. "Shepherd? Focus."

I turn and see Charlie moving back and forth, opening the bedroom closet and inspecting the whole space from different angles. I follow him back out to the hallway to a linen closet that he opens long enough only to shove his hand in to the back and study its ceiling before shutting the door.

"Any other closets?"

Dazed, I indicate the closet next to the front door.

This closet too he slides open and begins to examine, but he's already shaking his head, doubting the possibility of finding anything. Still, he continues the search anyway. Nothing. Frustrated, he slides the door shut.

He surveys the living room and I ask, "What about the basement?"

I lead him to the stairwell.

"I don't think Miranda came down here much," he says, studying the basement TV room. "No hiding spots for freak shows in masks here."

"That's good," I say, "because at this point I'd probably throw you in their path."

"I accept that," he chuckles.

In the laundry room, Charlie pushes aside a box. It leaves an outline of dust. Looks like nothing's been moved in here for quite a while. He studies the room's nooks and crannies before moving on to the bathroom.

"Yuck," he recoils, having stuck his head inside. "She never uses this place. No soap or shampoo… not even a towel." He steps out and opens the door to the office. "But there's lots of places to hide stuff in here, actually."

I shrug. "Charlie, I don't think we're going to find anything."

He scrutinizes the room, checking plastic bags full of clothes and opening the drawers of the filing cabinet. He picks up a dirty plastic container and gives it a sniff. "Whew. Stinks like… tuna? And hot sauce."

He sets it back down and studies the walls and ceiling here too.

I wish he'd hurry up. Too much time has gone by. "Are we done yet?"

But he's onto something. "Don't you see it?" He points up.

I shake my head, so he drags a chair over.

"This tile is way too dirty," he says. "Dirtier than the others." He reaches up and pushes the ceiling tile up and over with his knuckle. He steps precariously onto the chair's armrest so he's tall enough to reach inside. "I feel something. I just can't quite…" He pulls his arm out and reaches over to the next tile and tilts it up.

Plop.

A small wad of cash sealed in a clear zipper-lock bag falls to the floor.

"Oh, man!"

"Yes!" Charlie exclaims as he slides the tile back and hops off the chair. "*This* is why Terry was trying to get back in the house! He couldn't tell Miranda and she'd probably already given him all his stuff."

Charlie picks up the bag. It's filled with two stacks of fifties and hundreds.

"How much do you think there is?" I ask.

"Probably close to five thousand. That's a lot of spare cash, especially for a mechanic. Maybe our missing man had a side job."

"Charlie?" I'd like to continue this conversation, but we're running out of time.

He reads my mind. "Fine. Let's go."

"What are you doing with the money?"

"We're taking it."

"What? No. Leave it behind."

"This is our only clue to Terry's disappearance."

"So let the cops find it."

He sighs. "Look, I know they're suspicious about what he was into, but they'd have already come snooping around if they had anything solid."

He goes upstairs and peeks out the window. "All clear." He turns and hands me the cash. "Just in case, you take it."

"What? No!"

"Come on," he pleads.

"Put it back, Charlie."

"Shepherd, you know me. I'm taking this either way. But you're faster than me and if the cops are out there, I'd rather not be holding dirty money when they catch me and turn up my priors."

I hate when he puts me in this position. But we've been through enough that I feel I owe it to him to cover his ass. I take the bag of cash from him, pull back my sock, and slide it inside, hoping that it won't be too noticeable when I cover it with my pant leg.

"Oh shit, can you take this too?" He hands me a tiny baggie. "It's for Diane."

"More drugs? What is with you?"

"Relax. I didn't buy it this time. I just picked it up where I found it."

"Which is?"

"Near Man Bun."

"Off the floor?"

"Well, sort of."

"You picked his pocket?!" I can't believe this guy.

Charlie touches his nose, points at me, and smiles. I have the urge to hit him again.

"He'll never know where it went. Just stick it in your shoe, okay?"

I hear my brain saying that there's not much difference between a baggie full of cash and one with a quarter-ounce of pot, but none of this makes me happy.

"Come on, Shepherd. We've got to roll."

I flatten the baggie and slide it into the sole of my shoe.

"Thanks, man. Much appreciated." He goes to the door. "Still clear. Let's go."

chapter 46

We step into the backyard and pull the door shut behind us. The smell of smoke hangs over the neighbourhood. Hunched over, we strike out across the yard, through Miranda's fence and out into the alley. We're halfway down the lane when we hear a voice yell, "Stop!"

I freeze and so does Charlie.

Why'd I listen to him? When will I learn?

"Turn around, slowly." Two cops, a man and a woman, walk toward us from the end of the alley.

Charlie raises his hands and takes a step forward.

"Don't you move!" the male cop yells.

I feel sick. I'm not sure how small town cops operate, but situations like this are never good. I do note that the cops aren't in a defensive position, though; their arms are relaxed by their sides. Still, I don't want to make any wrong moves.

The plastic bag full of money sticks to my leg, digging into my skin under my damp pant leg. I have no clue if the drugs are still in my shoe—I can't feel the baggie. I hope it fell out somewhere in the backyard where it won't easily be spotted.

Charlie is visibly shaking. "I'm sorry, officer," he says. I've never seen him this way. "My friend was looking for me 'cuz we had a fight and I got pissed off and walked away."

The woman cop turns to me. "And what was the fight about?"

I wish I could play the part with the same elevated fear that Charlie is able to conjure, but I'm too scared to focus. "Uh, a girl."

"And it's just a coincidence that we have a fire burning one street over from where two teenagers happen to be out for a walk?"

Charlie sighs. "No, officer."

Wait, what?

"I think maybe my cigarette started it."

What the hell is he doing? I've never even seen him smoke. Does he know what trouble we'll be in? I take a breath, intending to say something and the cop looks from Charlie to me.

"It was an accident," Charlie continues, a bit louder now, not giving me the chance to interrupt, "I was pissed and smoking and I think the cigarette I tossed might've started it."

The female officer moves in closer to me. "Is that what happened?"

I hope my poker face is working because I'm sweating bullets.

"Officer? Honest, I can prove it," says Charlie, who keeps pulling their attention away from me, but my mind spirals— how can he prove it? Oh God, this is so bad.

"May I?" When she nods, Charlie slowly lowers his hands and reaches into his pocket to pull out a pack of cigarettes and an expensive metal lighter. He tosses them on the ground.

Where did those come from?

"And what about your friend, here?" Both officers glance over at me, assessing.

I can barely meet their eyes.

"Please, it was my stupid mistake," Charlie insists. "He was just trying to find me."

The man ignores him. "How did you get here?" he asks me.

"We drove."

"Where's your car?"

"Down the street." My hands are still up, but I indicate the car's general direction.

"Can you take us to it?"

I nod.

The male cop walks behind us while the female cop stays beside me. Charlie seems to have diffused their concern, but I worry they may yet spot the wad of money in my sock and this makes me very nervous.

The female officer takes out a notepad. "What are your names and your parents' names?"

"I'm Anthony Shepherd. My dad is Ben and my mom is Keya."

"Do you have ID on you?"

"It's in the car."

"Do you live nearby?"

I was hoping they wouldn't ask that since we have no good excuse for being in this neighbourhood. "No, we're staying across the lake."

When I glance over, I see both officers staring at us, but Charlie keeps up the act and says, "Again, officers, sorry. This is my fault. We were checking out the town, I brought up the girl, we got in the fight. Then I jumped out of the car and he had to chase after me."

I don't know if they believe it—I don't know if any of us do—but they let it slide for the moment.

"Well, Anthony, we're going to take your friend in and ask him a few more questions. We want to be sure he didn't start the fire on purpose."

I wait for Charlie to say something, but he doesn't argue. In fact, he says nothing at all and even seems to agree with the plan. And since he hasn't given them a reason, they haven't handcuffed him... yet.

We emerge from the alley and I point the officers to where my car is parked on the street, but instead of following me there, they stop at the corner of Miranda's street. Smoke no longer rises from behind the houses and one of the fire trucks is just pulling out down the street.

"Can I have a number to contact your parents, Charles?"

"Unfortunately, they're not around."

The officer addresses me. "Is he staying with you?"

When I say yes, the officer asks for Dad's number, adding, "We're going to call your father when we're done with him, okay?"

I answer, "Okay," because what else can I say, but I can't stop thinking of the world of trouble we're in. My parents are fairly reasonable, but I don't think either of them will appreciate having to pick Charlie up from jail. And I hate the idea of having to lie to them about all this.

As Charlie and the officers walk to their cruiser, he turns to me. "I'll talk to you shortly. Tell your folks I'm sorry for the trouble."

"Yeah, no kidding. You'll be okay?"

"Hey, these officers are really nice. I'm more than okay."

And for the first time, I wonder if he planned this all along.

chapter 47

I walk to my car and peek down the alleyway. The remaining fire crew continues to hose down the smoldering wood and ash of the shed, but nothing around it is burnt. Charlie seems to have pulled off a very controlled burn.

The cops drive by, with Charlie in the backseat.

He's smiling.

I climb in Dad's car and inhale a long breath, pull out the bag of money and slide it under the seat. I can't leave it in the car or my parents will find it, but I don't want it on me. When I get to the cabin, I'll need a place to store it before we go back to the station.

I drive out of town, running through the various conversations I could have with my parents about what happened. I think the less I say the better. The trees zip by as I drive past the turnoff to the resort and travel over the bridge toward the cabin.

Ring ring. The sound of my phone over the car speakers startles me. Although I keep the phone on, it rarely rings when I'm at the lake. My buddies send me the occasional text message, but when I'm away, I'm mostly off the social grid.

Ring ring.

I study the console display. The number is familiar, but I'm not quite sure who it is. I hit the pickup button on the steering wheel. "Hello?"

"Hello, Anthony?" The authoritarian voice of Detective Gekas cuts through the speakers and I feel my whole body go tense. It can't be a coincidence that she's calling so soon after Charlie was picked up by the local police. "Anthony?"

"Sorry. Hello, Detective Gekas."

She'd only called me once after finding Sheri to see how I was doing and to tell me that she'd contacted victim services to make sure I had the proper assistance. I appreciated her kindness back then, but I'm suspicious of her reason for calling now. I want to know what she knows, but at the same time I'd really like to toss the phone out the window.

"How's your summer going?" she asks.

I can't tell if this is small talk or if she's sniffing out the situation.

"Good."

"You're keeping busy?"

"We're at the cabin."

"You and your family?"

Does she suspect that Charlie's around? She must. Should I tell her? I'm not sure. "Yes. We come here every summer."

"That's nice," she replies. "It's good to get away from the city."

"It is."

"Have you heard from Charles, Anthony?"

And there it is. Time to either fess up or shut up.

"Yes. He's visiting us."

"Really." She doesn't sound surprised. "When did he get there?"

"A few days ago. You know Charlie—I think he might've hitchhiked." I need to quit supplying her with unnecessary information.

"Yes, I do."

"I think he's having a good time. He's sort of a city boy."

Shut up, Tony!

"I've been thinking of heading north myself…"—Don't come here, don't come here—"but it can be difficult to get time off."

"Sounds rough," I say.

"So, you're okay?" she asks.

"Yes. I am." I say it with a smile, hoping to sound legit.

"Glad to hear it, Anthony. Now then, do you want to explain to me why, moments ago, I received a phone call about Charlie from your local police?"

Shit.

"Umm…" World-class liar, I am not.

"Anthony, why is Charlie being questioned about a fire he may have started?"

"It was an accident?"

"Anthony."

"He— I—" I quit talking to stop digging my own grave.

"Anthony, you need to be honest with me. You two aren't getting yourselves involved in the missing person's case up there, are you?"

Yup, she knows everything and my silence isn't helping.

"You know, Anthony, after everything that happened last fall, my name is all over your and Charlie's files. Something happens involving the two of you, I'm going to know about it. And you two aren't vigilantes or superheroes or detectives, either. What happened before was luck, and even so, you made a mess of things and we were very fortunate that we were able to put him away and that you didn't get anyone hurt, including yourself."

The line goes quiet and I wonder if the connection has dropped, until she speaks again.

"I'm grateful for what you and Charles did. But I need to know that nothing bad is going to happen to you."

Holy shit, I think Gekas just thanked us *and* gave a damn about our well-being.

"Do you understand? Whatever you boys are up to, you need to stop."

"Okay."

"You have to give me your word, Anthony."

Crap. I know Charlie, and promising Gekas that he'll drop the search for Terry won't mean a thing.

"Anthony?"

"Yes. I give you my word."

"Thank you. Say hello to your parents from me."

"I will."

"Goodbye."

I hear the *be-boop* of the hands-free system disconnect, and I let out a long sigh.

chapter 48

I'm almost at our cabin, but first I take the quick detour over to Diane's. Getting rid of some of the illegal stuff I'm carrying around before the horrible task of telling my folks that Charlie's in jail is the first step to getting out of this mess.

I climb out of the car, baggie in hand, and make for the raccoon statue. I'm almost there when—

"Anthony?"

Oh, man. I don't have time for this.

Diane's coming around from the back of her cabin. Her skin has been cooked by the sun and her unkempt, white hippy hair is tied up, though it flops down like a mop. Her long denim dress swishes through grass and pinecones as she approaches.

"It's been you?" She seems surprised.

"No, not really. My friend, Charlie…"

"Oh, the young gentleman from the other day?"

I don't think he's ever been described in those words. "Yes, he thought you could…" What? Smoke a bowl? Toke up? Ugh… get me out of this.

"Well, tell him thanks."

"I will."

She flexes her hand in and out of a fist. "When it's warm, it doesn't hurt as much. But when the cold arrives, it hurts like a hell dog."

"Charlie said your… medication helped."

"Indeed. Last week's rain made me feel like someone was yanking at my bones, and with Terry gone, I had no way to stop it."

Wait. What? Hearing his name come out of her mouth is a shock. "Terry?"

"Such a worry that he's missing."

"You knew him?"

"I was his elementary school teacher," she says, smiling. "He was always in trouble. Always a follower. But he had a good heart. Used to like staying around and cleaning the chalk brushes after school." She pulls herself up straight and I see the pain and stiffness of her back in her face. "Your friend is like that too. Good, but I see the trouble in him."

The thought of Charlie in jail makes me tense and my mind goes back to work on how I'm going to explain it to my parents.

"Well, I should be going," I say, then realize I haven't handed over the little baggie of pot in my hand. I cross over to her, holding my closed fist close to my side. She senses my awkwardness and takes it from me, much more cavalier about the exchange than I am, not worrying who sees us.

"Tell your friend thank you and that I hope he finds what he's searching for."

Huh? Find what? What does she know that I don't?

She nods to her ATV and says, "And if you boys ever want to take it out for a spin, you let me know. I'm not riding much these days."

Are you kidding? After I talk to my folks, we'll never be allowed out of the house again.

chapter 49

I pull into the driveway and Ollie greets me at the car. He's always accepting—and at least I know he won't judge me over what's about to happen. I give him an appreciative head scratch before I step onto the deck and go around the corner.

Mom and Dad are stretched out on the outdoor couch, each with a mug of coffee, their feet tangled together. Dad's reading a book while Mom's playing solitaire on a tablet. They're clearly relaxing in the sunshine. And I'm about to throw a grenade into the middle of it all.

"Good day exploring?" Mom asks.

You don't know the half of it. "Sort of."

Dad gazes up from his book. "Well that doesn't sound very good."

"No," I say, steeling myself, "not exactly."

"Did Charles not get his wallet?" Mom moves her gaze from her tablet to where Charlie should be standing next to me. "Wait, where is Charles?"

Here we go.

"That's a great question, Mom."

They both shift in their seats and stare at me, no longer playing footsies.

I hang back, deciding what to say next. "You see, here's the thing—" I start.

"Did he run off again?" Mom asks, a note of concern in her voice.

I shake my head.

"So he's still here?" She seems puzzled.

"Yes."

"Is he hurt?" Mom's questions are increasingly intense and I'm not sure how to deflect them.

Dad takes Mom's hand. "Let him talk, Keya."

Mom gives Dad a frown that I've seen a few times before, but she soon softens.

"Charlie's fine," I say. I take a seat across from them. My leg is sweating against the plastic bag of money I now wish I'd found a hiding place for before coming out here. Only way out of this mess is through. "He's in jail."

Their calm vanishes. "What?!" they say in chorus.

"We were hanging out in town and—"

The screen door of the cabin swings open and Heather steps out. "Did you say Charlie's in jail?"

I try to interrupt her interruption, "I'm trying to explain—"

"This I've got to hear." Heather plunks herself down right between Mom and Dad.

"Like I was trying to say, we were in town, hanging out..."

As I do my best to explain, the three of them stare at me. I'm pretty sure they're not believing any of my story.

"See, Charlie met a couple of girls yesterday…" I shrug like this should be self-explanatory, but their expressions tell me it isn't. "And he got their numbers and wanted to call them today"—the hole I'm digging is getting bigger—"but it turns out the numbers they gave were fake. So then we were checking out their neighbourhood."

"Their neighbourhood?"

I realize I'm stumbling. "Uh, yeah, we dropped them off the other day."

Mom nods, but I know she's not buying it. I need to change things up and fast.

"Okay, it's all a lie."

Heather leans back, looking vindicated, and I wonder just how deep her suspicions run.

"I— We—" I struggle to find a balance between the truth and fiction. "Charlie was smoking—"

Mom's eyes narrow and I dread finishing the sentence, though I do anyway.

"—a joint. He was smoking pot and he tossed it. He thought it was out. I guess he was wrong."

I figure a lie that makes Charlie out to be a troublemaker is more believable than one that makes us look like idiots.

"It, uh, started a fire," I say, breaking the silence, "and when we saw the smoke, we freaked out and ran and two cops stopped us."

Mom crosses her arms. Oh, we're in so much trouble.

I don't stop talking, hoping if I say enough she'll quit glaring at me. "Charlie stepped up and took the blame. He didn't tell the whole truth—he told them he was just smoking a cigarette—but he didn't want to get me into trouble." I reach into my pocket and hand the cop's business card to Dad, who seems to be the only one not ready to explode. "The officer gave me this. He asked you to give him a call."

Mom doesn't move at all. "Ben, why don't you go in and find out what happened?"

Dad takes the card from me and reads it, flipping it from front to back, before heading into the cabin.

Heather shakes her head. "I knew he'd do something like this."

Mom doesn't take her eyes off me and I hold her gaze despite how awful I feel. I try to look apologetic—it's not hard; I feel terrible for lying—and remind myself to stop talking now. Charlie's right: I might just be the worst liar in the world. I find myself counting backwards in my head, but I can't tell if I'm counting down the seconds until Dad comes out of the cabin or if it's my mind totally lagging in this situation.

When Dad comes out he speaks directly to Mom, the woman who holds my future in her small and mighty hands. "I spoke to Constable Brandon and he repeated what Anthony just told us. There was a small fire and Charlie has taken responsibility for starting it. Charlie will have to spend the night, given his history, but they also need to confirm that his legal guardian will release him to me."

This seems to distract Mom from her anger. She appears to be thinking about it.

I may yet live.

"Mom, I know Charlie's not a saint, but he's also not a bad guy. He does a lot of dumb stuff, but I trust him. I think he cares."

Dad sits down across from Mom. "Keya, I know this isn't what we expected when we agreed Charlie could stay with us, but perhaps we can look at this as an opportunity to help him. We could send him back to the city, but I think we should make a different choice."

My parents are both good people, analytical and strong. Maybe it will be okay. She studies him, knowing what he wants.

Finally, she leans forward on the couch and takes my hand. "Do you trust him?"

"Completely," I say, realizing I mean it.

"And there's nothing else going on?"

I know the right answer. I know I should tell her about Terry and at least some of what we've been up to. Hopefully Terry will be found soon and we won't have to lie anymore.

I shake my head and say, "No. Nothing else."

Mom doesn't let go of my hand and I know she's trying to read me and decide whether or not I'm telling the truth. All I can think is that I'm a terrible liar. And a terrible son for lying to her.

I force myself to hold her stare and stay neutral. It must be enough because she nods and releases her mind-meld on me, but there's something in her eyes when she says, "Go in, clean up, and help your father with supper."

"Okay." I stand and walk toward to the deck door.

"Anthony?"

I turn back. Mom's sitting on the edge of her chair, an apprehensive look on her face.

"I know that you and Charlie bonded over the tragedy last fall. I get that. And I don't want to stand in the way of your friendship. I think you're a good influence for him. But we also want you to be safe."

"Okay."

She seems to have come to a decision—I can see it in her face—but all she says is, "Go on inside now."

As I go into the cabin to wash up before joining Dad in the kitchen, I think about how lucky I am. Charlie and I could've been caught coming out of the house, the fire could have been bigger, I could've been taken in with Charlie, and now my parents aren't freaking out as badly as I expected.

I'd like to hold on to this lucky streak and not jinx it—but I'm pretty sure Mom hasn't believed anything I just told her.

chapter 50

In the morning, Mom and Dad are up early. I smell the coffee and toast from my bedroom, so I don't procrastinate but get up and go straight to the kitchen.

"Good morning," Mom says, her tone neither chipper nor grumpy.

"Morning."

"Toast?" Dad offers.

"Sure."

He puts two slices in the toaster and turns back to his coffee. We don't say much. The toast pops. I butter it, eat it, and wash it down with a glass of orange juice.

"We're leaving in a few minutes to deal with Charlie," Mom says.

"I'm coming." I bite my lip after it comes out. "I mean, would it be okay if I came?"

Dad and Mom do that thing where they just give each other a blink and it's a whole sentence.

"Sure, you can ride along."

I rush to the bedroom to change my shirt and spot the suitcase I jammed the bag of money into last night. I'm worried Heather will snoop while we're out, so I quickly assess the options. I've never really had to hide anything before. Knowing I don't have much time, I slide out the bottom drawer of the dresser and push the money to the back before pushing the drawer back in.

Moving quickly, I wash my face and brush my teeth, then hustle out to the car.

chapter 51

I sit in the back seat and we drive in silence. It occurs to me that today is Wednesday, the last Wednesday of the month, in fact, and I'm five hundred kilometres away from Sheri's grave. I hate not being there to remember her, but I feel worse for having forgotten amid the buzzing rush of the past few days.

"Hey, Dad, how about some music...?" I ask, hoping for a distraction from my thoughts.

Mom stops him. "You know, I'm enjoying the silence."

Dad glances at me in the mirror. "Me too."

This is terrible—I'd rather be doing chores. It's a new sort of torture, leaving me alone with my thoughts and worry as I watch the countryside fly by.

Finally, I can stand no more. "Are you going to send Charlie home? He's really not a bad guy, despite this."

Silence.

"I think being out here in nature may be really good for him," I try again.

Nothing.

"Okay. Well, just my opinion."

I give up and shut up. I should know better than anyone that once they've decided on something, it's unlikely they'll change their minds.

The rest of the trip feels like forever and when at last we pull up to the police station, I'm grateful. But Mom and Dad just sit there, not leaving the car. It's the first time they've ever had to pick someone up from jail—I'm guessing that even at her worst, Jodi never did anything like this.

Then Dad takes Mom's hand and she flashes him a brief smile before opening her door.

I start to open my door too, but Mom quickly shuts me down. "Nope. You're staying here."

I know not to mess with her when she's using that tone. "Okay." No point in pushing my luck. I'm just happy that they're even willing to help Charlie out.

They walk across the street and into the police station, and again I wait for what feels like an eternity.

When they finally come out with Charlie by their side, he seems fine, like they've just picked him up from summer camp. He doesn't look like someone who's just spent the night in jail. He squints in the sun, but he's smiling and talking like he's trying to tell them a story.

Mom's not having it, but Dad listens and responds.

They cross the street and pile into the car. Charlie scoots into the back seat beside me.

He leans forward. "I don't suppose we could grab a coffee?"

"No," Mom answers curtly.

"I can pay?"

"Charles, I said no."

He settles back into his seat. "Fair enough, Mrs. S."

Dad pulls out and we head for home.

Charlie looks over at me. "Hey."

I smile weakly. "Sleep well?"

"Not my greatest ever, but I'm not going to complain."

Mom turns on the radio—opera—and she cranks it loud, drowning out any conversation we might have. Even this doesn't appear to faze Charlie; he merely closes his eyes and listens, his eyebrows moving in harmony with the highs and lows of the woman's plaintive cry. Between songs, he even has the balls to say, "This is fantastic, Mrs. S. That's Maria Callas, right?"

When she doesn't answer, he listens some more then nods to himself. "Yeah, I'm pretty sure it's Maria Callas."

And that's Charlie Wolfe: punk-ass, petty criminal, opera lover, and thorn in my mother's side.

chapter 52

Charlie talks all the way home. No one picks up the other end of the conversation, but it doesn't stop him. He covers every subject that comes to his mind: how the internet is similar to a forest's ecosystem, what he noticed in his second reading of *Infinite Jest*, or most surprisingly, how he believes the local police service need more officers and funding.

Mom stares out the passenger-side window and Dad keeps watching me in the rearview mirror, so I purposefully keep my eyes forward. I can't tell if Charlie's oblivious to the tension in the car or whether he's doing all of this intentionally, but he seems determined to share his every thought.

When we arrive home, Heather's tanning in a chair, Ollie's at her feet. He sees us and sits up but doesn't come over. Even he knows something's about to go down.

Mom gets out of the car and walks to the house. "Charles and Anthony," she says over her shoulder, "can you come inside, please?" She holds the door and waits for us.

Dad goes to the stove and sets the kettle to boil while Mom takes a seat at the table. She motions us over and indicates that we should sit too. Uh oh. Tea time.

I'm aware of what's about to happen, but when Charlie raises an eyebrow of curiosity, I just shrug.

Dad brings over four cups and a selection of tea and puts it all down on the table.

Charlie pushes his away. "No, thanks."

Mom pushes it back. "Actually, you will."

Charlie's brow furrows. He isn't used to this.

"I'm really more of a coffee person—" he tries.

"I understand that, Charles, but right now, I'm offering you tea. Do you have any allergies?"

"Not that I know of," he answers.

"Let's see," she says, slowly going through all the choices. "Something relaxing. A nice chamomile." She nods her approval. "Have you ever had this?"

"No," he says, with that charming smile of his, "but I'm willing to try something new."

Good job, Charlie. It goes quicker if you cooperate.

While Dad brings over the boiled water to fill each cup, Mom dunks a bag in each one but holds onto them, checking her watch and letting them steep. Tea is a ritual, a process that requires time and patience, and I think that's why she insists on it for these heart-to-heart discussions.

"Charles, the police told us the fire was an accident," she says.

He nods.

"And your cigarette started it?"

"Yes," he says.

"And that's it?"

"Yes," he repeats.

She pauses, watching him, waiting.

I can see him trying to read her, but she's deadpan. Unlike when I was questioned, he keeps his mouth shut and smiles.

"Nothing else you want to add?"

"Nope," he shakes his shaggy head.

"Charles?"

"Yes, Mrs. S.?"

"Anthony already told us."

"Oh." He doesn't look at me. "Okay." He points to the tea, "It's been two minutes. Can I have mine now?"

Mom looks at her watch, surprised that he's aware of this fact. Maybe she's also realized that he's not going to be as much of a pushover as I am. She relents and hands over his cup.

"If it was only a stupid mistake…" She pauses, hoping he'll bite.

But he merely nods and takes a big gulp of tea. "Wow, this is pretty good—"

Mom cuts off his compliment. "Did you start the fire on purpose?"

"No," he answers quickly.

"Charles?"

"No, ma'am."

"Are you two up to something?"

"No." Now his answer seems a little *too* quick.

Mom turns on both of us now. "We know someone's missing around here. We're not oblivious to that fact."

Shit.

"If you two are involved in anything to do with that, then that's it for both of you. Do you understand?"

I'm surprised to hear us both quickly respond "Yes."

"But if you're telling the truth—" She seems to be going over it in her head. "And the officers did say it was an accident…"

"You have quite a list of priors, Charlie," Dad interrupts, "and by picking you up, we have now taken responsibility for you, to make sure that you're safe and that we can manage your visit without causing any more problems for the police—"

"Or us," Mom interjects.

Charlie casts his eyes down at his cup. "I understand."

"This is your one chance. Can you be a good citizen of Shepherdtown?"

Charlie takes another long sip. "I'll do my best."

"That's all we ask."

"Okay."

"Nevertheless, no more wandering, no more unnecessary visits to town, no more run-ins with the law. You are on lockdown until further notice. Do you understand?"

I'm sure Charlie has never before been told these words by a parent and I don't know if Mom fully understands what she's asking of him. I hope Charlie understands that my parents are doing this because they care about him and that he fully appreciates how much shit he's in. Although he can disappear like a ghost in a city full of delinquents, he really stands out here.

"I get it. I'll keep things on the down low."

"Good. Now take your teas and go outside."

I stand, but Charlie takes the pot of hot water and tops up his cup. Mom and Dad stare at us and I want to go, but now Charlie has something to say.

"I'm sorry, Mr. and Mrs. S., for everything. I do appreciate all that you've done. I really do. Needless to say, the idea of parental concern has never been really front and centre in my life, so I've never really known what it's like to let anyone down before."

Mom's face softens and she reaches across the table to squeeze Charlie's hand. "Okay. Go on, you two. We'll call you for lunch."

chapter 53

Charlie and I go outside. Heather's still tanning in the chair, seemingly asleep, but I know better. She's heard everything. We move past her and walk down to the shore with our cups of tea.

Charlie sits on a log, keeping himself at a distance from the water, while I drop down on the dock facing him.

I expect us to sit in silent consideration for at least a minute, but Charlie doesn't wait.

"So, you'll never guess who I met in jail?"

"Charlie!"

"What?"

I point toward the cabin, "After everything you just promised?"

"But Shepherd, we can still talk."

I lower my voice. "You just lied to their faces."

"So?"

"Doesn't it bother you?"

"Of course it does," he says. "And I know you feel bad about it."

"Definitely," I say.

"Good, because you should." He slides closer to me. "Now, guess who I met."

"No."

He sighs, annoyed, but my lack of interest doesn't stop him from blurting, "Little Joe! I know, right?"

I'm pretty sure he doesn't even need me for this conversation.

"Charlie, we aren't doing this."

"Why not?"

"Because you just told Mom and Dad—"

"Nothing. I said I understood what they were saying, that I'd stay on the down low, and that I won't wander far from the cabin. I get all of it."

I get where he's going with this. "But you didn't promise not to talk about it."

He taps his nose.

Even if I said I wanted no part of this, he wouldn't listen. And if I give him this, he'll find another way to bend the rules. Once he sets his sights on something, there's no end until he finds the answers he's looking for. Either I sit on the sidelines, or I do my best to keep him out of trouble. And yet somehow I think that he actually believes he'll be able to keep the agreement he's made with Mom and Dad.

"Fine," I sigh. "Who's Little Joe?"

"Terry's buddy? The guy who got arrested."

Right. I remember Charlie telling me about him after our visit to Donnie's. Then I realize. "Wait, did you actually go to jail just to meet him?"

He picks up a stick and digs in the sand. "See, he was the guy who probably had some answers—"

"You went to jail on *purpose*?" I can't believe it. "Do you know how insane that is?"

"It's not like I haven't done it before."

He's right.

During our search for Sheri, Charlie had himself tossed in jail so many times that Detective Gekas eventually had to kick him out.

"You aren't normal," I say.

"*Pffft*," he scoffs. "Terry was trafficking."

"What?"

"Little Joe got him the job. He would go across the lake once a month and meet up with some people. He'd give them the cash from sales in a bunch of coolers and they'd give him the drugs for the next shipment in an identical set. Then he'd exchange the drugs with the dealers for cash, then rinse and repeat."

"Holy shit."

Charlie nods.

"Little Joe was pushing the stuff to kids, and I'm guessing the goons that showed up at Donnie's after he was arrested might be from the front end of that delivery system."

"But why?"

"Tying up loose ends?"

I realize what he's getting at. "Are you thinking they murdered him?"

Lake water filters up from below the sand to fill the channel Charlie's dug. "Maybe. When it comes to drugs, it's usually about money. Terry tried to get more, they wanted to give less, who knows? But maybe he pissed someone off and they dealt with him."

"But no one will figure that out until a body washes up on shore."

"Who says they dumped him in the lake?"

"What? You think they buried him?"

"Why not? He disappears and there's fewer questions." He looks out at the long stretch of shoreline. "Trouble is, with this current, Terry's body could be anywhere."

That's when it dawns on me. "I might know where to start."

chapter 54

I confirm with Mom and Dad that it's okay that we take a walk and, not surprisingly, they don't agree too easily.

Mom interrogates me, "How far?"

"Just around the cabins."

"No more, no less?"

"Yes!" I catch my excited tone and dial it back. "I'll take Ollie with us."

Dad stops reading his book. "Let them go. The worst that can happen is they get eaten by a bear."

Charlie scrutinizes Dad's face. "Are you serious, Mr. S.?"

Dad lifts his book to cover his face, not answering. I'm sure if I pulled it down, he'd be smirking.

I glance back at Mom and she makes up her mind. "One hour."

"Deal."

chapter 55

I really didn't want to tell Charlie about my conversation with Diane. I'm positive he'll take the hour Mom gave us and get us into even more trouble. On the other hand, letting him follow this lead might just shut him up and maybe we'll figure out what happened to Terry. Who knows? Maybe I can even go back to relaxing at the cabin and being a normal teenager again, doing whatever it is we do—playing sports, hanging out with friends, talking to girls—not chasing murderers and having dead girlfriends.

Ollie tugs me along, happy to join this adventure with us. I barely have to lead him—he appears to know exactly where we're going.

"Why didn't you tell me that you talked to her, Shepherd?"

"I don't know? Maybe somewhere between you being tossed in jail, me telling my parents that they had to bail you out, then the two of us being grounded, it sort of slipped my mind."

"And your mom was convinced there was more to the story."

I hesitate, then confess. "I *may* have told her you had a joint, not a cigarette."

"What!?" he explodes.

"You didn't give me many options, man!" I defend myself. "I couldn't tell her what we were really up to—and she sure wasn't going to buy that story you gave the cops."

"Actually, Shepherd, I'm just impressed you lied so well."

With all my blunders during Mom's cross-examination, I never considered that I might've actually pulled it off. Unfortunately, lying to my folks doesn't make me very happy.

"Yeah, well, hanging around you does that to a person."

"You're welcome."

"That wasn't a compliment."

We walk up to Diane's and hear the sound of metal clanging. We move around to the back to find the old woman perched precariously on the bumper of her truck. She's under the open hood, her arm shoved into the machinery of the engine.

"Lost my damn socket wrench!" she shouts at us. "I don't suppose one of you has long enough arms to get it for me?"

Charlie points at me. "I think this tall drink of water is your best choice."

"Again, what century are you from?" I mutter.

"I'm timeless, man," he muses as I begrudgingly hand Ollie's leash over to him before helping out.

Diane adjusts her angle and points. "If you try reaching up from below, that'd be great."

I drop to the ground and crawl under the front of her truck, dirt and pine needles digging into my back. I'm sure my shirt will no longer be white by the time I'm done.

"So, Tony mentioned that this missing guy, Terry, was one of your old students," Charlie says.

Through a crack between the engine and something I think is attached to the front axle, I can make out her smile. "Yup, quite the troublemaker he was."

Charlie gets to the point. "And he used to bring your medication?"

She points me to a ledge near the back, under the engine, but answers him. "Yes, he was kind. Didn't always charge me, and when he did, I always thought he was asking less than full price."

"Did he come over often?"

"No, only once a month or so. That was enough."

I feel around the contours of the engine block, my fingers sliding along sharp edges and gears. I'm sure I'd break something if any of them were moving.

"Did he only come around to deliver stuff?"

Diane's face drops and I can tell her guard is going up. "His business wasn't any of mine."

Ollie crouches down to see what I'm doing. I touch the smooth, loose edge of Diane's wrench and flick it with my middle finger. It tumbles down beside my head.

Charlie presses her, "Did he come by when he was making a pickup?"

Diane sits up and the shadow she cast above me vanishes. I barely hear her answer. "Terry was always good to me. No need for you boys to go digging around out there."

Out where? Where was Terry going?

Charlie shuffles his feet beside the front tire. "Diane, this is important. Do you know where he went on his route?"

I drag myself from under the truck, grabbing the wrench to hand it to her on my way out. Her face is tight and uncertain and I know she's struggling with how best to answer.

I offer, "If it's somewhere close, we want to see if we can find anything." I don't really want this, but I know Charlie won't let it go unless we try.

"The gossips around here will drag his name through the mud," she hesitates. She twists the wrench in her hand, mulling over her answer. She glances at us, scanning our faces, deciding if we can be trusted. "But you two have been so kind, bringing my pain relief."

I can feel Charlie's eyes on me—I hadn't told him that I'd given her the other baggie of pot.

She's lost in memories now. "He was a troublemaker, always making dumb choices, but he was a good boy. He only wanted to be liked. One time he came to me, asking for gas for his boat—he had run too low to get across the lake. The tank was too heavy to carry back, so I loaded it on my four-wheeler and took him to his boat. He was anxious about me staying around for long. He asked me to leave."

The *scritch scritch scritch* of the wrench stops and she leans against the bumper. "I'm not sure what he got himself into, but I fear the worst for poor Terry," she says with genuine concern.

Charlie asks, so gently it surprises me, "Where did you take him?"

"Old Fire Tower Road, north of here."

I know the place.

chapter 56

Diane offers us her four-wheeler to drive out to Old Fire Tower Road—it's too far to walk and it definitely breaks the limits of our house arrest. I urge Charlie to come back to the cabin with me so we can get permission.

"You know they aren't going to let us go," Charlie says.

"They might," I reply, but he can probably hear how unconvinced I am.

"They're already suspicious of everything we're up to," he says, building his case.

"Maybe we can tell them we just want to check the place out. You know, like an adventure—"

"You and me and an adventure probably doesn't work out in a way that would make your parents happy."

Charlie's got a point.

"Shepherd," he says finally, "I'd rather ask forgiveness than permission."

I'm pretty sure that's how he generally operates. I weigh the options. Pro: we might find one more piece of the puzzle that is the missing man. Con: I burn pretty much all the trust I've built up with Mom and Dad over the years.

But I do want to see an end to this. I don't want to admit it to Charlie, but I really want to know what happened to Terry. And when I think about it, there's no apparent danger in going to Old Fire Tower Road. Plus, this far from town, there's probably not much Charlie could do to make matters worse—unless he starts another fire and burns down the forest.

Still, I feel a swirl of nausea when I say, "Come on, let's do this. The longer we think about it, the later we get back."

Charlie hops on and takes the wheel. I unhook the leash and drag myself onto the ATV. "Drive slow so Ollie can keep up."

"Are you kidding? He's going to love this run." I think Charlie's as excited by this ride as Ollie.

At least some of us are.

chapter 57

I guide Charlie down the backwoods path that leads to the fire tower. It's about four kilometres away, cutting through the bush. The spruce and birch rise high and close above us, shading the forest floor from the sun with a soft green veil. As we get further from the cabins, the tall trees fall away, and small aspens and chokecherry bushes build into a thick, tangled mass.

Ollie keeps up with us for most of it and we only have to stop whenever he veers off the path to chase a fresh scent. After a little bit of calling, he pops back out of the trees, usually ahead of us, ready to find the next new thing, his tongue hanging out of the side of his mouth.

We drive until the forest opens wide and young pine trees that are only half the size of the trees surrounding them appear.

"What happened here?" Charlie yells over the roar of the engine.

"Forest fire, maybe twenty years ago. This is the edge of where it burned."

The path winds along a hill and we manoeuvre up the tight switchback road. At the top, the metal base of the old fire tower rises into the sky. Beside it is a log cabin, but the whole area is locked up tight with a chain-link fence that has barbed wire at the top.

"They closed this place years ago, but Dad used to bring my sisters and me here all the time and tell us all about the life of the forest ranger."

"Forest ranger?"

"Yeah. They'd stay here on their own, watching for fires, reporting conditions—"

"On their own?"

"Yup."

"They'd stay here all the time?"

"Well, they'd work shifts, sleep, eat…"

"Could they read? Listen to the radio?"

"I guess so."

Charlie marvels at the idea.

"No internet, though," I say, snapping Charlie out of his daydream.

His smile fades. "Yeah, I suppose that wouldn't work."

I laugh. "Whether you like it or not, you should have *some* sort of connection to the real world."

"Maybe in another lifetime, son," he utters wistfully, climbing back on the ATV. "Another lifetime."

chapter 58

Old Fire Tower Road skirts the top of the hill and travels back down toward the lake. We follow it, both of us noting that there are clear signs of recent use: fallen trees chain-sawed and moved to the side, and low-hanging branches that must've been broken by a large vehicle passing through.

Charlie pulls to the edge of the drop that leads down to the water and turns off the four-wheeler. Ollie trots behind us, ducking in and out of the trees, and I have to call to him. He comes racing, shooting past me and splashing into the water. I follow him while Charlie stays at the top of the ridge and surveys the area.

"You that worried about suckers?" I goad.

"Nope, simply taking in the scenery."

I figure I should do the same and take a step back to view my surroundings. If this was where Terry came to do the exchange, it offered good cover. The long shoreline curved around, keeping any transactions—or murders—hidden.

"This doesn't make sense," Charlie calls down to me.

Ollie hears his voice and races back up to him.

"What doesn't?"

"Notice the logs." He points toward a spit of land jutting out into the water and the large trunks pushed up against it. "The currents push everything into this bay. If you were trying to dump a body, you'd have to push it out past the point. It wouldn't be the most ideal way to get rid of it."

"So, what would you do?"

He studies the location. "Either get on the other side of that beach," he says, glancing back over his shoulder, "or go farther down past the bend."

"But that would require planning, arranging…"

"Exactly. If they came out here with the intention to bump him off and make it seem like he drowned, the logistics alone wouldn't work."

"So they knock him off and simply bury him," I suggest.

"But why kill him at all? Unless it was unplanned or accidental—"

"Why couldn't it be?"

"It opens up too many possibilities. He vanishes, then people start searching for him. Wouldn't that eventually draw attention to the very place you're doing business?"

"What if Terry brought a gun? Tried to double-cross them and take the money *and* the drugs?"

Charlie shakes his head. "After everything we've heard about him? He gave drugs to old ladies, planned on proposing to his girl, and had no clue she was cheating on him. He was an idiot, and I feel sorry for him, but he didn't have it in him."

"Maybe those goons that people said were sniffing around the arcade were cleaning house? Maybe Terry messed something up and they decided to get rid of him?"

"Possibly, but then that destroys your whole supply chain. Setting up an operation like this takes a lot of work. If the plan was to cut ties with Terry, there are a lot more efficient and effective ways to make the transition to a new trafficker."

I hear Ollie barking in the trees.

"What happened then?"

Charlie points to the water. "Terry gets fired, dumped by Miranda, and probably gets drunk. But he has his other job to do, and goes across the lake." He turns back and points up the road. "The delivery people come and…" His brow furrows, frustrated by his lack of insight as to what might've happened next. "They kill him? But why? And if he just drowned, where is his body?" He shakes his head.

I climb up the ridge toward him. "Look, we've seen the place now. Let's go back and maybe save ourselves from Mom's wrath."

He doesn't move, just stares out at the lake.

"Ollie," I call out, but he doesn't seem to want to come with me either. I walk up to the treeline. Ollie's a ways in, digging and barking. "Come on, buddy. Time to go," I call again, but he's not listening, so I go into the bush after him, a little annoyed that he needs this much prompting.

When I see what he's got, I yell, "Leave it alone!" I have to get right up close to finally drag him away. "Charlie!" I call.

"What?"

I stare at the torn jeans, the white, bloated, rotting flesh exposed in the dirt. "I think we just found Terry Butler."

chapter 59

Our cell phones have no signal, so I go back to the cabin to call the cops, but Charlie elects to stay behind. He says he wants to be sure that nothing else happens to the body, but I'm sure he really wants to spend time studying the crime scene.

Mom and Dad aren't happy about our lengthy absence, but when I let them know what we've found, they stop lecturing and let me use the phone. While we wait for the cops to arrive, I tell my parents and Heather the version of the story that Charlie and I agreed on: Diane lent us her four-wheeler, I showed him where the fire tower used to be, Ollie took off, and we found him digging up the body.

Since we only left out a few key details and most of it was true, I didn't struggle too hard telling them this. None of my family believes me anyway—once you stop one serial killer, all the other dead bodies you stumble across no longer seem to be a coincidence. Still, Mom is strangely passive. I suspect there's a storm brewing that she'll unleash when the time is right.

When the police arrive, I ride out with them to the location. They stop at the top of the hill beside the base of the old tower and walk down. Right away, they're taking notes and asking questions about how we approached the area, where we walked, and if we had moved any of the freshly sawed trees—everything that Charlie and I had seen as signs of recent activity. Whatever headaches and predicaments he's brought into my life, I have to give Charlie credit for my new powers of observation.

Charlie is exactly where I'd left him, sitting on a log by the edge of the slope down by the water, but I'm certain he's been all over the area. They split us up and we go through our story question by question and I tell it exactly like I told Mom, Dad, and Heather. I skip over why we came out here to begin with and the whole discussion we had on the ridge, and I'm positive my story will concur with Charlie's version perfectly.

It isn't until they ask me if I saw anything else—plastic bags, duffle bags, or any other kind of container—that I'm certain they already suspect Terry's connection to drug-trafficking. I play dumb. The less we go down that path, the better it'll be for Charlie and me. We're just two clueless teenagers who accidentally stumbled across a dead body.

Suddenly, a cry down by the beach catches everyone's attention and a few cops race toward another cop who's down by the logs jammed against the spit of beach. Sure enough, after photographing and cataloguing it, one of the officers lifts a plastic bag above his head. I'm positive it's the money

Charlie and I found. I'll confirm it with him later, but I'm betting he found my hiding spot and planted the bag while I made the call.

After they're done questioning us, they take us up the hill to a car waiting to drive us home. Charlie and I don't say much on the way back to the cabin. I'm too nervous around the cops and Charlie knows from experience to stay quiet.

The hill isn't steep but it's long, and as I listen to the flit and chirp of birds in the trees around us, it occurs to me that we've solved the mystery. I can go back to my vacation and my normal life. I wonder if Charlie will stay or move on, but I'm guessing I already know the answer.

chapter 60

Cousin Rachel is impressed by Little Joe's kitchen—for a
dealer and scrap yard owner, he kept the place immaculate.

She searches under the sink and finds some dish soap and
a knitted washcloth in a drawer. She wets it, suds it up, and
washes off the blood and small bits of flesh caught on her
serrated knife. She's careful not to knick the cheap dollar
store gloves she wears so that she won't leave any DNA behind.

She rinses the knife off, squeezes out the cloth and hangs
it on the rack. She knows there may be traces still on it, but
it'll be dry before anyone finds it.

Outside, she gets into her car. As she starts the engine, the
police scanner squawks and she hears the chatter. Terry's
body has been found—and there is talk of drug money.

That's it, they're done here.

She calls her two guys and sends them home, anticipating
the long drive ahead. She'll get home late, but at least she'll
get to sleep in her own bed beside her husband and watch
her son's swim meet tomorrow.

She shifts the car into gear and pulls out of Little Joe's yard, driving out onto the highway. She goes over the bridge, moving past the turnoff to the old road where they used to do the exchange. Her priority was to clean up and remove any traces that could lead back to her bosses and she feels no loss or sense of nostalgia over the fact that she'll never return to the town of Estoria. Adapt or die, wasn't that the old adage?

Yet her thoughts drift to Terry. Although his death had caused her extra work over the last week—nothing she couldn't handle—he hadn't deserved to die. Whenever she cleaned up a mess like this, the real reason behind it usually became obvious. Most often it was due to greed or a bad relationship but Terry's old boss and ex-girlfriend, cold-hearted and duplicitous though they were, weren't killers—and it was clear, to Rachel at least, that Terry's death had nothing to do with a power play for the local drug scene. She doesn't really care—it isn't in her job description—but she makes a mental note to keep an eye on the local papers to see if the real reason finds its way to the surface. She doesn't care about Terry, but she'd like to know who cost the company a solid source of income—as well as an inconvenience to her busy schedule.

Cousin Rachel's car speeds down the highway.

There's one thing she does know, though: whatever happened to Terry, it had nothing to do with her.

part 3

chapter 61

The woman lies in the silence of the forest, watching.

The men in uniforms move up and down the hill. They'd found the body of the man she killed almost two weeks ago when he came to her shore. But he's no longer where she left him; he had floated with the currents to where the other woman and the four men with the white van had found him. She finds it strange that they buried him—they hadn't ended his life and certainly didn't seem to be his family.

She rolls over and the soft moss cushions her back. Her hair twists in a long, loose braid across her neck. The tops of trees brush against the blue sky; birds rotate in a cyclone above. She stretches out her arms and her fingers feel spongy mushrooms and smooth blueberries and the rough bark of trees. She digs beneath the cool earth, where the ants and worms crawl.

Her attention is drawn to a tickle on her cheek. At first she thinks it's a stray hair falling across her face, but then it moves. An insect—a small, smooth beetle—makes its way toward her nose before veering down to the top of her lip, where it pauses. With a quick flick of her tongue, she catches it and pulls it into her mouth, crushing it between her teeth before swallowing.

She rolls back and watches the men again. They've been here for many days and nights, but they don't wander too far, staying close to the path and the road. They're here because of what she did to that man—that stupid, stupid man who got too close. She hopes her patience will pay off and that they'll leave soon.

Because if they don't, she'll do whatever it takes to protect her family.

chapter 62

When we pull up in the police car, I'm sure Mom and Dad are going to freak, but Charlie takes the blame immediately. He tells them that it was his fault, that he knew they wouldn't let us go, but that he couldn't pass up the opportunity to go for a ride on an ATV. They aren't convinced and drag us into teatime. By the end of it, they're even more distrustful of our defense that we really weren't looking for Terry, that we just happened to stumble across him. We are put on lockdown in the cabin, restricted to only places where one of them, including Heather, can keep an eye on us.

So, over the next few days, we stay close to home, hanging out at the dock and reading. I persuade Charlie into giving the water a try and he finally agrees, mostly because his tough-guy persona doesn't work well with a fear of leeches. But it doesn't stop him from bringing down a container of table salt to the dock before going in and thoroughly checking every inch of himself every few minutes.

In the late afternoon we pick through the collection of board games and play a few, and in the evening, we return to the firepit to roast marshmallows. Charlie displays a calm temperament that I've never seen before, possibly due to the relatively healthy experience of being away from the city. Although I'm not used to this version of Charlie, I think it's a good thing. It's like we're really on vacation.

On the second day, the cabin phone rings and I answer it.

"Hello, Anthony."

I recognize her voice immediately. "Hello, Detective Gekas." When I say her name, Charlie stares at me, dumbfounded.

"Is Charles with you?"

I point at him and he shakes his head, waving his hands in the air in a way that tells me I should say no. I ignore him. "Yes, Detective."

He throws up his arms and slumps his shaggy head.

"Put me on speaker."

"Uh, I can't. It's a rotary dial phone."

There's a pause and I can tell Gekas is wondering why we're still using this ancient technology.

Charlie can't keep quiet and yells, "It's like living in the stone age around here!"

"Hello, Charles," Gekas says flatly.

I point at the receiver and wave him over. After a few awkward seconds, he finally comes over and the two of us lean in close to the handset.

"Hello, Detective," Charlie says.

"I hear you two have been busy," Gekas insinuates.

That's an understatement. We could play dumb, but we know she'll see through it.

"The missing guy they found?" I ask innocently, though not very convincingly.

She adds, "Don't insult my intelligence, Anthony. I know he happens to be a drug trafficker. Your names are on the report, and the fact that it was you and Charlie who found him doesn't come as much of a surprise, I have to say."

Man, she really does keep tabs on us.

"Promise me, you two," her voice is stern now, "that this is absolutely it. No more hunting for mysteries or playing detective. You gave me your word, Anthony."

"Yes, that's it," I say, though Charlie is noticeably quiet.

But Gekas isn't done. "Chasing after these kinds of people… leave it to the professionals."

"We will, Detective Gekas."

"Take care, you two," she finishes, then hangs up.

I look at Charlie, hoping he'll stay in vacation mode so that I can keep my promise.

chapter 63

By the third day of sticking close to the cabin, I convince Mom and Dad to allow us to go with Heather to the resort and hang out on a nicer beach. Since we can walk over to the restaurant and relax among other people, it makes me feel a little less like a prisoner.

Of course, Heather isn't too pleased with my suggestion and I have to bargain: I have to agree to do all of her chores for the next two weeks before she finally gives in. She's been giving Charlie the silent treatment for the last few days, but it doesn't seem to bother him. In fact, he often tells her that he agrees with her opinion of him, which, of course, only frustrates her more.

For the first two hours on the beach, Heather appears to ignore us, although I know she's watching our every move like a hawk. I eventually convince her to join us in the water, and she agrees, mostly because the cool water offers a nice break from the heat, although she does play some paddle-ball. Her ability to almost entirely shut Charlie out is amazing; she's spoken only one or two terse words to him, and those only when absolutely necessary. It isn't until the three of us take a break for ice cream that Heather's tough shell starts to crack.

"I'm buying," Charlie says, smiling. "Chocolate swirl?"

"Fine," I say, trying to cut him off before he twists his selection into a bad punchline.

He looks at Heather. "And I'm guessing you like to keep it interesting... so, flavour of the day?"

She glares at him but finally says, "Cookies and cream."

He snaps his fingers. "Right. Going with the safe choice." He bounds up the stairs to the concession window.

I peer at the menu board of choices. "Flavour of the day is tiramisu and you passed it up?"

"You trying to suggest something, brother?"

I grin. "Nothing. You might want to hate on the guy a little less."

She frowns at me. "I like cookies and cream."

"Sure you do. Tons more than tiramisu," I say sarcastically.

Charlie comes back with our cones and a handful of napkins.

"What'd you get?" I ask him.

"Pistachio. Everyone disses it, but it's a classic."

"It's simply misunderstood?" I offer.

"Exactly!"

It isn't until we're on our way back to the beach that Heather steals up beside him and whispers a quiet, "Thank you, Charlie."

We return to the blanket and munch on our cones in silence. I finish first and toss my napkin in the garbage before venturing out into the water again.

"Yo, Shepherd. Wait up," Charlie calls, sloshing through the water toward me.

I look back over my shoulder to where Heather's still sitting, finishing her ice cream. "You really like to push her buttons, don't you?"

"Who?"

"My sister."

He glances back. "What? No. Wait, I'm aggravating her?"

I scrutinize him, trying figure out if he's messing with me.

He cracks a smile. "Yeah, maybe a little. She really doesn't like me."

"Well, you do tend to get me in shit all the time."

He sighs "Yeah, but it's for a good cause." He looks across the water toward our cabin. "You think the cops are done processing the site?"

"Where we found the body? Probably."

"Think they believed the drugs angle?"

"I think the big bag of cash you left probably helped."

"Yeah, about that. You need to hide stuff better."

"You didn't leave me much choice."

"Yeah, yeah…" He stops as a wave splashes up against his trunks.

I can tell he's nervous about what might be lurking below the surface. "You're going to have to accept your fate sooner or later and dive in," I say.

"I'm starting to feel sorry for you, Shepherd. Even us poor kids had the chlorinated city pools, while you were forced to swim in creature-infested waters."

"Well, thank you for the sympathy," I say before diving deep into the water and popping up halfway to the buoys. "Come on, man. The fish aren't going to bite."

"Maybe. But the leeches will."

"Your fear of this lake is stupid."

Charlie squints at me, the sun bright in his eyes. "All right, here's the deal. I'll race you to the buoys, and if I win, I get to do something I want."

I stare him down. "Within Mom and Dad's rules?"

"Whatever they'll allow us," he agrees.

He's got to have something up his sleeve and I know he'll twist my words to his advantage, but so long as Mom and Dad have the final say, I can probably keep us out of trouble.

I barely get the chance to say, "Deal," before he dives and swims fast toward me. I turn and plunge into the water myself, making long, swift strokes. I'm hoping that he's not going to catch up, but the bigger waves out this far smack into me and slow me down. I drop further under the water, trying to make headway against the current, but when I come up for air, Charlie's right there on my tail.

Hard as it is to believe, I might not win this.

Charlie's got strong form and punches through the waves with ease. I haven't got much left in my arms and instead focus my strength in my legs, kicking hard. We're side by side as we near the buoy and reach for it at the same time.

"Tie!" I yell.

"Thought I had you," he says, breathing hard.

"Yeah, not so much."

"Fine." He leans back and floats on the water, staring up at the sky.

I've been mulling it over and now I get to the point. "You don't think Terry's death had anything to do with drugs, do you?"

"Nope."

"And we're not done yet, are we?"

"Nope."

"Damn."

chapter 64

The trip back from the lake is unreasonably quiet. I sit in the front and Heather drives, while Charlie stares out the back window. The more I think about Terry's death, the more I agree with him.

For starters, the whole crime scene didn't make sense. Charlie was right: the body *was* way too close to the exchange location. If Terry's suppliers intentionally offed him, it would've been smarter to bury him farther out in the woods or, better yet, dump his body in some remote place. Staring out the window, I see a dozen other locations that would've been better: old back roads that disappear into the forest; sandy cliffs close to the water; overgrown rivers that wind out along the edges of fields; nearly collapsed old farmhouses—hell, even weighting the body and dumping it in the middle of the lake would've made more sense. So why bury him so close to the beach they had made their drop site?

I want to ask Charlie, but it'll have to wait until we're out of Heather's earshot, so the question just churns in my head.

Maybe whoever killed Terry was in a hurry, in which case I could understand the choice to bury him quickly. But he hadn't been reported missing until last Saturday and even then the posters said he'd been missing for a week already. Which means that whoever killed him had nearly two weeks to dispose of his body, plenty of time to do whatever they thought was necessary to cover up the crime.

Charlie leans forward in his seat. "Do you think your parents would let us take the canoe out?"

Heather eyes him in the mirror. "And where would you be taking this canoe?"

"I don't know. Along the shoreline?"

She studies him. "You're done chasing after missing guys, you know."

He nods, smiling. "Of course."

"Any other mysteries you might want to share?" she asks, glancing over at me and catching me off guard.

"Well, Charlie *was* telling me there's a high incident of UFO sightings—" My grin is sarcastic.

"And don't forget that ghost road…" Charlie puts in.

"This isn't *The Mystery of Skull Island*—" she says with a look of exasperation.

Charlie perks up. "There's a Skull Island?"

She glares. "Okay, enough."

I look back and see the flash of Charlie's smile.

Yup. Definitely a button-pusher.

chapter 65

"Why do you need the canoe?" Mom asks.

"Because we're going stir crazy here!" I say.

"You're the ones who put yourselves in this position."

She's got a point. Everything she says makes sense. I've been burning bridges ever since Charlie showed up. Well, lighting them on fire, anyway.

"Anthony, we can't keep doing this."

"I know."

"Do you? Do you really understand?" She waves Dad over. "We worry about you. We worry about your safety."

Dad sits down beside me. "Everything Charlie does seems dangerous."

"It isn't, though. He just…" I don't really know how to explain it to them. "He actually cares." Their faces tell me they aren't convinced. "Really, he does. Only, he goes about it all wrong."

"That's an understatement," Dad mutters.

"Ben…" Mom stops herself. "The longer he stays, the more we realize we don't really know him. We don't know if he has your best interests at heart."

I think he does, but I don't say anything immediately, and I wonder if I really believe it.

"Anthony, I know what he did to find Sheri may have saved lives, but—"

I have to say something. "I think he lost someone in his life and he's doing what he can to make up for it."

She considers this. "Maybe, but chasing after people isn't going to help him bring them back."

Dad leans in. "And while he's chasing after these monsters, who's going to get hurt?"

That hits me hard. "I don't know."

Mom pulls me close and gives me a hug. I feel big and awkward in her arms, but that doesn't stop her and I'm sure if Charlie is watching this, he'll give me a hard time about it later.

Dad comes in for a hug as well. "I'm glad you asked permission. We'll let you take the canoe," he says at last. "But don't go far."

Mom glances at him. "And no going where the police are. Let them do their job."

"Okay."

chapter 66

Charlie and I pull the canoe out into the water. He hops in the front and I take the back so I can steer.

As we push off into the calm surface, Charlie says, "This is how it should be done. Float above all those slimy little monsters."

I rock the boat. "Oooh! Hopefully, we won't tip."

"You do that and I'll be sure you don't come out of the water alive."

I actually believe he might make good on this threat, so I counter, "But if I'm dead, you won't have someone to solve mysteries with."

"Yeah, then I could show my real potential for... pulling off the perfect crime!"

I splash water at him with my paddle. "Like not burying the body where it might be found?"

He nods. "I don't think whoever buried Terry expected two guys and a dog to be nosing around."

"There had to have been a dozen better places—"

"Whoever buried him didn't kill him."

I'm surprised by Charlie's statement. "You sound certain."

"Because I am."

I want to understand Charlie's reasoning, but he won't explain anything to me until he's ready.

He points with his paddle, "Head to the right."

"I promised Mom and Dad we weren't going anywhere near where we found the body."

"We're not."

He's telling the truth. We move past the jut of land with the stray logs where Charlie dumped the bag of money.

"So, where are you taking us?"

"Further upstream."

"Why?"

He doesn't stop paddling, but he slows down. "The day we found the body was Wednesday, right?"

"Yes."

"The last Wednesday of the month. When you visit Sheri's grave."

Now my paddling stalls. "How…?" I remind myself that this is Charlie. "You really need to not be so weird all the time."

Charlie lifts his oar out of the water and turns around on the bow seat. "Hey, it's my lot in life. I accept it." The canoe starts to drift with the current. "My point is that last week was the third Friday of the month and Terry disappeared the week before."

"Okay?" I don't know where he's going with this.

Charlie sighs. "Remember? Miranda told us that he used to go out to the lake with his buddy every third Friday of the month like clockwork, which I'm assuming was the regular night he did his drop-offs."

"Right. But he went out on the lake the week before that."

"So the delivery goons wouldn't have been there."

"Then who killed him?" I ask.

"Exactly."

Once we get past the place where we found Terry's body, Charlie lifts his paddle out of the water and lays it across the bow, scanning the water and the shoreline. He's looking for something, but I'm guessing he won't know what it is until he sees it, so I don't bother asking. I stay quiet and keep paddling, hoping to help the cause.

As we move farther away from Old Fire Tower Road, the land rises above us and steep sand cliffs block any access to the woods. Roots stick out in snarls; large birds have built nests in their hollows. Ahead, a section of cliff has collapsed; grey mud forms a long narrow triangle down to the lake.

"Must be an underground water system," I point.

"Look at you, Shepherd, using your observational skills."

It feels like a diss. "You know, you don't have to be a prick *all* the time."

He doesn't respond and continues studying the shore.

The edge of the cliff drops down to the water; thick undergrowth restricts access to the trees beyond. The water is getting shallower, and when I look over the side of the canoe, I see minnows race in a long line through the thin seaweed that stretches far past us.

A strip of sand appears on the lakefront and a thin beach comes into view. We coast along in less than two feet of water. Lengthy streaks of purple and golden sand ripple below us.

"Do you know what makes it that colour?" Charlie asks.

I know the answer, but I'm not talking.

"You pouting back there, Shepherd?"

"You can't have it both ways, man."

"Fine. I'm sorry," he says.

But I'm not going to make it that easy.

Finally he turns to me. "Seriously, your insight is invaluable."

"Why is it almost everything that comes out of your mouth makes you sound like an asshole?" I gripe.

"I don't know. It's what makes me my own unique butterfly."

He wins. I can't help but laugh. Still, I have to add, "You know, my parents have almost had enough of you."

"Happens to most people sooner or later."

"You could try a little harder," I suggest.

"Yeah…" He doesn't sound convinced. "But that takes effort and I only have so much to go around."

"Don't be surprised if they kick you out at some point," I say bluntly.

"*Your* parents? Never. They like me too much. I got a feeling for these things." He faces the front of the bow again and takes up the oar. "So, are you going to tell me why the sand is purple?"

This guy never stops.

"Fine. Geologists don't know for sure, but they think it's garnet deposited by the glaciers—"

"Wait, shut up. Look!" He points and, although I'm annoyed, I see what he's showing me.

Three blue coolers lie on the beach ahead.

chapter 67

We pull onto the shore and drag the canoe above the logs.
Charlie walks over to the first cooler and studies it before
prying it open with a piece of drift wood and his shoe.

Water pours out.

"I think it's a dead end, man."

He goes to the second one and pops it. More water.

"Told you. Somebody just abandoned them."

He ignores me and goes to the third.

He cracks it, but I can't see what's inside from my angle.

"Boom," Charlie says.

"What?"

He reaches in and pulls out a sopping wet convenience
store bag with a white envelope inside it.

"You've got to be kidding me!" I exclaim.

He peers inside the envelope. "Oh, it gets better." He pulls
out two pieces of drenched paper that tear as he pulls them
apart. He hands one to me.

"Paycheques?" The ink is indecipherable, but I can just make out the account-holder's name: Huber Motors. "You think these are Terry's?"

Charlie nods. "We found his money—maybe he tried to pay off his suppliers with them?"

I shake my head. "Every time you think the guy can't get more pathetic, he goes one better. Or worse." I survey the rest of the beach. "So, you figure he was here?"

"Seems like it. The question is why? The meet-up was back there," he motions the way we've come, "near Old Fire Tower Road." He climbs up the small bank toward the trees. "The undergrowth is pretty thin around here."

Beep boop bing.

Charlie pulls out his phone. "Seriously, of all places, *this* is where I get reception?" He scrolls through his messages, momentarily distracted.

I scramble up the bank after him. "Do you think Terry was meeting someone else here?"

"Maybe." He stares at his phone as he steps further into the trees.

"Charlie?" I call out, trying to distract him from his phone, "what do you see?"

He doesn't answer.

"Charlie!"

He glances up at me, annoyed.

"Will you focus? What do you see?" I gesture around.

He sighs, then slides his phone back in his pocket and walks parallel to the beach, examining the ground and the trees. Occasionally he looks further into the woods or back toward me. I decide to go in the opposite direction, following his lead.

Nothing really stands out.

The trees are mainly pine. Small leafy plants cover the ground. The occasional mushroom pops through, and blueberry and raspberry plants grow in small clumps in the brush. A deer path winds deep into the forest, but when I look back toward the water, I see that the trail ends by an immense fallen tree. I walk toward it. The bark on the top side of the tree is worn smooth, and I take a step back to assess it before sitting on the tree's polished surface. I think the lights of the resort across the lake would be visible from here at night.

A tuft of white plastic sticks out from a little hollow beneath the tree trunk. I lean down and tug, pulling out a white plastic garbage bag. I unwrap it to find a half-burned copy of *The Great Gatsby*.

"Shepherd!" Charlie yells, standing ankle deep in the water. "Look." He reaches into the water and pulls out a pair of glasses, the unbroken lenses glinting in the sunlight.

"Someone lost them?" I ask.

He sloshes toward the boat. "I don't think it was just someone." He reaches into his bag and pulls out the notice he got from the police officer at the dock. Terry's wearing glasses in the photo.

He compares the frames in his hand with the glasses in the photo. "They sure look the same."

"There's more," I say, taking him to the fallen tree. "It's like someone's... thinking spot. And it doesn't end there." I hand him the book, showing him where I found it, and he flips through the charred and torn pages.

"It's like someone hid it," I say.

Charlie looks down the deer trail into the woods. "How far back do you think that path goes?"

"No clue."

He wraps the book in the bag I found it in and crams it back into the shallow hole. "Want to walk a little and find out?"

I doubt I've got a choice.

chapter 68

Before diving into the forest, Charlie slips the glasses into his backpack and throws it over his shoulder.

"Dude, no one's going to steal your bag," I say.

"Are you kidding? It's got all my valuables in it."

"Like what?"

"I don't know. My phone, my bear-banger… you know, the essentials!"

I shake my head as we follow the path that winds deep into the woods. It zig-zags back and forth, and our direction feels random. The bush grows thicker and overgrown and we need to duck several times under low-hanging tree branches and force our way through bush that spreads across the trail. At several places, the path splits or crosses with another deer trail, and the more options we find, the more chance we have of getting lost. I try to keep track, but the constant shifts and twists make it a challenge.

"Do you know where we're going?" I eventually ask.

"Not really," Charlie says, "but I think I know where we've been."

I'm not sure I trust him on this. His skills in the forest haven't been stellar so far.

"Look," he says, pointing toward the sun, "as long as we keep it on the left, we should be okay."

"But this path goes everywhere."

"It must end somewhere," he says, logically.

He's got a point, but still. "What if it's just a deer trail and the damn animal has no clue where the hell he's going? Maybe he's just looking for berries and avoiding wolves."

"You really think so?"

"Why not? There's no real pattern—"

"I mean, wolves? You really think so?"

I stare at him. "What is with you and wildlife? Bears, wolves, leeches—?"

"People I can usually understand. They want something and will do whatever they can to get it."

I shrug. "Same with animals."

"Yeah, but with people, they want to be happy or have some importance in this universe. With animals, they just want to eat and have sex—"

I chuckle. "Sounds a lot like people to me."

"Maybe," Charlie ponders, "but they typically don't want to eat *me*."

"I think you're being a little paranoid."

We continue on and the bush gets even more dense. Charlie and I push through enveloping leaves and branches, walking blindly, barely able to keep track of the thin path as it winds through the overgrowth.

Finally, we come into a tiny clearing no bigger than the size of a car, and I stop.

"How much further do you want to go?"

Charlie shakes his head. "Wherever this path is going, I don't think we're getting to the end of it anytime soon."

"If it's even a path," I say, leaning back to look up at the clouds that have slowly gathered above. The wind has picked up and the tops of the trees sway back and forth. "And those clouds don't look good."

I can tell Charlie is tempted by curiosity to keep going, but he appears to be as frustrated as I feel. "Charlie, I think you're right; this path was made by deer wanting berries and other deer to have sex with."

He squats low, looking at the trail as it disappears into the undergrowth ahead. Even when we look behind us, we can hardly tell where we've come from.

"Fine, let's go back," Charlie says.

chapter 69

The walk back is challenging. It doesn't help that we're frustrated at not finding anything. I scan my surroundings and don't recognize any of it—it feels like a brand new forest.

"Are you sure we're going the right way?" I ask.

"Maybe," comes the reply.

"Uh, Charlie?"

He stops. "I'm not really sure, but it sort of feels the same. As long as we keep going along this trail, we should be fine."

My confidence is not bolstered by his words, still less when the path splits in two and he pauses.

"You don't know which way to go, do you?"

"Give me a sec." He stares at each of the paths and I'm not sure if he's thinking or guessing. He points. "This one."

"You sure?"

"Yes."

"Really?"

"Yes." I don't believe him and he notices it on my face. "Fine!" He digs into his bag and pulls out his phone and turns on the compass app.

"You getting a signal?" I ask.

"Don't need one. It has an onboard magnetometer."

I don't know whether this is true or not, but with no better option, I follow along.

We twist along the winding trail. The clouds continue to roll in and darken the sky. There's not even a hint of sun to keep on our right to lead us to the canoe.

"I think we're going to be rowing back in the rain," I grumble.

"Ah, no worries," Charlie, always the optimist, says. "It won't take us that long."

But I don't particularly enjoy the idea of getting wet and cold, so I pick up the pace. "Let's hurry a little."

"Patience, Shepherd, or we'll lose the path."

And so we trudge along to the low rumble of thunder in the distance. As we push through a dense patch of bush, the trail opens to a more sparsely populated pine forest. Leaves and branches rattle in the wind, which has kicked up a notch or two over the last few minutes.

"This looks familiar," Charlie says.

"You still don't know where we are, though, do you?"

"No, but we're getting closer," he waves his phone in the air, "and going in the right direction."

I can see from here that he's not even on the compass app. "Wait. What are you looking at?"

"What?" He tucks his phone in his hand. "Nothing."

"Are you on the internet?"

"A signal popped up. I took advantage of it."

"You didn't put it in standby mode? You're killing the battery for a couple of dank memes?" I feel like I'm scolding a child.

"I was looking for us on the map."

"And?"

"Well, it took forever to load and when it finally did, all I got was our dot in a whole mess of trees."

"And you probably burned through half the phone's charge doing it."

"Shepherd, you worry too much. We're almost back to the canoe. And besides, I don't need a compass. I've got you." He taps me on the chest with the back of his hand as if to reassure me.

"What's *that* supposed to mean?"

He grins. "You know your way around the woods and shit."

Why does he only offer a compliment when he's pissing me off? "Whatever. Turn off the internet."

He sulks, "Fine." He fiddles with his phone. "It's off."

I glare. "Really?"

"Yes." He shows me that it's in airplane mode, but the phone is already nearly dead. "Geez, Shepherd, I give you an opportunity to show off your skills and you dump all over it."

As much of a punk as Charlie can be, I can't deny that his faith in me is reassuring.

I see my first hint of the lake. "Come on!"

We shove our way through the brush, beelining for the water. The trees give way to the beach and as soon as I hit the sand, I realize we've got problems. "Where's the canoe?"

Charlie halts, looking around. "This the right place?"

"Positive. That's where I found the book." I point to the fallen log, then look out at the lake. "The water's a lot rougher now, but I still don't think it could've pulled the boat out."

Charlie and I see it at the same time, but he reacts first—the canoe is out on the lake, rapidly being carried out of sight by the current, and he drops his phone and backpack and charges into the waves after it. By the time he's deep enough to swim, our best mode of transportation is gone.

"Charlie!" I holler at him. "Get back here—now!" If the current is strong enough to take the canoe, he shouldn't be out in the water.

I'm amazed when he actually does what I ask, stopping this pointless, dangerous rescue attempt and turning back to shore.

I take another look at the sky. There's a flash of lightning and another rumble of thunder. This time it sounds closer.

Charlie wades back up onto the beach a minute later. "Let's quit dicking around and get moving," He's wet to the chest but clearly determined to take action.

"Where?"

"Back to the cabin."

"I'm not walking," I say. Is he nuts? It'll be nearly impossible to follow the lakeshore all the way back.

He grabs a stick and squats in the sand, smoothing a space with it. "This is where we are." He draws an X, then another X a bit above it. "This is your cabin. And this is the lake." He draws a wide curve. "If we cut straight through the woods, we'll reduce the distance by half."

I'm sure he knows what he's talking about—he does love his maps—but I hate the idea of leaving the beach. "We don't know what's between us and the cabin, though. There could be swamps, ravines—who knows what."

Charlie shrugs. "We've got the compass, for awhile anyway. We can navigate around anything."

"We're going to get soaked."

He looks up at the dark sky. "That will happen either way. Come on, Shepherd. We can't overthink this. We have to go. Now."

"Dammit. Fine." I follow him into the woods and, hopefully, back home.

chapter 70

For the past half-hour, we've trudged through a mire of fallen trees and deep trenches. Every step of our journey seems blocked and we often have to retreat to find a new way through. Then the rain begins. It goes from scattered sprinkles to a full downpour in seconds and even with the canopy of trees, we're soaked.

"Charlie," I say finally, "it feels like we're lost."

He turns, scouring the landscape, hoping to find some hint of our location.

"We could go back—"

"Which way?"

"We came from over there—"

"What does the compass say?" I notice it's not in his hand. "Where is it?"

"In my bag. It, ah, died a while ago," he mumbles.

Shit, this is not good news. "What? When?"

"Must've bricked when I ran into the water to get the canoe."

I think back. "That doesn't make sense. You left it on the beach." I lock eyes with him. "You turned cell service back on, didn't you."

He doesn't answer immediately. "I got a signal. I was just trying to download a proper hiker's map for this area when it stopped. I thought it would help guide us. I just didn't think it would be so hella big."

"You killed the phone."

Charlie ignores me, swiping the damp hair from his face, looking at the high ridge that rises behind us. "Maybe we could work our way back up there, find our bearings—"

I'm pissed. "And how do we get back up there? And which way? You ruined our one chance to find our way out of here."

"Hey, I was trying to help."

"By screwing us even more?" I yell. "Charlie, we don't even know if we're going the right way anymore."

"Well, can't you figure that out?" he yells back at me.

I stare at him in disbelief. "How?"

"I don't know. Don't you know some forest trick?"

"Huh?"

"Yeah. Like, from your grandfather, maybe."

"Such as?"

"I don't know. Reading the moss or leaves or something?"

"What are you talking about?" He *is* nuts.

Charlie sighs. "There's got to be a way to tell directions out here."

I point to the rain clouds. "Yeah, it's called the sun, but we don't exactly have that. I nod at his bag. "Don't you have anything else in there that could help us?"

He shakes his head but goes through it anyway.

"Jackknife, notebook, pen, small hammer," he says as he digs a little deeper, "there's a bandanna, a lighter, my lock-pick kit… a pair of socks, my bear-banger, the Tannerite, and the road flare."

He's like Mary Poppins. Only without the umbrella.

"How can you carry so much shit and have nothing for cover?" The rain's falling on my face and running down the back of my neck and I'm getting cold. "Look, we need to find shelter—"

"But if we keep moving—" Charlie protests.

"No, we need to stop—"

"Maybe find an open hill, signal for help—"

"Charlie, we need to wait this out."

"We could use the lighter to start a fire and warm up."

"Are you kidding? It's too wet to burn anything."

"How about the flare? Maybe we could ignite something."

"What if we need to get someone's attention?" I snap back. "It's daytime now, but we might be out here all night if we can't find a way home."

"But if we start a fire, somebody might see it—"

"Sure. Or we could burn the whole forest down. Sounds like your kind of thing."

"Hey, are you still pissed about the alley?"

"No, I'm pissed about *everything*. You always do this sort of shit, charging in wherever, doing whatever the hell you want without listening, and then it all goes to hell for me."

"I'm in this too, you know!"

"Yeah, but your parents don't give a rat's ass what happens to you."

I've gone too far.

"Shit, sorry."

"Nope, you've got a point."

I can tell I've hurt him.

"Come on, Charlie, I'm just cold and tired. I want to be back at the cabin."

"Hey, you're right. It doesn't matter." He starts walking again.

"Charlie, wait—"

"Shepherd, enough." He glares at me, rain dripping into his eyes. "You know what? You're not perfect. You can be a real asshole too."

"What are you talking about?"

"You know, I tried hanging out with you after we caught Sheri's killer. I went to your games, even when you didn't invite me. I went to the dumb parties you and your friends went to, and watched all the people drink too much and talk about boring, stupid shit." He gets up in my face. "But when did any of them do anything for this world that fixed something, that saved someone? Huh? When? You may not like me or the way I do shit, but at least I try."

I can barely process everything he's just said, as he marches off into the foliage.

I chase after him. "Don't… Wait!"

He keeps moving through the trees. "No, Shepherd, you just keep doing whatever the hell it is you do and I'll go my own way."

"Dammit, Charlie, slow down! We need to stay together."

He stops. He's a fair distance away by now and his head is down. He's got to be bitterly cold too.

"If we split up, it'll makes things worse. Please, stay. We'll get through this better if we work together."

He turns and comes back, slowly. "So what do you want to do?"

I look around and see a towering spruce with a thick, wide base. "Let's get under there."

He shoots me a questioning look but complies.

We worm our way under the branches, close to the trunk. There's very little room to move and we have to lie on our sides close together.

"This is a little closer than I ever thought I'd have to be with you, Shepherd."

"Same. You said you had clothes in your bag?"

He nods.

"Hand it to me." I dig through it, take out his socks and bandanna, wriggle out from beneath the spruce, and tie his stuff to the tree in case someone passes this way. I crawl back underneath.

Charlie shivers in his wet tee-shirt and jeans.

"You're freezing," I say.

"I'll deal with it."

"Dude, your body doesn't care how tough you think you are."

He knows where I'm about to go with this. "No, Shepherd—"

"Seriously, if we get closer, our body heat will keep us both warm."

"No—"

"If this rain keeps up until nightfall and the temperature drops or if no one finds us right away—"

"No."

I can see in his eyes that he gets it but doesn't want to admit it. "Charlie, quit being an asshole. It's for your own good." I raise my hand as much as I can in the cramped quarters. "I promise I won't tell anyone."

He glares at me. "Fine. Just be careful where you put your parts, okay?"

"Fair enough."

chapter 71

For years, the men had been moving further into her forest.

At first, she approached them, their strange, unnatural odour was so different from other animals. But they quickly proved themselves untrustworthy and dangerous. They'd come here, acting friendly with food and other offerings, but then some would desire vile and disgusting things and try to take them at any cost. She learned not to hesitate, not to pause in protecting herself from them, from their ways and wants. Soon, it seemed easier to stop them before they even spoke their lies.

This last one she killed had brought others and she could only hope that in time they'd leave her alone. But now these two boys had moved into her territory, cutting through the forest without thought or direction, coming closer and closer to her home. She didn't like it.

She would have to send a message.

As clouds float over the canopy of trees filling the thick, dark sky with the strong scent of rain, she leaves them, escaping their stink and filth. She pads through the woods until she finds a path and squats at the base of a large tree, pushing her toes into the soft earth.

Now she must wait for her prey.

She closes her eyes and separates the layers of sound. While the others find the forest peaceful and relaxing, she hears a beautiful symphony of noise. Trees creak; leaves rustle in the wind. Squirrels chatter and insects scratch around her, while above a woodpecker beats out a rhythm. A chickadee and a swallow have found themselves a copse of nearby birch, while a seagull squeals high above in the sky. Somewhere behind her another bird she can't quite identify flits over the forest floor, and she spies the flash of a critter, likely a marmot, scrounging for roots ahead of her. She breathes deeply, quietly, not wanting to intrude upon the music that surrounds her.

A crow—that damn fiend—arrives to pester the rest.

She tunes it out, closing her eyes and turning her head toward another utterance, a rough *pat pat pat* coming through the trees. A raindrop hits her cheek and then another and another. The shower sweeps in, silencing all other sounds. It doesn't hinder her pleasure but rather adds a new percussive movement played against every surface in the forest.

She tilts her head and sticks out her tongue, drinking the water from the sky. Eyes closed, she feels the rain running through her swollen braids and across her face to stream down the front of her shirt.

She rocks slowly back and forth taking it all in.

Crick.

Her heart skips a beat and she draws her knife.

Snap.

Her quarry is approaching and patience is the key to a successful hunt.

Years of practice have honed her skills. The first few times were brutal and difficult and, younger then, she had hurt herself as much as the animal. She used to make a much larger mess, but now she's careful and efficient. She keeps the animal pure with a quick kill and other animals stay away because less blood sprays than it used to.

She opens her eyes. In one smooth thrust, she digs into the chest of the young white-tailed deer at the end of her knife. Its front legs buckle as she pushes through the muscle of the animal and into its lung. It snorts in pain, and after a hard shove, the creature is on its side.

The rain pours into her eyes, but she doesn't break focus. She pushes her knee into the deer with all her weight, pulls out the knife and slices through the muscles of the neck until she cuts through the jugular vein. The beast's short, panicked breath puffs against her arm as it looks up at her, squirming under her hold, blood spurting out, thinning as the rainwater washes it onto the mossy forest floor. The deer blinks once, twice, then its eyes glaze over though they remain open. It is still.

She waits until she's certain the animal is dead, then rises, catching her breath. Steam rises from the passive creature as its flesh cools in the soft rain.

But she's not done.

She kneels again, taking it by the throat with one hand to pull its head back and expose the neck. The knife plunges in again. A back leg kicks, likely a nerve spasm—she ignores it. The tough tendons and vertebrae resist the knife at first, but she is strong. She tears off the head and tosses it aside; it lands with a splat on the wet ground beside her. She rises up and carves a line from throat to underbelly and without pause reaches into the animal and pulls out its organs. The entrails reek, but this doesn't stop her.

Standing in the pouring rain in front the carcass, stained to the elbows with blood, knife in hand, she looks at her workmanship. She bends down to sort through the mass of guts, picks up the heart in one hand and reaches for the head with the other. She'll be back for the meat shortly. First she must let the boys know they are no longer welcome.

chapter 72

It's a long, rainy afternoon for Charlie and me—and an even longer night.

Although the tree provides reasonable cover, water drips on us constantly. Fallen spruce needles dig into our arms and clothing. We empty out Charlie's backpack and open it wide to use as something of a cover, but we're both cold, although much less so than if we were each shivering alone.

We talk very little and sleep even less. I drift in and out but never feel like I fully fall asleep. Mom and Dad will be freaking out that we're not home, I'm sure, so for some time, I worry that someone might be looking for us and that we'll miss them. so I keep waking at every little sound.

Charlie's restless too; he never stops moving in his attempt to get comfortable. Finally, he settles and I think he's fallen asleep because he's mumbling quietly, whispering what sounds like "selfie," but I'm sure that can't be right.

At some point, I open my eyes and find Charlie solidly asleep. It's dark and the steady roar of the rain is gone. The only sound is the soft patter of water dripping off the leaves. There's a *crunch crunch* of an animal moving around our tree and I hope it doesn't plan to poke around underneath. I stay still and barely breathe, waiting until I hear it move off. It's only then that I relax and try to get back to sleep.

chapter 73

Charlie's movements wake me. It's morning. I follow him, blearily scrambling out from under the tree. Although the sun's not up yet, we can see enough to tell there isn't a cloud in the sky. Charlie checks his phone. 4:30 a.m.

"I didn't even know this time existed," he says.

There are two large black garbage bags, split open and spread between the branches of our tree to provide cover from last night's rain.

"Charlie, was this you?" Even as I ask, I know he didn't have any in his backpack.

"I'm resourceful, but even I can't pull a garbage bag out of my ass." He points behind me. "And I'm guessing you aren't responsible for that?"

I turn and see what he's looking at: the severed head of what I'm pretty sure is a deer, staring wide-eyed, hung by the antlers in the branches of a nearby tree. On the ground below it is its heart.

A chill runs down my back. "Um. Time to go?"

"No argument here."

We leave immediately and I look at the shadows of the trees to try and get a sense of where the sun is. I point. "That's the direction of the cabin, so the lake"—I shift my arm to the east—"must be over there."

Charlie shivers, "And the warm sun, correct?"

I nod.

"I vote we head for the lake."

"I couldn't agree more." At least we could go back to my original plan and follow the shoreline back to civilization.

The walk over uneven land hasn't gotten any easier, especially now that the ground is soaked from the rain. We battle through trees and over and around fallen logs; branches jut up and redirect our path more often than not. The leaves, grass and moss are heavy with moisture and it doesn't take long until our feet are as wet and cold as the rest of us. A large bog blocks our progress and we travel further north to get around it.

As we struggle along, the sun rises high in the sky and the air is heavy with humidity. My clothes have started to dry out from the rain, but I'm drenching them again with sweat, I'm grimy from the less-than-ideal sleeping accommodations, and I can feel my endurance waning. But I can't stop thinking about what we found this morning.

Charlie beats me to it. "How do you think those bags got there?"

I glance over at him. "I'm more concerned about the severed deer parts."

"Couldn't it have been a bear?"

I shake my head. "Bears don't hang their leftovers from trees like offerings. This thing was only missing a bow and a card saying Happy Birthday."

He thinks about this. "So then why the bags *and* the head?"

I don't have an answer for this. Charlie retreats into his thoughts, his attention diverted from the situation at hand. It's unsettling that something this unnatural is happening out in these woods. Maybe we *are* dealing with aliens.

I also can't seem to escape the nagging thought of something Charlie had said yesterday: that he'd been at the games I'd played and attended the same parties as me. How had I not seen him? How many times had he been around without me realizing it? Had I really been so oblivious?

"Charlie?"

"Hmm…?"

"I don't hate you."

He chuckles and leans against a tree, taking a break. "Really, Shepherd. We're at the ass end of nowhere. We've got someone or some*thing* decapitating deer for our viewing pleasure, and you're worried about whether or not I think you hate me?"

Sounds pretty stupid when he puts it like that, but I press on. "Well, I don't."

"All right," he nods. "Well, thanks."

"I'm serious."

"Okay, great to hear."

"And I'm sorry about what I said to you yesterday."

"What a relief."

"Come on, man." Charlie's never one to make things easy.

"What do you want me to say? You're forgiven." He places a hand over his heart.

Now he's just pissing me off. "You know what? You're an asshole too."

"That makes us two assholes."

"Fine, we're a couple of assholes, lost in the woods—"

"With some batshit crazy person leaving animal remains—"

"Right. Still, I wouldn't have it any other way," I tell him.

"Oh, so you're saying you *want* me to be lost in the woods with a psycho who leaves severed heads as gifts?"

"No—! Not *you*... us—"

"You *like* being stalked?"

"No—" I finally get it: he's messing with me. Again. "You really *are* crazy!"

He smiles. "There you go, Shepherd. Now you truly understand me."

I toss my head back. "You— I just—" He's waiting for me to finally explode. "You're really enjoying this, aren't you?"

He smirks. "Tormenting you? Of course."

I sigh and finally laugh. "Charlie, you're aggravating! And I am truly thankful that you're lost here with me!"

"Thank you, but it looks like you're wrong about us being lost."

I look to where he's gesturing and see open sky through the trees. We step out onto a ridge. Down below us is the lake shining in the sun.

chapter 74

We slip back into the trees and descend the ridge, thankful that the lake isn't far away. We crest another hill and go down again, and the trees open onto long grass and bushes. We shove through them, brambles and branches scratching our arms, and it doesn't take long before we're at the edge of a small, sandy bank that drops into the lake. We jump right in with our shoes on. The cold water feels awesome against our hot skin.

I try to get my bearings. I think we're somewhere between Old Fire Tower Road and the cabin, but beyond that I have no clue where we came out. We slog through the shallow waters, skirting fallen logs, water splashing around our pant legs. By this point, it appears Charlie is long past caring about leeches or other creepy crawlies, but I don't draw attention to the possibility in case it changes his mind about being out here.

A short while later, we see a boat out on the lake, but they're too far out to notice us. Soon, another boat passes by, followed by a few more, and eventually we flag down a couple of early morning fishermen, Americans who've travelled north to catch jackfish.

"You boys lost?"

"I don't suppose you can take us to Dyson's Point?" I ask.

"Where's that?"

Once the fishermen help me get my bearings, I guide them back toward our cabin. Charlie is unaccustomedly quiet on the trip. We stop at the main landing where we are greeted by a couple of police officers.

"Anthony Shepherd? Charles Wolfe? Come with us."

It takes us both a few minutes to understand that we aren't so much in trouble as we are the centre of great concern—with good reason. Last night, Mom and Dad issued an all-points bulletin for us, and when some boaters found our canoe half submerged in the middle of the lake early this morning, the police expected the worst. Our arrival at the dock comes as a major relief.

Even though we're nearly dry except for our feet, the cops offer us blankets and take us in their patrol car back to the cabin. Mom and Dad look like they haven't slept all night, and as they hurry to us, I can tell they've been crying. I hug them both and my parents pull Charlie into the circle too. He seems to tolerate it. Heather runs up the path from the lakeshore and gets between me and Charlie in the family hug we've got going on.

Of course, the police want to know what happened. We tell them how we pulled to the shore to rest and do a bit of exploring. How when we got back, the canoe had floated away and we tried to walk back to the cabin before the rain hit—and it's all true, with only a few details missing, like the fact that we might've found the actual place where Terry drowned. Since, to them, we're no longer just a couple of dumb kids who stumbled across a corpse but two teens with one too many run-ins with the law over the last few days, they question our actions. Why did we go canoeing? How far did we go? Where were we in relation to the site where we found the body? Why did we pull into the beach that we did? What did we do at night?

The questions continue for half an hour, and while Mom and Dad sit beside us, they stay quiet; more than anything, I'm sure, because they want to know the answers themselves. We push through the interrogation, and although Charlie answers some of the more loaded questions, I've grown accustomed to telling half-truths and can even sense how he might respond to them sometimes. Eventually, the cross-examination ends and the officers leave, happy not to be dragging the lake for a couple of teenagers who got lost in a storm. We thank them for their help—even Charlie shows his appreciation—and they go on their way.

Now, Charlie and I are left with the biggest challenge—dealing with Mom and Dad. Surprisingly, they go easy on us. Heather doesn't even have harsh words for Charlie. The two of us find ourselves amid an eerie calm as we wait for the bottom to drop out, but it never does. Frankly, I'm not upset by this fact and hope that if I don't poke the beast, I can escape the wrath.

Charlie, though, is strangely quiet for the rest of the day and is unusually attentive and helpful around the cabin. He sets the table, helps clear it, and silently dries the dishes while

Dad washes. In the evening, he sits with us by the fire and roasts marshmallows before going up to bed early, and when I decide to do the same, I find him reading Ernest Hemingway's *A Farewell to Arms*.

"You okay?"

He nods without looking up from the book.

"You thinking about this morning?" I ask.

"No, not really."

"You sure?"

"Yup. Do you mind letting me read?"

"Sure."

I climb into the bottom bunk and lie down. At some point, he turns out the light and I'm left in the dark wondering what's going on.

chapter 75

Sunday morning arrives and I drag myself out of bed to the fragrant smell of coffee and bacon. When I step into the kitchen, I find everyone awake, including Charlie.

"Good morning," Mom says, beaming.

"Morning."

"We didn't think you were getting up," Dad says.

"Well, sleeping under a tree in the rain the other night was less than exceptional."

"You have a greater appreciation for your mattress?" Dad asks, trying to be funny, but it's too early to have a sense of humour.

"Uh-huh," I mumble, grabbing a fresh cup of coffee.

Charlie pipes up. "About that... can we have tea time?"

Everyone stares at him.

"Well, not tea time, but maybe coffee time?" he clarifies.

"Charles...?" Mom's not sure how to proceed.

"We typically..." Dad's speechless as well.

"I understand all that. It's just you guys haven't said anything and I think we should talk about it."

What does he think he's doing? For once, we're not in trouble.

He takes a seat at the table and waits expectantly until Mom and Dad comply. Now it's only me and Heather standing and I don't really want to plunk myself into this situation.

Charlie looks over at my sister and I'm not entirely shocked when she pulls up a chair, clearly eager to see whatever's about to go down. I resign myself to the fact that I'm not going to win this one and sit down too.

"What's on your mind, Charles?" asks Mom.

"Well, first I want to take full responsibility for us getting lost," says Charlie.

Mom and Dad exchange looks with him before Dad says, "That's good of you to say, but it seems you've been doing that a lot."

"What Ben means to say is that Anthony is responsible for his own actions and hasn't been accepting that fact," says Mom.

Great, Charlie, *now* look what you've done!

"You can't keep apologizing for Tony," Dad adds. "He's as much to blame for what's happened as you."

They wait for me to respond and I feel a bit clueless. Finally I say, "You're right, it hasn't been all him." I hope that's enough, but they seem to want more. "It's definitely not only Charlie's fault."

Mom says, "No, it hasn't been—"

"But yesterday wasn't our fault at all." I feel defensive.

"We're not blaming either of you—"

"We thought we had secured the canoe—"

"We understand. And we're very grateful that you're home safe."

Charlie intervenes. "Actually, I have to thank Tony for that. If he hadn't been there, I would've been screwed."

Mom and Dad consider this as he continues.

"Tony wanted to stay along the shoreline and I argued that we should cut through the woods until I got my way. Then, when I got us good and lost, he had the common sense to hole up under the tree until the storm passed and we could get our bearings. He was levelheaded every step of the way."

Mom reaches across the table to take my hand.

Dad says, "Well, Keya and I have been talking and we know things can't keep going the way they have been. Charlie, you aren't used to our expectations and we're pretty sure you're going to continue doing things your own way. Nothing we say or do is going to change you."

Mom continues the thought, "If we ground you, you'll find some way to break the rules. Every time you make a promise, you either take it to the very edge or break it altogether. And every time you leave this house, we're never sure what danger you might be getting into."

I can see Charlie brace himself for the very real possibility that they'll toss him out.

"However, you and Anthony have always come home safe. And we know you protect each other, look out for each other. And like we said earlier, he needs to take responsibility for his own actions. That's why we've decided that we need to put a little faith in you. We're not going to keep punishing you or keep you locked in the cabin. But we want you to be more honest with us. Tell us where you're going. Because, whether you want to accept it or not, Charles, we care about you too—you've become part of our family."

My parents' words really hit some deep part of him and for one of the only times since I've known him, Charlie is speechless. He gives a brief nod, then asks to be excused and wanders down to the water.

I decide to give him some space. My mind is buzzing with questions from our adventure in the woods. Who does the book belong to? Who left us the garbage bags and severed head? Is it all the same person? And is there a connection between any of these questions and Terry's death?

chapter 76

At lunch, Charlie comes up from the shore when he's called, but when we're done and cleaned up, he turns to Heather. "Would you be interested in taking us to the resort?"

Heather pauses. "What's in it for me?"

"Hot sun, cool water?"

"What about just hanging down by the dock?"

"Too much seaweed. And..."

She smiles. "You're scared of leeches."

He nods, still embarrassed. "How about all the ice cream you can eat? My treat."

"Will I have to babysit you?"

He raises his hand in an oath. "I promise to behave myself, not to run off anywhere, and to tell you where I am at all times."

She raises an eyebrow, but I think he's being genuine.

"Please?" he begs. "It's a nice day and I'd just like to swim for a bit."

Heather looks over at me. "How about it? Are you going to conduct yourself accordingly?"

I suspect Charlie has an alternative plan, so I don't volunteer any promises. "Sure."

After Mom and Dad give her the go-ahead, she says, "Fine. Be ready in ten."

chapter 77

Charlie spends most of time in the water while I sit beside Heather on the beach. He swims out to the buoys and back several times, and now I understand why we tied in our race the other day. I don't think I expected him to be so committed to swimming. In fact, the more I watch, the more surprised I am that he didn't beat me.

"The longer I spend with him, the less I understand him," Heather says.

"You and me both."

"I really didn't like him—I really *don't* like him. He's aggravating, obnoxious, pretentious, dangerous, a miscreant…"

I don't argue.

"And then he does the nicest damned things…"she says, looking out at him in the water.

"He's his own mystery." There's an understatement.

"And I wonder how much of it's bullshit."

"Which part?" I ask her.

"All of it. I mistrust almost every aspect of him."

"Including the bad parts."

"Especially the bad parts!" Heather exclaims.

I smile, understanding how irritating he really can be.

"Did you two really lose the canoe?"

"Yes."

"The wind came along and took it away?"

"Far as I know, yes."

"But nothing else happened?"

I think before answering because I really don't have another explanation. "I don't think so."

The answer is vague and she studies me. "Is there something you're not telling me?"

The book and the deer head flash through my mind. "No."

She peers back out at Charlie and I feel bad that I've lied to her, but the fact is I don't have any real answers. It bothers me. I don't know for certain how the canoe drifted out into the lake. Maybe whoever left us the deer parts was responsible, or maybe we simply had a run of bad luck and didn't drag the boat up high enough and the waves took it out before we got back.

My head swirls from the heat and the uncertainties. I rise and tell Heather I want something to drink. She nods and I walk up the beach, leaving the two of them behind.

chapter 78

The convenience store is at the base of the hill beside the ice cream shack. The air conditioning is on; it feels good. I grab a large bottle of water from the refrigerator and take it to the till.

While the cashier rings it in, I glance down at the local newspaper. The headline reads VOLUNTEER MISSING. I unfold the paper and scan the first paragraphs of the article. "Rita Dobson, 56, local wedding photographer, assisting in the search of the recently deceased Terry Butler, has been missing since last Monday…"

My heart beats faster. I buy the paper and take it with me. I skim through it quickly as I walk and jam it into the nearest garbage before Heather can see it.

As I approach, she spies me. "Hey, baby brother. All good?"

I realize I haven't even opened my water yet. It sounds like a crack of thunder when I do and I take several gulps, covertly scanning the water for Charlie. "He's still out there?"

"The enigma wrapped in a puzzle sealed with a roll of annoying packing tape? Yeah, he's out there."

I spy someone swimming hard toward a buoy and assume it must be him. I toss my bottle of water down beside Heather. "I'm going to swim out, see how he's doing."

She looks up at me, squinting in the sun. "Maybe the cool water will do you good."

"Maybe," I mumble, wandering down to the water. The waves splash around my toes and it's refreshing, but my mind is fixed on getting to Charlie quickly, so I don't savour the feeling.

I see his head bobbing in the water and I dive in and swim toward him with my best front crawl. When I arrive, he's treading water.

"Yo, Shepherd. Finally got off your lazy ass?"

"Someone else is missing."

"The photographer?"

It doesn't surprise me that he knows. "Yeah."

"Yeah." He stays afloat with ease, water splashing against his chest.

"Do you know where she was last seen?" I ask.

He shakes his head and it feels good to know something he doesn't.

"West of Old Fire Tower Road. Right where we were lost."

As soon as I tell him, he swims back to shore. I follow. He climbs out of the water and plunks down on the blanket beside Heather. "How about that ice cream?"

"Actually, I'm good."

"You sure?"

"Yeah. But thank you."

He pulls out his phone scrolling through it pauses and stares up at me. "What's up, Shepherd? Relax and stay awhile."

What's he up to, though? He seemed anxious to get to shore, but now he just wants to sit on the beach? Why isn't he more interested in the missing photographer?

I consider dropping down beside him but decide to go back into the water instead, Rita Dobson's disappearance buzzing in my brain as I plunge in. I swim out until my toes can barely touch bottom then twist back to watch my sister and Charlie sitting on the blanket.

The woman went missing west of the road, right about where we were lost. Terry was buried at the end of Old Fire Tower Road, but he was likely murdered where we found his glasses and the coolers, as well as the burnt book. Those two areas aren't linked to each other—unless you know about the deer head and the garbage bags we found after the storm. Although it was raining and hard to see in the dark, it's doubtful that we wouldn't have noticed them when we first arrived if they'd already been there. Someone had to have been out in those woods, and it's likely the same someone who attacked Terry and the missing photographer.

The question was who? And why had they spared us?

chapter 79

I return to shore where Charlie and Heather are shaking the sand off the blanket.

"Are we heading back?" I ask.

"It's close to supper. If we go now, we can help make it," Charlie says, jamming our stuff in the bag.

Again, this generosity suggests that he's more interested in helping around the cabin than figuring out what's going on in the woods.

He looks up at me, "Right, Shepherd?"

I resign myself. "Sure." I help pack up and carry stuff to the car.

Charlie flips through his phone while he still has reception. "Have either of you been to the library in town?" he asks. "I'm almost finished *A Farewell to Arms* and want to read some more of his stuff."

I laugh. "You're nearly done? Didn't you just start it last night?"

"Shepherd, some of us actually enjoy reading."

It's a dig, but I let it slide.

"I don't even know where the library is," Heather says.

Charlie looks at his screen. "Central Avenue, open Tuesdays to Saturday from nine to five. Unfortunately, they don't have their catalogue online unless you have a library card. Do you think your parents would let us go to town so I could pick something up?"

Heather is immediately distrustful. "What are you really going for?"

"Another book."

"And?"

"Getting my hands on some sharp modernist writing?"

"Charlie—"

"It's a library, Heather. How much trouble can I possibly get into?"

"You don't do anything like a normal person. You always have another plan."

I'm sort of proud that my sister has figured him out.

"Nope. I just want to look through their catalogue and pick up a book."

"And you'll return it? Not steal it?"

He feigns indignance. "Of course!"

"And nothing else?"

He pauses before saying, "I will probably use the internet. 3G is nice, but I'd like something a little faster."

She studies him and we both know she's not done with him.

He raises his hand in a solemn oath. "I promise I will go to the library, check out a book that I will return when read, and maybe use the Wi-Fi. I may ask your brother to take me to Cup of Joan's for a coffee and try to get him to get the coffee lady's phone number…"

Heather gives me a look.

"…and I think that's it." Charlie ponders the to-do list in his mind before looking over at me. "Oh, and maybe get a newspaper to find out what's happening in the world."

"A newspaper? Because the world wide web isn't thorough enough?" My sister's observant nature impresses me again.

"What can I say? Sometimes I like kicking it old school." He gives her a big smile and winks.

I feel the depth of her sigh.

chapter 80

We get back to the cabin and Charlie follows through on all his promises. He helps with supper, which he successfully convinces Mom and Dad to let us make. Even though the rest of the family is outside, he doesn't say much. After supper, he asks us all if we want to play a game of Risk and everyone agrees. I hold my own in the game for a while, occupying North America, but the balance of power soon shifts and Dad and Charlie wipe me out, then Mom, then Heather. The two of them battle it out for nearly another half-hour until Dad finally gets Asia and Australia and quickly finishes Charlie off. By the end of the game, it's late. Charlie grabs his book and sprawls out on the couch by the good reading light.

Since he doesn't mention anything, Mom eventually brings it up. "Heather says you were asking about the library in town?"

Charlie glances up at Mom. "Yeah, I was thinking about it."

"You wanted to pick up a book?"

He nods.

"And maybe get a coffee?" she asks, looking over at me and smiling.

I can see Heather's told her about Laurie. Dammit Charlie, why did you have to bring me into it?

"And then you two will come back to the cabin right after?"

"Yeah, with the drive there and back, a little bit of looking around for a book, and maybe a quick stop at Joan's, I'm hoping it will only take us a couple of hours. Is that okay?"

Mom queries Dad with a glance and he contemplates his answer before leaning forward to say, "If we let you go, we are putting our faith in you to keep your word."

"I understand," Charlie says.

I'm barely in this conversation.

"But if you break this promise, that's it. We can't keep banging our heads against a wall, expecting you to work with us. We'll make sure that you get on the bus safe, but we'd have to ask you to leave."

"Understood."

I hope Charlie means it.

chapter 81

Charlie doesn't talk to me that night and it isn't until we're in the car alone the next morning that he finally says something.

"Do you know how lucky you are, Shepherd?"

"What do you mean?"

"To have a family that gives this much of a crap about you?"

"I do." The more time I spend around Charlie and understand the life he must live, the clearer this becomes.

"In fact, I've never known anyone luckier than you."

It takes me a second to realize what he means by this—that he's never met any parent as loving as the two of mine.

"Explains why you're such a boy scout."

"Can you just stop?"

But he shakes his head. "Serious. If I had parents like yours, I'd be all normal and well-adjusted."

I can't help but laugh out loud. "I don't think you could ever be normal and well-adjusted."

He looks disappointed. "You really don't think I'm going to keep my promise, do you?"

"Nope."

He sticks out his hand. "Wanna bet?"

"What? That you'll do exactly as you say?"

"Yes. To the exact letter."

This feels like a bet I can't lose, but because it's Charlie, I'm suspicious. "To the library, borrow a book—which you won't steal—use the Wi-Fi, look at a newspaper, and maybe grab a coffee?"

"Well, I *was* planning on stealing the book, but I'll check it out from the front desk. And I might look at a few newspapers and have a doughnut with that coffee."

"No stealing, no breaking and entering, no drug dealers, no killers—"

"I can't promise we won't come across dealers or killers—the place seems to be crawling with them. But I do promise not to antagonize any of them."

"If you can do all that, I will buy you that doughnut."

"If I do all that, you can buy me a half-dozen."

"Deal."

chapter 82

We arrive in town and I follow Charlie's directions to the library. It's an old brick building with touches of recent renovations around the windows and front door. We try the door—it's a few minutes after nine o'clock—but it's still locked.

"I don't understand how small towns operate. Closed on Sundays, sometimes Mondays, and even when they say they'll be open, they may or may not be."

"It's called a relaxed way of life."

"But how does anything get done?"

"What does it matter? You haven't been in that much of rush lately."

"What? You mean the past couple of days?"

"Yeah. After I told you about the photographer—"

"Rita Dobson."

I'm embarrassed to have forgotten her name but am even more surprised that Charlie knows it.

"Hey, I do my research."

"Well, you sure didn't seem too concerned yesterday."

"The second I rushed out of the water and wanted to leave, your sister was on to us. I had to act without acting."

"How very Zen of you."

"Just biding my time. But here we are. We need to focus. The glasses, the book—"

"Rita, Terry—"

"And possibly the dead deer and the plastic bags—"

"They're all connected."

"Yes."

"So where do we start?"

"We figure out what's out there?"

"Not much. Forest. Swamps. Deer. Bears. We saw it all the day we got lost."

"But there's got to be something else, something we're missing, so let's find out." He rattles the library door handle again. I think he really expected it to open.

And sure enough, an older woman appears around a corner inside the library and comes to the door. She says something, but we can only hear her muffled voice through the glass, so we shrug and shake our heads. She searches through her key ring until she finds the right one and unlocks the door.

"We're not open yet."

Charlie looks at his phone. "Don't you open at nine?"

She looks at her watch. "Hmm, would you look at that." She holds open the door, stepping out of our way. "Well, come on in, then."

She leads us up the stairs and we wait beside the front desk until she gets behind it. There is a wood name plaque with "Gladys" engraved on it beside a small dish of pale green mints. Charlie digs into it and pops one in his mouth, chomping down on the hard candy.

Once she's seated, she says, "Not used to seeing a couple of young fellows like you on a fine summer's day. What can I do for you?"

Charlie gets right to business. "Well, a couple of things, Gladys. I'm wondering if I can get a library card and—?"

"Slow down, one thing at a time." She turns to a filing cabinet behind her and rolls out not one but two drawers before finding the application form she wants. She sets it down in front of Charlie and hands him a pen.

He spies the computer beside her. "Don't you do this electronically?"

"Oh, I could," she shrugs, "but this way I get it all correct and can do it at my own pace."

We look around the empty room. "So, while you're typing that out, we can look around?"

"Certainly. But you can't take anything out until I issue you a card."

"And you can't issue a card until—"

"I assign you a number—"

"Which I'll get after you finish typing it out?"

"Now you're understanding."

Charlie forces a smile. Gladys isn't going to make this easy for him. He leans down and fills out the sheet.

"I don't suppose you have any sort of map section?" I ask.

Gladys stares at me and I worry that I may have derailed the task at hand. After a long pause, she asks, "What are you looking for?"

"Local maps. Maybe landscape?"

"Topographical or RM?"

"What's the difference?"

She scowls at me again. I guess she doesn't have the patience for my ignorance. "You could check the 900s."

I shake my head and search the walls for some sign as to where to go.

"Shepherd." Charlie nods toward a doorway. Beyond it is a room filled with wooden bookshelves with the Dewey Decimal classification written in black, flowing calligraphy on old paper and attached to the end of each partition. I give the two of them a thumbs-up—Gladys is definitely not impressed—and head into the room.

The numbers on the shelves are ordered from left to right so I walk to the back. It's musty in here, and in the corner are small bluish-green machines that look like hundred-year-old computers. The shelf at the end is where the 900s begin and I study it. Although the shelves are tall, many are only halfway filled. There's a geographical atlas of the province at the front of one of these and I narrow down my search to that shelf. There are road maps, travel guides, books full of historical maps, geographical maps, geological maps, and other books describing the origins of nearby towns. Finally, at the end of the stack, I locate the book Gladys was talking about: a topographical atlas full of maps detailing the physical features of every inch of the town and its surrounding the area. Beside it is another book containing photocopied RM, or rural municipality, maps that also names everyone who owned land around Estoria at the time of publication. I grab them both and carry them to a table.

I'm halfway through the topographical book when Charlie comes over.

"How goes it? Do you have your card?" I ask.

"Gladys tells me it'll be another ten minutes. Have you tried the Wi-Fi?" Charlie winces to show his disapproval.

"That bad?"

"I think it might be dial-up."

"What's that?"

He gives me a look. "It means I have a better chance of surfing the net when I'm lost with you in the woods than standing right beside this building's router. Tell me you have something."

I show him the two books I've pulled out.

He takes the one with the RM maps and flips through it. "Interesting. Looks like most of these forests are on provincial land owned by the government." He shows me a jagged, pixelated shape beside the lake. "See, even the road to your cabin is owned by the political regime."

He searches some more. "Nope, there's nothing, no roads or buildings out where we were lost." He slides the book back toward me. "Here's your resort," he shows me where it cuts a small hole in the mass of provincial land. "It's separate. But everything west and north of there"—he flips over the pages to prove his point—"is all government property. No one lives out there."

He grabs the topographical map out of my hands and examines it. "Here's Old Fire Tower Road and there's the hill where the fire tower used to stand." The lines that circle the tower seem to represent the shape of the hill it's actually built on. Charlie runs a finger west along the coastline. "We probably found Terry's glasses somewhere around here and travelled inland here." His finger trails up a quarter of the page and stops. "But from there, I have no clue how far we got." He runs his finger back to the shore then looks for where the resort is. "So then we travelled somewhat in this direction—"

"Until the storm hit, then we can't be certain," I add.

"Right." Charlie says, studying the map. "There's nothing out there, though. It's just hills and valleys."

"And trees." I pull the book over to me and look at the place where we found the glasses. I move my finger past where Charlie traced our path until I come across a creek that winds its way from the north, then turns west toward the lake. "This whole area burned in that forest fire twenty years ago. Nothing could have survived it. And even if it did, the firefighters would likely have found it."

Charlie's face lights up. "Maybe they did."

chapter 83

Charlie jumps up and goes to talk to Gladys. "Do you keep web archives of the *Estoria Journal*?"

I think he's already talking above her level of technical comprehension, but she throws a hardball right back at him.

"We have everything on microfiche. Is that what you're asking for?"

"Uh…"

She glares and waves Charlie over to a stack of thin file drawers.

"What year do you want?"

"Not sure. About twenty years ago, there was a forest fire?"

"Ah, yes, the summer of '94."

She tugs one of the drawers open and it's full of cartons the size of matchboxes. She runs her finger over them until she finds the one she's looking for and pulls it out. Guiding him over to the machine in the corner that looks like an old computer, she flips a switch and the screen lights up like a digital projector.

She opens the box, pulls out a roll of film and slips it on a peg, unrolling it and guiding it through the machine before hooking it to a spool on the other side. She cranks a handle and images and text zip past on the screen. It takes me a second to realize that it's the newspaper.

Charlie whistles. "Whoa, this is just like a spy movie. Are you really James Bond, Gladys?"

She isn't amused. "Each roll has two months on it. The fire started in July and burned until August."

She continues spinning through the reel until she arrives at the front page of the July 21st edition. The front-page headline reads: WILDFIRE RAGES. Below it is a photo taken from the bridge of a thick, dark cloud rising above the forest, blocking out the sun.

"That looks like a beast," Charlie says. "It says it took out almost fifty thousand acres of woods."

"They actually thought it would skip over the river and take out Estoria," Gladys says as the memory comes back to her. "They brought in water bombers, the army, almost everyone."

"What started it?" Charlie asks.

"Lightning."

"Why didn't they catch it sooner?"

"They should have, but it was dry and the winds pushed it far and wide before anyone arrived."

"Did anyone die?"

"I remember a couple of firefighters got caught when the wind shifted…"

"Any civilians?" Charlie asks.

"Not that I ever heard of."

"There weren't any settlements or businesses out that way?"

Gladys is suspicious. "What exactly is your interest in all this?"

"Curiosity," Charlie says mildly. "I like to know about the places I visit."

"Well, there's more about it in the history books."

This piques Charlie's interest. "Can you show me those?"

She sighs. "You know, I haven't even had my coffee."

"Gladys, you do this for me and I will get my friend here to buy you your coffee."

She brings over *Keepsakes and Memories: A History of Estoria* and Charlie hands it to me. I hunt through its contents while he spins through the microfiche.

It turns out Estoria was a part of the early fur trade, a meeting place where First Nations and Europeans bartered their goods. By the mid-1700s, a line of trading posts had been built along the river, including a spot just east of Estoria where the bridge now stands. A fort was later constructed and eventually burned to the ground when trading was no longer profitable. In the early 1900s, settlers came and homesteaded in the area, and stores and lumber mills soon followed. When the railroad arrived, the town was established where present-day Estoria now stands.

I flip through accounts of the first schoolhouse, the first grain elevator, and the first railway station. There are stories about curling bonspiels, hockey teams, and elections. It's interesting in its own way, but nothing seems relevant to our search—that is, until I find a personal account from Barry Pederson, the last forest ranger to occupy the Estoria fire tower.

I slide it over to Charlie and Gladys catches sight of it. "Ah, yes, Barry…"

Charlie looks over at her. "Do you know him?"

She gets a funny look on her face and I wonder if they'd been sweethearts or something. "He'd come to town for dances and all us girls wanted our chance with him."

This amuses Charlie. "Quite the ladies man?"

"He could cut a rug with his footwork," she agrees, and she actually giggles.

"Did you two ever hook up?"

Gladys scowls at Charlie. "He was *always* a gentleman."

Charlie turns away from her. "Uh, huh…"

"Anyhow," I say, interrupting this strange line of questioning, "it says he served with the Forestry Department for over thirty years."

Gladys nods. "He worked at the fire tower until they shut it down in 1978."

"What happened to him?"

"The damn government moved him to town and into an office. He was none too happy about it. Still misses the woods."

"Still?"

She glowers. "Of course. He's up at Spruce Vista."

Charlie and I stare at her.

Gladys looks exasperated by our ignorance. "At the nursing home, up on the hill."

chapter 84

Charlie and I have spent almost an hour at the library, and step out to call Mom for an extension. "We're running a little behind."

"That doesn't surprise me," Mom says over the phone.

"Well, Charlie says the library is better than he expected."

"Really?"

I look through the glass doors to where he's standing at the front desk, checking out another Hemingway novel. "Uh, yeah. You know how he is. Get him talking books and he doesn't shut up. He's friends with the librarian now and everything."

As if she can hear me, Gladys looks up at me and glares. Fortunately, Mom has seen Dad and Charlie chat it up about books, so I'm not stretching the truth too far.

"I suppose he does like his literature. How much more time do you need?" Mom asks.

"Half-hour to an hour?"

"Hmmm. That seems like a lot."

I throw myself under the bus. "He thought that maybe we could sit down for coffee and visit with Laurie for a bit."

Mom's quiet on the other end of the phone, chewing on the options. "All right. One more hour, then home."

"Thanks, Mom." I hang up as Charlie steps outside.

"All good?" he asks.

"Surprisingly, yes. Like I always say, communication is a positive thing."

He rolls his eyes. "Ready?"

"Uh-huh. A quick visit to Spruce Vista?" I ask.

"You know it isn't a part of our bet?"

Curiosity eats at me. "How about I allow it this one time?"

"You sure? Wouldn't want you to feel cheated."

I nod and Charlie smirks. We jump in the car and drive up the hill to find the town's last forest ranger.

chapter 85

None of my grandparents made it to a nursing home. Mom's parents lived in their home until Grandpa died and then Grandma passed away only a few months afterward. Dad's parents lived on the other side of the country and when the time came, they moved into seniors' housing, which allowed them independence and daily visits from assisted living. So when I step into Spruce Vista, I feel unsettled.

Although it has a lot of windows, the place is unusually dim, with rows of fluorescents spilling cold light down the hallways. Across from the entrance is a hall with a shuffleboard table and a piano where several residents are arranged in a circle and secured in their wheelchairs. An open doorway leads to a carpeted room where relatives visit their loved ones in hushed tones. A memorial made up of the pictures of a man and a woman who have recently passed away stands on a table between the two rooms, surrounded by flowers. We need some directions, but I don't see a front desk or even a listing of the residents.

"I think we're going to have to ask someone," I say.

Charlie is extraordinarily quiet, just like he was on the boat after we were found, but he spies a nurses' station down the hall and walks toward it. I follow. He approaches a dark-haired nurse a little younger than my mom.

"I'm wondering if you can help us find Barry Pederson?" Charlie asks.

"And you are?"

I expect Charlie to come up with some complex lie, but he surprises me. "My name is Charles and this is Anthony. We don't actually know him, but we read about him being a forest officer back in the day, and we're wondering if he'd tell us about it."

She considers Charlie's request. "He doesn't get many visitors these days."

"We promise not to stay long."

She laughs. "That's what *you* think. Come with me."

She guides us back the way we came, past the entrance. We travel down a long hallway that turns left, moving through an open room filled with residents and a blaring television. An old man reaches up to cop a feel of the nurse, but she brushes him away without even acknowledging him.

We continue down the hallway, and as we pass one door, we hear the moans of an older woman. None of it affects our guide, or Charlie for that matter, but I can't help but feel a chill.

As we pass another doorway, a wheelchair shoots out, but the nurse grabs it before it hits her shin.

"Dorothy, we've asked you to stop doing that."

I see a woman grinning at the edge of her bed, an oxygen mask over her face, one hand resting on the tank. We take a final turn and the nurse leads us to a closed door.

She knocks. "Barry, are you awake?"

Without waiting for an answer, she enters the small room. It has only a bed, a dresser, a closet, and a door to a bathroom. A radio is playing 1950s rock 'n' roll, but Barry's nowhere to be seen. She does a quick inspection before heading out into the hallway again.

"He does this sometimes." She goes down to the end of the hallway and looks into another resident's room. A woman is napping in bed while an older man with a white beard, red suspenders, and different-coloured socks relaxes in the rocking chair.

The nurse takes him by the hand. "Come along, Barry."

"Just waiting for my dance."

"Let Helen rest."

As she leads him into the hall, he hears the music playing in his room and he shuffles his feet. "Come along, Katheryn," he says, slipping his other hand onto her shoulder.

She doesn't stop him but instead dances him toward his room. As I watch the two of them shake and shimmy their way along, I can see what Gladys was talking about. Barry must be seventy or eighty years old, and he's still got moves that would put some of my friends to shame. I'm scared he's going to blow a hip—or his whole body—but his enthusiasm for the music is infectious.

The nurse manoeuvres him back through his door as the song ends. He finishes with a flourish, then says, "If I were a little younger, I would have dipped you, Katheryn."

It seems Barry's given her a workout and she has to catch her breath. "It's good you didn't—I might not have made it back up!"

Barry notices us. "Stay clear, boys. Katheryn is *my* dance partner."

"Actually, Barry, they're here to see you."

"Really?" His face lights up at the possibility of visitors.

"They heard you used to be a forest ranger. Would you like to visit with them?"

"Well, indeed." He gestures to the door. "Boys, why don't we step into my office."

chapter 86

Barry's office is a sunroom at the end of the hall. It's filled with shelves of books and magazines. Two women work together, sewing a patchwork blanket.

The nurse sets Barry up at a table in the corner with a couple of romance novels sitting on top. He helps her pull up two more chairs for us, and as she leaves, he calls out, "Katheryn, please come back for us in an hour."

Since we need to leave town before then, I catch up to her. "Excuse me, Katheryn, we only need about fifteen minutes with him."

She smiles, but there's pity for her patient in her eyes. "He thinks I just dropped you off at the fire tower."

"What?"

"When he said come back in an hour, he thinks I'm bringing the boat back."

Seems like Barry's not fully out of the woods himself.

"And my name's Susan. I'm not sure who Katheryn is, but he's been calling me that since the day he arrived."

I sit down beside Charlie, not sure how to explain to him that this may not go the way we planned, but Barry kicks things off right away. "So you boys want a tour of the tower?"

I catch Charlie's look and shrug.

Barry taps the table between us. "This here is the Fire Finder. We use it to identify the precise location of a fire." He stands the romance novels on their ends and turns them so that he can peer along their spines. "We look through the apertures to sight the fire and read the degrees off the compass. But you notice these notches?" He points to the lettering on the spine of the book. "These work like an alidade to give us a rough distance of the fire. Ideally, I'd work with Roy to find the intersection." He pauses, pleased with this explanation.

Charlie's curiosity gets the best of him. "Roy?"

Barry looks out the window beside him, squinting at the light. "Over at Flame Creek Fire Tower." He waves.

I don't know what he's looking at, but all Charlie and I can see is a maintenance worker riding a lawnmower across Spruce Vista's lawn.

"Barry, how long have you worked at the fire tower?" Charlie asks.

This stumps him. "Five... five years...? Fifty...?" He looks down at the table.

Since Gladys already told us he'd worked there thirty years, we know he's way off. Charlie takes a different approach. "Is it true they're thinking of shutting the towers down?"

Barry's brow creases and his eyes mist up. "That's what they're saying. Already closed down a bunch in Ontario. Fear they're going to come this way soon."

He must be thinking it's sometime before 1978.

"Must've been quiet out there?" I ask.

"Yeah, but you keep yourself busy. Lots to do. Hauling water, getting food, cleaning and maintaining the tower, the instruments, the radio—"

"Do you go into the woods much?"

"I go all the time. Just north of here is a nice patch of blueberries and down by the water you can find saskatoons—"

"Anything to see out there?"

"Oh, sure. Moose, deer, bear, fox, coyotes. I got a couple of squirrels to come all the way up to the deck outside. You want a tour? It's beautiful. Especially this time of year."

It's becoming apparent just how disconnected Barry is from the present.

"Anything else?"

He thinks for a minute longer than he should. "Nope."

Charlie pushes a bit. "I hear people are always seeing UFOS out here."

Barry scoffs at the idea. "Hell, people get their heads full of the craziest ideas. I've been here for ages and all I've seen are some weather balloons. Half these folks probably see a falling star and think it's aliens."

By now the sewing ladies have tired of our talk. They get up and leave the sunroom.

I decide to change the direction of the questions. "What happens when you spot a fire?"

"Well, Roy and I position it, then we call it in."

"You don't go and fight it?"

"No way. We call in the fire fellas to deal with it and we offer radio support to the water bombers."

"You see many bad fires?"

"Not during my time but there was that one a few years back," Barry says. It dawns of me that we've skipped ahead in time as he continues, "I always said if we'd been on the ground instead of trusting a bunch of machines in the sky, we'd have caught that sooner."

"Were you in the office back then?"

"Ah, no. Retired from that job in '90 before it happened."

So he was out of the service for four years when the fire hit.

"I saw the pictures," Charlie says, "it was pretty big."

"Oh yeah, it was scary. Really worried about them."

We both catch it, but I let Charlie take the lead. "Who? The firefighters?"

Barry pauses, the switches in his brain firing, trying to figure out what he's just said and what we know. He doesn't answer.

Charlie asks again, "Which folks were you worried about, Barry?"

He looks around and seems to realize he's not in the fire tower anymore. He shifts uncomfortably in his seat, studying us. "Who you boys again?"

I lean forward. "Barry, do you know about someone out in the woods by the fire tower?"

He breathes out slowly. "I said I'd never tell anyone."

"I think it might be time you did." This is bold of me, but I think it's time to step things up.

Until this moment, he's been looking around the room, distracted by every shift of sunlight through the windows, every loose thread on his sweater, every speck of dust on the table, but now he looks me in the eye.

"I suppose I've kept this secret long enough."

chapter 87

"Back in '74, these city folks came out to see me at the tower. Just showed up, didn't call or nothing. One morning, I wake up and look down and see this mustard-coloured van outside my cabin. I didn't know where it came from. When I go on out and look through the windows and curtains, I see this young couple sleeping butt-naked in the back."

He takes a moment, arranging the books, fiddling with the plastic bracelet that has his name stamped on it, before carrying on.

"Now, I get couples coming around all the time, looking for some privacy in the woods or on the beach to make out, and I ain't got no problem, with what people do. In fact, I don't even blame them for wanting to do it." He looks past us at a nurse and gives her a wink, sharing an approving nod with us.

"But I never had them pull right up to my door and do it. Well, I bang on the roof to wake this couple up so I can run them off, but after dressing and apologizing, they say they're here to talk to me.

"Turns out this couple came from out east. A couple of professors from a university out there. Making their way across the country, camping in their van, with one big plan. They dreamed of one day having themselves a family and decided that city life was no longer for them. Things were getting rough in the city, not only because of crime but because the police were even shooting unarmed folks." He glances at me and unfortunately I understand what he means.

"Anyways, before they leave the city, they open themselves an atlas, close their eyes, flip the pages, and end up sticking their finger down on my lake. In fact, they drop it right on my road and decide to drive all the way here.

"Now, out here, it's just about me and no one else…" He gestures to the room and it's evident he sees something different than we do. "Sure, there's a few folks who built some places by the lake, but unless you know which old logging road to turn down, you'll find yourself stucker than mud in the middle of nowhere."

Barry laughs. "My goodness these two don't know what they got themselves into. Read a couple of books—you know the type, 'I went to the woods one day because I wished to live deliberately'—thinking they'll build themselves a home out of logs. They ended up selling most of their stuff to start new in the wilderness."

He goes back to studying his bracelet, eventually taking a novel from the pile and slipping a corner of the cover between the plastic band and his skin. He works the book back and forth like he's trying to cut through it.

"What did you tell them?" I ask, trying to keep him focused.

"Well, the first thing I tell them is they're on government land and they can do no such thing as live out here. They try to reason with me, ask me who they can talk to, what forms they can fill out, that sort of thing. They even offer money, hoping to talk me into their way of thinking, but I tell them I'm not the person to talk to. They yak themselves blue in the face and when I won't give an inch, they pack themselves into their van and I think that's that."

He shifts in his chair, stretching his back, taking a deep breath.

"A few weeks ago, I see a little smoke rising above the trees from the west. Nothing big, but I can't figure out where it's coming from, so I haul myself out to see what's what. Sure enough, I come through the woods and there's the couple still living out of their van. The place is a real mess. They set themselves up a camp but are driving to town in their van for supplies. They're buying all this canned stuff and dumping the remains. They're smart enough not to keep things close and attract bears, but it don't take long for wild animals to arrive and start sniffing around. The critters get so bad, the couple starts driving their van over to their dumping pile to get rid of the garbage.

"Well, I say I'm going to report them to the local officers and they say they'll drive away before I call. So I get them gone and figure that's now the end of it, but sure enough a couple of months go by and I'm inspecting fire lines way out west and what do I come across but that mustard-coloured van. It's far deep in the woods this time, along an old trapper's line, and the tires are flat and there's a layer of dirt and sap that's thick as crust on this van, but no sight of them. I'm thinking maybe they left it there, but maybe they gave it one more try, despite my saying to leave.

"I hunt around a bit, but I got a job to do and it doesn't include chasing a couple of damn city folks, so I head back. But the whole thing works into my mind like a bug and I start searching the woods. I take out my map, break it into a grid, and every couple of days, go out and search a few miles. It takes me only a few weeks before I find them, not far from where they left the van, but you wouldn't believe it—they'd gone and done it."

"What?" Charlie asks.

"Built themselves a home. Now, I'm not saying it's pretty—I think there are more holes in it than there is wood—but they put a roof over their heads. They got a little bed made of cloth and leaves, stumps for sitting and eating, and even a split log shelf on the wall to put their books. But they're skinnier than homeless dogs because they barely caught themselves any food and are only living on a bit of fish and berries they scrounged up.

"I tell them I've got to report them and they say please, please, please don't, and I say they're going to kill themselves out here and I can't have that on my conscience, and they say they're hurting no one but themselves."

Barry stares at us, looking tired.

Charlie urges him on, "You didn't report them, did you?"

Barry shakes his head. "They were happy. Despite their skinniness and their awful home, they'd gone to the woods and done 'lived deliberately.' I can get it. I understand. The woods have a way about them, their own time, their own schedule, their own rules. I like going into town and listening to the bands play and dancing with the ladies, but I need to go home at the end of the night and look up at the stars and the northern lights and see a world all its own."

"What happened next?" Charlie asks.

"I make an agreement with them. I won't tell anyone, but they have to promise to take my help. I set up a drop box at the end of the road and dump food and supplies in it at the end of the month and they pick it up. Nothing too big. Some fruit and vegetables, a blanket or two, maybe some traps." Barry shrugs. "Never saw them, never bothered them. I figured, out of sight, out of mind, right? Anyone asks, I can deny everything.

"Well, for about six months, I'd go to the drop box, find it empty, and fill it up. Then one day, I come out, open it, and it's still full. I get worried, so the next week, I check again. Still full. I think maybe they don't need my help anymore. But I also think maybe they died, so the next week I go, I'm ready to head into the woods and look for them, but I decide to check the box one last time. I open it and it's empty except for a book. That damn fool Thoreau book that sent them out there to begin with, and when I look it over, someone's scratched with charcoal the word 'Thanks' on the inside cover.

"Well, after that, I leave them alone. Every once and awhile I think about them, but the longer time goes by, the more they slip from my mind. It isn't until this damn fire burns through the area that I think about them again. So after it's done, I head out to look, but there's no trace of them, not even of their cabin."

"Did you ever find out what happened to them?" Charlie asks.

He shakes his head, looking sad. "I didn't even know their names."

chapter 88

Barry leans back and we know he's done. He looks exhausted, like the secret has kept him running all these years. He doesn't wait for the nurse and shuffles out of the sunroom to his room. We follow to make sure he gets there safely.

"Do you believe him?" I whisper to Charlie as we trail behind.

"I'm not sure."

"He barely knows what year it is now. Maybe it's all in his head."

"Maybe. But time was his trouble, not the facts."

The nurse comes down the hall and she takes him by the arm. No more dancing for him. It appears he's ready for bed.

As we're walking to the exit, Charlie says, "I don't think he's ever told that story before in his life."

"He's never had to," I agree. "No one knew they existed."

We step outside and go to the car. I can't stop thinking about what Barry has told us. "If that couple *was* out there, maybe they're still alive."

"Maybe they're the ones that killed Terry and the photographer—"

"Rita Dobson—"

"Yeah, because they just wanted to be left alone."

As we climb inside the car, he looks at me. "Not just alone."

"What do you mean?"

"They wanted a family." He has a distant look in his eye before he comes back to the present and glances at me. "But right now you owe me doughnuts and Gladys a coffee!"

"Fine, but only because you behaved."

"See, you can take me out around people every once in awhile."

"Just like Ollie," I say with a grin.

He smiles as he stares out the window. "Hey, just be happy I didn't hump the furniture."

chapter 89

We pull up to Cup of Joan's. Charlie doesn't move from his seat but pulls out his phone.

"You're not coming?"

"Nah. I'll just siphon the Wi-Fi from here while you go in." He peers up at me through his perpetually shaggy hair, "Besides, I don't want to crowd your moves."

I shake my head and get out of the car. I can't stop thinking about the college couple in the woods and I'm only half aware of my surroundings as I enter.

Laurie's at her usual spot behind the till and I head right to the counter.

"Charlie not with you today?"

My mind isn't on the here and now and I am slow to nod to the window. "He's out in the car. I owe him a half-dozen doughnuts—and can I get three coffees too?"

"You're becoming my best customer." She pauses, coyly tucking her hair behind her ear. "Not that I mind."

By the time I register what she's up to, I've waited too long—any response will be awkward. I make it worse by forcing a smile as I pay for the coffee and doughnuts and rush out of the cafe. I'm thankful Charlie is in the car and didn't see my failure to flirt. Still, I'm not entirely bothered. Although Laurie is attractive, my heart's not yet into it.

Before I can even get my seatbelt on, Charlie's taken the box of doughnuts out of my hand and cracked it open. He scans the options and decides on a cookies and cream. He takes a bite and I've never seen anyone enjoy a doughnut so much.

"You good?" I ask.

Charlie doesn't answer immediately, chewing and clutching his phone tight.

"Good Wi-Fi. Good doughnuts. Good times," he cries out. I worry he'll punch the roof he's so enthusiastic.

He takes another bite, swallows, and looks like a happy man. "All right, let's take Gladys her coffee."

chapter 90

Charlie isn't in the library for long. In no time, he comes back out and hops in the car. I can tell by his face that something is up.

"What?" I ask.

He tosses a mint into his mouth—he must've snagged another from Gladys's bowl—and crunches on it. "Just drive."

As I throw the car into gear and pull away from the curb, Charlie pulls out a small reel of film.

"You stole a microfiche?"

"Yeah, but before you freak out—"

"A little late for that!"

"Fair enough, but I'm just borrowing it."

"Borrowing? As in stealing then returning?"

"Well, I guess if you put it that way..."

I slow the car to make a u-ball.

Charlie turns to me. "Come on, let's just go. Your parents are waiting on us.".

"No way. We made a deal. Hell, we made a *bet*—"

"Yeah, we made a bet and I won and you closed it out by buying me doughnuts. The contract is done."

"Charlie! You can't go around stealing shit all the time."

"Hey, I'm trying to keep a promise to your parents, but more research is needed."

"On what?"

"The university couple."

"Barry couldn't remember their names, if his story is even true. How are we going to research anything about them?"

"Maybe we don't have to."

chapter 91

Before leaving town, Charlie has me stop at the local pharmacy. He's in and out quickly and we're soon on our way back to the cabin.

"What? Did you steal something from there too?"

"I *bought* this, thank you very much," he says pulling out a magnifying glass.

He opens up the roll of film and squints at it through the glass lens. As the car bounces along, I can just make out the handwriting on the box the microfiche came in: "May-June 1996." Of all the films in the library, why that one?

And it's like he reads my mind. "I've been thinking about everything," Charlie says. "There's Terry and Rita and the book, the bags, and the deer."

"Uh-huh?"

"And I've been wondering if we've been thinking too small."

"What do you mean?"

"We've been focused on the present, but we haven't considered the past."

"Like when the couple arrived?"

"Exactly. They might have arrived sometime in the '70s, right? If what's going on now is connected to them, what else has happened that might be connected to them?"

"You aren't talking about aliens again, are you?"

He taps his nose. "Remember that farmer who mysteriously disappeared a long time ago?"

"The one who they say still mows his field?"

"That's the guy. While you were inside getting doughnuts and sweet-talking Laurie, I did some research and found out that's only half the story. Turns out, he *did* show up again, a few towns over, shacked up with a lady-friend. Needless to say, his wife wasn't too happy about it. So nothing to do with our hippy couple. But those two hunters that got lost? Well, the one hunter that returned? He said that after they got separated, he—get this—holed up in the shell of a yellow van in the middle of the forest."

"Holy shit, Barry's story really does have some truth to it."

Charlie nods.

"Don't tell me you've solved the ghost lights too?" I ask.

"Nope."

"Then what's with the microfiche?"

"The only other unknown."

I look at him.

"The missing kid," he says.

"The one from the '90s?"

"Bingo."

chapter 92

Charlie scours the 1996 microfiche until he locates a news article about a missing girl, but even with the magnifying glass, the fine print is too difficult to read on the drive home. The rest of the research will have to wait.

Our arrival home—together and on time—buys us good will from Mom and Dad, and to solidify this, we spend a couple of hours with them. They challenge us to a game of ladder-ball and trounce us. When Heather gets back from the beach, Mom swaps with her to retire to the deck with a glass of wine. We get destroyed even worse; Heather's not going to let Charlie beat her at anything.

Our colossal losses mean that we're on the hook to make supper and set the table, and we agree, although I can't wait to read what's on the film and I'm sure Charlie is just as curious. Afterward, they send us out to chop wood and get the firepit ready while Mom and Dad wash dishes. Heather follows us down, so we're unable to talk, but Charlie keeps the mood relaxed by challenging my sister to a marshmallow-roasting contest with me as the willing judge. Heather finds some nice coals, and when Charlie sees her advantage, he crowds her spot.

"Hey, enough, or you'll ruin both of them," she cries out.

"All's fair in caramelized sugar and war," says Charlie.

"Wow, you really do try to ruin everything, don't you?" Heather says, but she's smiling.

When the golden and gooey marshmallows are presented, I make a show of studying their shape and colouring.

"You better be careful choosing the winner, little brother," Heather says. "After Charlie goes home, you'll still have to live with me."

"He has to live with you *and* eat that overcooked tripe? Why would you make him suffer twice?" Charlie goads, earning a scowl from her.

I taste them both. "Tonight we gather to measure the merit of the marshmallows. And although one might think they would taste the same, the honour of greatest toaster goes to"—I pause for dramatic effect—"Heather."

She cheers while Charlie boos. "The jury is rigged! I never stood a chance."

"Don't be a poor sport," Heather scolds. But she's still smiling.

"Fine, I'll let it go," Charlie says amiably, "but will you please afford me the privilege of one of your marshmallows since mine are so poor by comparison?"

She shoots him a dirty look but obligingly digs into the bag and stabs another one onto her stick.

"If I'm murdered in my sleep," Charlie stage whispers to me, "you won't have to look too hard for the guilty party."

chapter 93

After spending some time around the fire with the family, Charlie goes up to bed. I follow shortly after. By the time I join him, Charlie's already got the magnifier and microfiche in hand.

"It's hard to see."

I grab a flashlight and position it behind the film, projecting it onto the wall beside the bunk bed.

"Nice thinking, Shepherd."

I keep the light steady while he turns through the roll.

"There."

The image of a small child splashes over the wall.

He moves the film back and forth to focus it. "Pull the light back a little more so it's bigger."

I follow his instructions and the shadowy image of the newspaper fills half the wall. We read it together, but Charlie skips through it quickly, finding the important parts. He reads aloud, "'Police continue search for Joanna Grassing, age two, after she disappeared from her campsite last weekend…'" He scans down the page, "'…was berry-picking with her mother and stepfather while camping at Dyson's Point…' This happened on your home turf, here, buddy."

"Hey, I wasn't even born," I protest.

He reads some more. "'They weren't at the campsite but travelled west…'" He drops the roll as he thinks about it. "Right into the burnt area?"

"That's prime picking," I say. "Blueberries love scorched land. They thrive like crazy."

Charlie lifts the film up again. "Searchers scoured the area, working down to the water and across for a mile. A child that age, that size, could never have gotten far."

"Unless someone found her beforehand."

Charlie unspools the film until he stops at a headline: STEP-FATHER BROUGHT IN FOR QUESTIONING. He works his way down the page. "'Police question the parents of two-year-old Joanna after neighbouring campsites reported hearing an argument the night before her disappearance.'" He looks over at me. "This pisses me off so much."

I'm not sure if he's mad at the parents or the police for questioning them, but he doesn't elaborate. He reads a bit more before his hand drops. "It's certainly motive."

"For who? The step-dad?"

He glares at me. "No, the hippy folks."

"What do you mean?"

"Barry said they were done with mankind. What if they overheard the fight at the campground? Maybe the hippy couple think they can look after the kid better than her own parents."

"Or maybe she just wandered off…"

He ignores me. "So they think she needs protection—"

"Or she drowned. Or was attacked by a wild animal."

"They would've found a body." He rolls the film back. "Look, they brought cadaver dogs, searched the area, found nothing."

"Charlie, I think you're reaching."

"So where did she go, then, Shepherd?"

I don't have an answer.

"Okay, let's pretend: what if she survived?"

"She'd be what, twenty-two?"

"And she's still out there, living life in the woods."

"Killing deer and people?"

"But also reading classic novels and helping lost teenagers."

I'm not buying it. "It could be anybody."

"Agreed. Or it could be Joanna."

"Or the hippies. What's your point?"

"I think it's time you and I go introduce ourselves."

part 4

chapter 94

On Wednesday morning, Charlie and I get permission to take out the canoe, which is none the worse for wear even after being half-submerged, with the promise that we absolutely won't leave the shoreline or do any exploring in the woods. Neither Charlie nor I is interested in undergoing the same ordeal twice. But just to be safe, Charlie packs rain ponchos and a roadside survival emergency kit.

Our plan seems straightforward enough. Since Charlie has cell reception down by the water, we're going to wrap his phone in a plastic bag, along with my number on a piece of paper, and shove it into the hole where we found the burnt book.

"What if they don't know how to use it?" I ask.

"It seems they can read. Let's write out some detailed instructions."

Charlie writes everything simply and clearly, and includes drawings that detail how to locate the "on" button and how to send a call. He even includes a diagram for where to listen and how to speak into the phone. While I admire his skill at making a cellphone understandable to someone who's never used one, the more we explain, the more complicated the whole thing seems.

As we push the canoe out into the water, I have to ask, "How do we know this will even work?"

"We don't. We just have to hope we get lucky."

"But what if it doesn't?"

He shrugs. "I don't know."

I can see him trying to work through all the possibilities as he paddles, so I counter quickly. "We're not sitting around waiting for them, okay?"

"Why not?" He must have already been considering this.

"Run-ins with these people didn't work out so well for Terry or Rita."

"But if we wait in the canoe—?"

"For how long? And if they have weapons, like guns or spears or something? No way."

He surveys me with disbelief. "Spears? Really, Shepherd? Do you really think they're that primitive?"

"Who knows? They might ask us for supper and we might be the meal. The point is that we don't know anything about them and that's the trouble."

He lifts the oar and pauses, thinking it over.

I continue, "This plan with the phone is as far as it goes. Either way, after this, I think we need to tell someone and leave it alone."

"Like the cops?"

"Sure," I say, hoping to reason with him. "Gekas listened to us last time—"

"After repeatedly getting in our way."

I shake my head. "We weren't exactly the most helpful—"

"Well, you weren't—"

"Oh yeah, *you're* the model citizen."

He shrugs and paddles again.

"Charlie, you may not like it but whether we hear from the forest people or not, I'm going to tell someone." I know he hates handing control over to others but I'm hoping that if I draw the line, he'll be reasonable.

"You really think I'll let you wear the big boy pants?"

I just keep rowing, but I can feel him studying me.

"All right, Shepherd. You can have your way this time."

We paddle up to the beach, and I stay in the canoe while he climbs out. As I watch him walk up the shore, it occurs to me that if someone really is out here, they very well could be hiding in the woods, watching us right this moment. In fact, if they're as dangerous as it seems they might be, they could rush either of us and there wouldn't be much we could do.

"Hurry up," I say as Charlie approaches the tree line.

He looks back at me. "You worried we're going to get attacked?" He scans the woods. "You know, it's possible. They could get you with an arrow, or maybe I step into a snare, or some naked man could rush out and drag me off into the trees." He leans down beside the fallen tree and checks to make sure *The Great Gatsby* is still there.

"Shepherd, would you leap out of the boat and come save me from the naked man?" He tightens the bag with the phone, smoothing its surface, and slides it in beside the book. "What would you do? Grab the flare out of my bag? Or maybe the bear-banger? Would you chase after me and try to scare them away? I don't know if that'd work, but I sure hope you'd at least try." He jumps down the bank and splashes back toward me, then drags himself back into the canoe.

"All good?" I ask.

He picks up his oar. "I think so."

As we row away from the beach, he looks back at me. "Seriously, would you risk your life to rescue me?"

"I don't know. I guess so."

"Cool." He starts rowing again, "Because I wouldn't hesitate to save your sorry ass."

I don't need to question whether or not he's telling the truth.

chapter 95

She sees them push away from the lake's edge just as she arrives.

The deer's head warning didn't seem to have worked. They've returned and they'll likely come back again. There is no choice—she must follow them.

They row their canoe along the shore and she pursues them, out of sight, silent, in the shadow of the tree line. When the trail grows too thick, she retreats into the bushes, but she can still hear them, a constant chatter like noisy squirrels.

They draw her further away from her home and closer to their world. The sounds of the forest fall away and the disruptive noise of civilization and mankind interferes with her thoughts. She hears the loud roars of boats that belch smoke and leak foul-smelling fluids, and the buzz of motorized carts that rip and tear apart her forest.

A vibration of fear rises from her core. It catches at her heart and makes her breathe hard, like she's chasing a rabbit. She dislikes being this close, but instinct tells her to carry on, to track the boys, to remove the threat, to keep the forest her own.

They float ahead, but a cabin built on tall wood piles at the top of a ridge stands in her way. She comes to a halt. Light pours out of it—too much—every window is an eye that studies her. She shrinks low and creeps between the spruce trees and cool shadows like a lynx approaching a grouse.

The boys pull their boat alongside a dock and a dog rushes toward them. Dogs are smart and, like her, can hear and smell things that these people can't—but they're also a threat, alerting people to her presence and protecting them from a perceived danger.

She crouches down onto her belly, not wanting to be seen by the creature. The boys and the dog walk up the path where they meet more people—an older man and two women—and they all talk and laugh. This makes her angry and she exhales a slow growl, regretting it immediately. The dog hears her and it rises, moving to the edge of the property, clearly intent on searching her out. She stays still and silent, watching from the low grass, knowing that it senses her but doesn't yet know exactly where she is.

The dog barks and pushes into the trees, hoping to flush her out. She wishes it would go away because if it gets too close, she'll have to hurt it.

Now the older woman is yelling. "Ollie! Get over here!" but the dog doesn't stop, so the woman calls it again. Finally it halts in confusion and looks back at her.

The younger woman says, "It's probably a raccoon."

"Aren't they nocturnal?" one of the young men asks.

The dog, Ollie, hasn't left his spot and the hairs on the back of his neck are raised, but the woman shouts his name one last time and he goes back to the people, dissatisfied.

They walk into the cabin, taking the dog with them, but she remains. She watches them move around inside their ugly, extravagant home, talking and laughing, and a faint image floats across her memory.

It's time for her to go, to leave this world of noise and waste and return to the rivers and the trees, the starry skies and the wind in the leaves and the forests where the animals walk. She retreats, moving back in stealthy silence, not taking her eyes off the building and its bright lights and many windows.

Although she dislikes the world of man, this journey beyond her boundaries hasn't been in vain. She's found the den where her quarry lives. And if the time comes, she knows how to hunt them down and snare them.

chapter 96

For the next few days, we wait patiently.

The biggest weakness in our plan is Mom and Dad's choice of cell phone carriers. Although Charlie's phone has great reception, mine doesn't always pick up a cell tower and the best solution is to hang by the water, where we only get a signal strength of three bars.

We also haven't really considered what to do if the phone actually rings. We can't exactly answer it with the family around, but they're sticking to us pretty tight. Somewhere in the back of my mind I know this is a good thing—I come from a close-knit family and usually I like it—but right now, it really sucks.

None of this seems to faze Charlie; he just keeps busy. After returning from the phone drop, he decides to chop wood for the firepit, even though Dad points out that we still have plenty. After lunch, he cracks open his collection of Hemingway short stories and hangs out at the dock, but I can't tell if he has the phone with him and there's no way to ask since

Heather is sunbathing out there too. At supper, he's helping Mom and Dad get food ready and I can't get him alone to find out where he left the cell until we're prepping the firepit.

"Relax. I've got us covered."

"What are you talking about?"

He points. "See that rock over there? No signal. Then that tree stump? That's about where we get two bars. As long we keep the phone somewhere around there, we're all good."

"You left it lying out there? Dude, that's my phone!"

He ignores my dismay. "I'm also known for borrowing stuff that doesn't belong to me." When he realizes I'm not impressed, he adds, "Chill. I stuck it under a piece of wood—it'll stay dry."

I shake my head. "Tell me you don't plan on leaving it out there tonight?"

"No, we'll bring it in."

"And? What happens if they call and we don't answer?"

He runs his hands through his shaggy hair. "Hopefully, they'll leave a message."

chapter 97

Thursday rolls around and the phone still hasn't rung. We walk down to the water to check again. No missed calls or new messages. I can tell Charlie's a little disappointed.

Someone's behind us. We turn around to find Heather standing there. "Hey, do you guys want to go over to the resort?"

Charlie glances at me. "Sure." He seems enthusiastic and I'm guessing he's thinking there'll be better reception.

Unfortunately, Mom and Dad decide to tag along. I have nothing against them participating in our day at the beach, but it definitely complicates things.

I watch the bars drop to nothing as we travel away from our cabin toward the main road. I look out the window to divert attention from my phone, but Charlie's rocking out to Dad's musical selection.

" 'This Town Ain't Big Enough for Both of Us'? Classic!" he yells over the singer's high-pitched voice.

Dad peers into the rearview mirror. "You actually recognize this?"

"Absolutely! Sparks, 1970, right?"

"'74. Charles, you never cease to amaze me."

Dad cranks it up and the two of them sing the rest of the way to the resort.

We draw people's attention at the beach. No matter where we go, Mom and Dad always get at least one person staring at them since Dad is as white as they come. Heather and I usually attract the least notice, but with Charlie trailing along as our newest shaggy-haired blond relative, onlookers can't quite put all the pieces together.

We set up near the water. Mom stretches out on the blanket beside Heather, but Dad is eager to get into the water.

'Don't forget your sunscreen, hon," Mom warns him.

"I'll do it when I come out of the water."

"You say that now, but do I need to remind you—"

He knows she's going to keep bugging him until he follows orders.

"And just because it says it's waterproof, doesn't mean you don't add more later," she lectures.

"Yeah, yeah…"

Charlie and I make sure the phone is turned on with the volume up and that it's safely stowed in my bag before we wade out to play paddle-ball. Once he's followed Mom's rules, Dad joins in to persuade us into deeper waters.

"If we go out a little further, we can dive for some shots."

I love that Dad acts like a teen sometimes, but right now Charlie and I need to stay close to shore—and the phone.

"Nah, Dad. This is good."

"You playing it safe?" he chides me. "Can't stand the challenge?"

I recover a hard spike from him and he has to hustle. "I think it's the other way around, old man."

He catches the ball with the tip of his paddle and lobs it high in the air. I have plenty of time to get under it and send it back to him, but he's ready and swings hard and I don't have enough time to catch it.

"Man, Shepherd, your dad's got you going in circles," says Charlie.

I glare at him as I grab the ball. "Well, once I lose, I'll let him kick your butt instead."

Charlie grins. "Sounds good."

"All right, let's finish this," Dad calls out.

"Settle down," I say, nodding toward Mom further up on the beach and raising my voice a bit so she can hear me, "your lady doesn't need you showing off—"

Charlie jumps in. "Maybe he's just worried he'll burn if he doesn't get more suntan lotion on soon?"

"Hey!" Dad sputters, "it was *one* time—"

"Only one time *this* year," Mom says, "then there was the year before that."

Dad catches Charlie laughing and points at him. "Hey, just because we let you out on good behaviour doesn't mean I won't find cruel and unusual punishments for you."

"All right, Shepherd," Charlie calls, "can you please hurry up and lose so I can have a crack at trouncing this"—he catches Dad's scowl—"this very fine and distinguished gentleman."

"Don't expect mercy just because you didn't call me old.'"

"Wouldn't dream of it!" Charlie taunts.

Dad and I play a little longer, but he destroys me, then beats Charlie seven-three. After a particularly rough dive into shallow water, Charlie throws in the towel. "I give up. Your years of experience upon this earth have bested me."

Dad shakes his head as Heather wades over. "He does that, doesn't he? Never shuts up, then annoys you with one of his back-handed compliments."

Charlie pulls himself up and we all go back up the beach to Mom. "Well, then, I offer ice cream to everyone as a truce."

Mom seems honestly surprised by Charlie's offer. "You know you don't need to, Charles."

"Mrs. S., after all you've done for me, it's the least I can do."

She smiles. "Well, that's very kind. All right, but I'll take an iced coffee instead of ice cream."

"Awesome." As he reaches down to toss me my bag for safe-keeping, he looks over at Heather. "Coming, sis?"

She dusts sand off her legs. "Sure, so long as you never call me that again."

"Fair enough."

chapter 98

Charlie takes the lead at the ice cream shack. "I'll take an iced coffee, a small saskatoon berry cone, a small mint chocolate chip, a small black cherry pie, and lastly, one cone with a scoop of chocolate fudge brownie, a scoop of banana pineapple, and a scoop of maple bacon, dipped in chocolate with sprinkles."

Charlie catches sight of our expressions. "What? I never really ate breakfast."

Mom shakes her head, but Heather and I laugh out loud.

Ring ring.

Charlie and I glance at each other. I dig into my bag and find the phone. The call display says SERGEANT PEPPER—it's definitely an incoming call from Charlie's phone. I step away from the group to answer it.

"Hello?"

I hear a sort of scrabbling in the receiver, like someone's covering the mouthpiece. Then silence, then nothing.

"Hello?" I ask again, but when no one speaks, I pull the phone away from my ear. CALL ENDED, it says.

I walk back to my family.

Although I'm sure Charlie wants to know, it's Mom who asks, "Who was it?"

"Don't know. Wrong number, I guess."

This is good enough for Mom, whose drink has just appeared at the takeout window, but I catch Charlie's scrutiny. I shrug. We'll talk later.

Our ice cream cones are ready, and Dad grabs his mint chocolate and Heather's saskatoon berry, while I grab mine. Charlie's monstrosity comes out last.

I watch as he digs into it. "Damn, that actually looks good."

He grins. "I know, right?"

We make our way back down the hill to the beach, but Charlie and I hang back a bit.

"What happened with the call?"

"Nothing. No one was there."

"No one?"

"Well, someone, but they didn't speak."

"Makes sense. Cell phones might be totally new to them if they've been stuck in the woods since the '70s."

"Think they'll call back?"

"I hope so—"

Ring ring.

Here we go again. I answer. "Hello?"

Silence, followed by the same muffled sound, the scratch of rough skin against the edges of the speaker, then more silence.

"Hello?" I say again.

A tiny voice whispers, "Hello?"

Charlie and I slow to a stop and thankfully my family doesn't notice. Charlie turns his back to them for cover and I switch the audio to speakerphone.

"Who am I talking to?" I ask.

More shuffling. Finally, "Tasha."

We look at each other. This wasn't the name we were expecting.

Charlie urges me to talk. "Hello, Tasha, my name is Tony."

"Tohhhny," she repeats, rolling through the middle vowel slowly.

"And I'm here with my friend, Charlie."

"Ch...ar...lie?" she says, reciting his name carefully despite the fumbling, scratchy sound. "Are you on the radio?"

"Pardon?"

"This is like the radio, but you're talking to me."

Everything she says is a small window into her world.

"Yeah. It's called a cell phone."

There's a long silence and we keep checking to make sure she hasn't hung up on us.

Charlie leans in. "Was it you who helped us in the woods?"

She answers his question with her own: "Was that you under the tree?"

"Yes."

"The two boys with the canoe?"

"Yes, that was us. And that was you?"

Another pause. "Uh-huh. I wanted you to stay."

I continue, "Tasha, do you live in the woods?"

"Are you the ones with the blue walls?"

I look at Charlie and he shrugs. "What do you mean?" I ask.

"When I close my eyes, I see… blue…"

I consider what she's saying. Is it possible she's Joanna, the girl who went missing in the '90s. "Were they *your* blue walls?" I ask.

"I think so."

"And you miss them?" I go on.

"Yes."

Charlie and I stare at each other.

I push on. "Do you live by yourself out there?"

"No."

"You live with someone else?"

"Yes. My sister."

Again, something new. "How old is your sister?"

"Younger."

Our minds buzz with possibilities—where did the other girl come from?

"Is it just your sister and you?" I ask.

"No."

"Who else?"

"Mommy." If this is Joanna, then "Mommy" must be the hippy woman.

Charlie asks, "Has she always been your mother?"

We get only silence and I worry Charlie's question has scared her off.

I try to move on. "Your mommy looks after you?"

There's another long silence before we hear a faint "Yes."

"And she keeps you safe?" I ask.

"Yes."

"In the woods?"

"Yes."

Charlie pushes it again. "Does she ever let you leave?"

She doesn't answer and I toss him a look of annoyance. I try to pick up the conversation again, to keep her talking. "Is she the one who gave you *The Great Gatsby*?"

"Yes. She has many books."

Charlie leans in. "Tasha, would you like to meet us?"

"I can't."

"Doesn't your mother let you leave?"

"I should go now."

"Does she keep you there?"

"I mustn't—"

"Does she hurt you?" Charlie blurts out and I punch him.

"No!" she cries.

I can tell he's pissed with me, but he still has the presence of mind to take advantage of her answer. "Has she ever hurt anyone else?"

"I don't think so."

"Are you sure?"

She doesn't answer.

"Would you—?"

"I can't—"

"Do you want to—?"

"No."

There's a *clunk* and I think she's set the phone down.

"Tasha?!" Charlie says loudly into the speaker, "Tasha?"

Silence.

When we don't hear anything further, I check the phone. Although she hasn't hung up, she's definitely no longer on the other end. After a few more seconds, we hang up.

We stand there, the disconnected phone between us.

"The phone will likely lose power soon if she doesn't hang it up," Charlie finally says.

"What should we do?"

"Not much unless we go get it."

"No, not the phone. Tasha?"

"What do you mean?"

"She might be the girl who's been missing for twenty years."

"Joanna Grassing?"

I nod.

"We don't know that, Shepherd."

"I know, but—"

"She might also be the person who murdered Terry and Rita."

"You seemed pretty convinced that it was her mother just now."

He shrugs. "Could also be her sister. We can't rule anything out yet."

I think about this. "We need to take what we know and let the police deal with it."

"And what are they going to do?"

"Go in and save her."

"How? We don't even know where she is."

"If we tell the authorities, they can bring in planes and search helicopters, maybe track her down while the phone still has a signal—"

"That girl and her family have stayed hidden this long. What makes you think anyone can find her now?"

I hate to admit it, but he's right. "So what do you suggest?"

"I think we need to find her ourselves."

I should've known. "Didn't you just tell me that any of them could be a murderer?"

Charlie grins. "That's why we'll do it all real careful-like."

"And just how do you plan on finding her?"

"The way she talked about the blue walls? I'm thinking Tasha *wants* to be found. I know I would."

chapter 99

Charlie and I don't talk much as we walk back down to the beach, but I can't help worrying about the whole situation. Our search to find the truth about Terry's death has only grown more convoluted. We've got another possible death—the missing photographer, Rita—and now suspect there's a girl missing since 1996 out in the woods. There are absolutely no guarantees that Tasha really is Joanna Grassing, and her sister may or may not be someone else's lost child. We also don't know if either of these two things is connected to the couple in the van. Worst of all, we don't know who Terry's murderer is.

Mom and Dad decide to stay around the resort until evening and this only raises my anxiety level. By the time we're eating supper at the local fish and chips place, both Charlie and I are far too distracted to enjoy the meal.

"Don't tell me I broke your spirits with paddle-ball?" Dad asks.

I glance up. Mom, Dad, and Heather all staring at us, so I force a smile and mumble, "No," but Charlie dives in head-first.

"Sorry, Mr. and Mrs. S., it's my fault. I've been thinking about Sheri."

Her name coming out of Charlie's mouth captures the table's attention.

"How long do you think I'll feel this much?"

"I don't understand, Charles, what do you mean?" Mom asks.

"Well, I didn't know her as well as you guys or Tony, but after spending the time looking for her, I got attached."

He picks up a fry, munching it before continuing, "I mean, I was pretty sure we wouldn't find her in time, but you know, I hoped that I'd be wrong." He takes a moment. "I guess what I'm asking is, how long do we keep thinking about those who are absent from our lives?"

I remember my earlier suspicion that Charlie has lost someone in his past and I'm guessing Mom and Dad are thinking it too.

"Charles…" I'm surprised that Mom doesn't have an answer right away.

Dad speaks up, "The closer we are to people, the longer we try to hold onto them."

That rings true to me; it feels like some of my memories of Sheri will never fade.

Dad goes on, "You know, I was never close with my father while he was alive. I didn't understand him and he didn't understand me. It wasn't until after he died that I began to grasp what he meant to my life. Now, I barely remember how he looked. His face, his features—when I try really hard, they all seem to slip away. But then I'll have these moments when I catch myself in the mirror… and suddenly, there he is, because I see him in me."

I don't think I've ever heard Dad talk about Granddad this way.

Mom takes Dad's hand. "I don't think we ever forget the people we lose. I think we'll always want them back."

"So, Mr. S., after all this time, you don't think your father has ever really gone away?"

"Only the details of my memories have lessened."

"So the idea of Sheri out there…"

"Will always be with you," Dad finishes.

Charlie nods at me and I realize what he's up to. Although I think he's sincere about Sheri, he's got other things on his mind too. One woman is missing and someone else out there has lost a daughter—Tasha or maybe the sister she told us about too—and right now, Charlie and I are the only ones who might be able to get her back. My only fear is that Charlie's past, his loss, will make him reckless and it'll get us both in trouble—or worse.

chapter 100

It's cool out by the time we get back to the cabin and Charlie volunteers the two of us to light the firepit while the rest of the family stays inside, giving us a few moments to ourselves. As we build up a small pointed stack of wood, Charlie walks up and hands me my phone. I don't remember giving it to him, but I no longer question these things.

"Dial the number," Charlie says.

On the screen is a listing for Denise Grassing.

"Joanna's mom?"

He nods. "She's two hours earlier, so you shouldn't be waking her."

"Charlie, I can't."

"Why not? You want proof that Tasha is Joanna, don't you?"

"Yeah, but—"

"Then call and ask her if her daughter's room had blue walls."

I slip the phone in my pocket and kneel to light the kindling. "Look, I don't disagree with you. I just think we need to be careful."

"Whether or not Tasha is Joanna, it doesn't change the fact that Denise Grassing is still missing a daughter. Or that another woman is missing."

"And you think only you can find them?"

"No, I think only *we* can."

The wood flares and I throw a few sticks on top.

"What happened to you, Charlie? Who did you lose?"

He glares at me.

"I'm serious. What's your deal?"

Charlie doesn't move, doesn't change his expression; his face flickers in the shadows of the rising flames.

"Because you lost someone, didn't you?" I go on. I'm certain he's deciding whether or not he trusts me enough to tell me.

As the fire grows, the heat builds. Charlie takes a step back.

I throw on a few bigger pieces of wood and come to a decision. "Okay, Charlie. I'll help you find Tasha. But one of these days—it doesn't have to be today or tomorrow—you need to be honest with me about your past."

chapter 101

After Charlie heads to bed, I take my phone, step out of the cabin, and walk down to the dock. I cycle through the list of calls and hit dial. I need a plan in place before I do anything else.

A sleepy voice answers and I pause for a second before plunging in. "Hello, Detective Gekas. It's Tony Shepherd."

"What time is it?" Her tone shifts abruptly, "What's wrong?"

"Nothing… yet. But I need a favour."

"What are you boys up to?" She sounds wide awake now.

"Nothing," I protest, "at least, not yet. But I do need to do something and I can't see the whole situation."

"What do you mean?"

"I think Charlie's not thinking clearly and I'm afraid he's about to do something stupid." I feel guilty for going behind his back, but I need to know. "Detective, do you know anything about Charlie's past?"

"What are you asking, Anthony?"

"Did something happen to him when he was younger?"

"You know I can't disclose private records."

Not helpful, Detective. I try again, "Has he ever lost someone?"

She gets quiet. "You need to talk to Charles, not me."

I know that's all I'm likely to get.

"What's going on, Anthony?"

"We're going to try and find someone tomorrow. Maybe two people." I can't say it more simply.

"Who?"

"A photographer that's disappeared and a girl who's been missing for twenty years."

There's a pause, then she says, "I know you think you're doing what's right, but there are people—"

"Detective Gekas, I think we're the only ones who can help."

"Tell the officials what you know—"

"I'll keep my phone on me, but I'm turning the ringer off."

"Anthony—!"

"If something goes wrong, track us with it."

I hang up on her protests. I set the phone to silent and when I go back up to the cabin, I disconnect the house phone. Maybe it'll buy Charlie and me enough time before all hell breaks loose.

chapter 102

I listen to Charlie toss in bed throughout the night, but when I wake the next day, I'm surprised by how revved up we both are. Once up and caffeinated, we strategize. There are a few things going for us. First, we have some idea of where Tasha might appear, and more importantly, she used the phone once—maybe she will again.

We pull out Dad's fishing rods and a small box of tackle. We don't know how long we need to be out, so pretending to go fishing will give us enough time to be away from the cabin for a while without anyone worrying.

When Mom sees us step out the door, she orders us to take sunblock and a hat.

Dad looks at him with sympathy. "If you don't do it, she'll harass you for years—"

"Well, if you wouldn't be so careless—" Mom says.

"It was one time—" Dad protests.

"More than one time. And quit acting like a baby. You whined the whole time your skin was peeling."

Charlie grabs a hat and sunscreen from the closet and stands beside Dad, holding the lotion out like he's in a TV commercial. "Only Solar Bronze can stop the UV light that damages your skin and leads to skin cancer. Look at this before"—he points to himself—"and after—he points to Dad—comparison. Terrifying, right?"

Mom chuckles as Dad pushes him away. "Go, fish, and get out of my hair."

Charlie grins as we step outside. "You know they're just fake arguing so they can have sex while we're out, right?"

"Dude! Gross." Not getting enough sleep hasn't dampened his attitude.

When Charlie spots Heather down by the dock, he informs her, "Keep your distance from the cabin for at least an hour."

"Why—?"

"Don't ask," I warn her.

"Why?"

Charlie winks and she realizes what he's suggesting. "Jeez, dude! You're sick."

Charlie lets out an exaggerated sigh. "Just trying to protect you young impressionable kids."

Heather spies our gear. "You two going fishing?"

"Gonna try," I say.

Charlie sets his rod in the canoe. "I seek the full lake experience."

She smiles. "What are you going to do when you have to stick a leech on the line?"

He stops dead. "You didn't tell me we had to do that, Shepherd." He looks at Heather, "You're joking, right?"

She just smiles and walks up the path.

"Shepherd?"

Now it's my turn to smile. "You know why Heather's a good fisherman?"

"Why?"

"Because she just caught you hook, line, and sinker."

chapter 103

The day is warm and bright, not a cloud in the sky. The water is calm—not one scrap of driftwood spoils its surface on our journey. Long strands of weeds sway in the gentle currents of the clear water. I catch a glimpse of a rippling flicker, probably a fish weaving between the waving grasses of the lake bottom, before it's gone forever.

"Remember that mysterious hitchhiker?" Charlie's question comes out of nowhere. "The one on the bridge who disappears when you see him?"

"Yeah. What about it?"

"It feels like we've picked up a couple of those."

"What do you mean?"

"All we seem to be doing lately is chasing ghosts."

"I was thinking the same thing yesterday. We started with Terry—"

"And now we've got Rita."

"And we're not even sure if either of them is connected to Tasha."

"Or Joanna."

"Or whoever we're dealing with—"

"*Whom*ever."

I look back at him. "Seriously, dude?"

"What? Proper grammar matters."

I laugh. "Fine. Whomever."

He nods in sage agreement, then gets serious. "But we have a lot of unknowns going on and I hate it. It would be nice if some of these questions had answers."

He pulls his paddle in, setting it on the gunwale. "I almost called that number myself last night."

"Why didn't you?"

"Didn't feel right."

"But you were hoping *I* would?"

"Maybe… no. It would've been like ripping the bandage off a twenty-year-old wound."

"But to have an answer, any answer…"

He nods. "A little less uncertainty would be nice." He picks up his paddle again and pulls it through the water. "I don't like going in when there's so much we don't know—"

"But everything comes back to these woods."

"And Tasha seems to be our only way in."

I slow the canoe to a crawl as we approach the bank with the fallen log.

"Let's keep some distance between us and the shore," Charlie says.

I'm in full agreement. The more space between us and whatever craziness is going on in the woods, the better.

chapter 104

Although we brought the fishing rods as an excuse, we might actually have a long wait until Tasha phones or appears, so I work on attaching a hook.

"Your sister was kidding about the suckers, right?"

I grin. "They work better than worms."

He cringes.

"Relax," I wave a hand at him. "I don't have any and I'm in no big hurry to deal with a fish anyway."

I hand him a rod and he fails at a couple of casts, splashing the tip of his pole into the water. Once I'm ready, I show him how to do it properly.

"Don't whip it. Clean steady motion, wide arc, then release." I demonstrate and cast my hook a good distance from the boat.

Charlie gives it another try and this time he pulls off a nice one.

"Good job. Now don't let it sink too much or you'll get caught in the weeds." I demonstrate reeling my hook back in.

We spend the morning casting, with a steady eye on the shoreline. The waves slosh against the aluminum hull, getting amplified and echoing as they do. Charlie settles into the bow and, what with the constant rocking back and forth, I think he might fall asleep. He probably would if it weren't for the constant whir and click of his fishing rod.

Occasionally, I set down my pole and pick up the oar, paddling us back into position when the currents carry us too far downstream.

When the sun is high in the sky, I check my phone. "Almost noon."

Charlie pulls off his hat to wipe his brow. "Damn, it's hot."

"Did you put on some sunscreen?"

"Yes, Mom."

"Hey, you come home looking like a roasted beet, it'll be both our asses."

"True." He slips his cap back on. "But roasted beets sound good right about now."

"Really?"

He shrugs. "I like my colourful veggies."

I laugh but stop quickly. Someone's watching us from the edge of the woods.

"Charlie."

He glances up, then reels in his line and sets down the pole. We study the person, but they're too far away and shadowed for us to see what they look like.

"What now?" I ask.

Charlie waves. The figure doesn't respond. He tries again. The person raises an arm in what might be a friendly gesture.

"Guess it's time to introduce ourselves," says Charlie.

chapter 105

We paddle to shore at a steady pace, not wanting to frighten whoever it is off. I try to work out all of the possible ways this could go wrong, but I don't stop rowing.

The closer we get, the more sure I am that it's a woman in her twenties. Tasha. She's hiding behind a tree, but even so I can tell she's short and slight, and her light brown hair is worn in a long braid.

"Tasha?" Charlie asks.

She nods hesitantly.

Charlie turns to me. "Shepherd, you need to talk."

"Why me?"

"She's already talked to you. Now say something."

I wave. "I'm Tony. We spoke on the phone?"

She watches me from behind the safety of her tree.

"And this is Charlie." I point to him and he waves.

My biggest fear is that we rush this and freak her out. I pull in my oar so that the canoe glides gently toward shore. Charlie looks over his shoulder and follows my lead.

The boat thunks against the sand in the shallow water and we don't move, just sit there and watch her. She's curled around the tree, keeping it between her and us.

"We're going to get out of the canoe now," I say finally. "Is that all right?"

She thinks it over before nodding her agreement.

Charlie glances back at me and we both climb out. We're now onshore, and things could go badly at any moment—we're pretty exposed here and it would be tough to get away safely. But I inhale slowly and deeply and do my best to stay calm; any sign of nervousness could spook her.

I lead the way up the sandy bank and we stand at the top, deciding our next move. Charlie walks over to the log and I see her face tighten. He ignores this and reaches into the hollow, pulling out his phone and the book. "Is this yours?"

The young woman nods again.

"Do you like to read?" he asks, studying his cell before turning it off and slipping it into his pocket.

Another nod.

"Is *The Great Gatsby* your favourite?"

"Yes." It's the first word she's said. Charlie's making progress.

"Yeah, it's pretty good," he agrees. "What do you think is the best part?"

Tasha slides around the tree into full view, leaning against it but still holding on tightly. Her eyes are brown and she's wearing a pair of jeans and an unzipped purple hoodie, neither of which fit her right. Her shoes are filthy and look like they might be too small.

"The green…" She freezes, like she's said too much.

But Charlie knows what she's thinking and finishes her thought. "The green light across the bay?"

She smiles and dimples appear in her cheeks—but she catches herself and stops.

Charlie looks out across the water before turning back to Tasha. "I bet you see lights across the lake at night?"

The dimples return and she nods.

"Do you ever want to go see them?"

A grimace crosses her face and she draws back behind the tree.

"What's wrong, Tasha?" I ask.

"We shouldn't talk about this," she says.

"Why not? Because of your mother?"

"We aren't allowed to leave."

"What does she do if you try?"

She ignores me, suddenly emboldened, and stands straight. "Man is wrong," she says forcefully, "you are men." It seems as if she's just realized this now.

She looks like she's going to retreat, but Charlie calls out, "Tasha, why is man wrong?"

"Man is the end of innocence; he is the darkness. Man is the Fall." She recites this flatly and I feel nervous, ready to take a step back myself, but Charlie holds his ground.

"You read that as well, didn't you?"

She nods.

"*The Lord of the Flies*? You have that book too?"

She watches him with interest, then nods yet again.

"Did your mother teach you these things?"

"Yes."

"She told you to avoid man?"

"Yes."

"Is that why she tells you not to leave?"

Tasha nods once more.

"Since we are men, do you want us to go away?"

She thinks about this, hiding behind the tree. There's a mushroom by her foot and she takes note of it. She kneels down to pick it, sniffing it before breaking it in half and popping it in her mouth. Finally, she shakes her head—maybe she's made up her mind that we aren't a threat.

Charlie sits in the dirt and I feel awkward hovering over him, so I sit down too.

Charlie speaks again. "You said you remember blue walls?"

"Yes…" We can see her mind turning, remembering something from the distant past. "I dream of them…"

"Do you think they were the walls of your room?"

I see conflict in her eyes.

"Mother tells me they're in my imagination only. That I should forget about them. And I try—"

"But you can't."

She shakes her head and I see sadness in her eyes.

I can't imagine what she's been through, but now I know exactly why we're here. "Tasha, I can't promise you that we can take you back to the room with the blue walls. But we'll try to help you get back to… to the woman who lived there with you."

She holds my gaze and I think she knows I'm telling the truth.

"Would you like to come with us?" I venture.

"Yes," she says, "but not without my sister." At this she turns and rushes into the woods.

Charlie gets to his feet quickly and chases after her, but I stay put. He turns back towards me, "What are you waiting for? Come on!"

"We can't!"

"Why not?"

"We don't know anything about her. She could be leading us into a trap and try to kill us!" I exclaim.

"Have you looked at her?" Charlie scoffs.

I admit she's small and likely couldn't overpower us, but none of this feels safe.

"She knows these woods way better than we do—"

"Which is why we need to catch up to her." He looks back to where the small speck of her purple hoodie is still visible in the deep woods.

"Go. I'll catch up," I say.

He glares anxiously at me. "Why? What are you going to do?"

"Go, keep up with her. I'll be right behind you."

Charlie throws me a questioning look, but at my hurried nod he takes off into the woods. I sprint down to the boat to pull it ashore, yanking it all the way up the bank. Whatever happens next, I want to be sure that we'll have a way home.

I pull out my phone and check the battery and signal. As long as it's on, Gekas can find it if things go bad.

It's 11:38 a.m. I scan the trees for Charlie. He's running down the deer trail we took before and I sprint after him.

I only hope we're not being led into danger.

chapter 106

The path twists and turns and I have to work hard to catch up to Charlie. Tasha moves between the bushes and beneath the branches far more easily than the two of us do, advancing just slowly enough that we can follow. There doesn't seem to be a plan or method to the path she takes and each time she chooses one direction over another, I can't figure out any particular reason why.

I keep an eye on the sun and the shadows that spill through the trees. We're travelling north-northwest, but I have no sense where we are in relation to the beach or our cabin. I'm glad I'm in charge of the compass this time—if it clouds over today, at least we'll know how to get home.

Our journey rises and falls up hills and across streams, and although there are several points where the land is marshy, Tasha takes us over conveniently placed logs without sinking into the bog. The wetlands lead to another small creek and we move quickly along its winding banks, but suddenly Tasha slows to a walk.

Charlie and I keep our distance and fight for breath.

"They always say living naturally is healthy," Charlie wheezes.

I'm thirsty and my voice comes out in a croak, "Why'd she slow down?"

We watch her move to a fallen pine tree that hangs over a small pool. As we step closer, I hear the trickle of water. She turns and waves at us to follow. We struggle to keep our balance on the log, but she slips swiftly between the prickly, cobweb-covered branches. We scramble across and eventually come to a small opening where the cracked stump meets a sharp embankment. Water percolates out of the soil, cutting through the sand and mud, and she cups her hand under it and drinks. She prompts us to do the same.

Charlie studies the water, seeing where it runs into the pool to form a coppery stain. An oily film reflecting a spectrum of colours floats on the water's surface.

"Is it safe?" he asks.

She nods and urges us to drink.

Charlie sticks his hand underneath and immediately smiles. "It's so cold." He fills his palm and sips. "But, wow, tasty."

I test it too. "Sort of metallic." It's refreshing in my dry throat.

Tasha smiles. The things she may have done to keep hidden in these woods makes me anxious about her intentions, but her kind gesture prompts my sympathy. Besides, if she intended to hurt us, wouldn't she have tried already?

This is the closest she's allowed us to get to her and I notice the little stray hairs frizzing out from her braid, her tanned, clean skin, and a faint musky smell. Despite having lived out here for so long, she seems healthier than most people her age. She's thin and weathered, but she doesn't have bags under her eyes or the little gut and blotchy skin from unhealthy, mass-produced food that people so often have.

She manoeuvres past us and hops back onto the tree trunk. She's on the move. I take a last quick sip of water, and Charlie and I follow her down the log and back onto the creek bank.

We travel further northwest and the stream eventually disappears as we turn onto another animal path. The bush is thick, and at several points all three of us have to crawl on our hands and knees, but even so, the trail is never blocked by any of the obstacles Charlie and I encountered when we were lost. Every path we take has been charted in Tasha's mind, walked, crawled, and refined to its most appropriate, most traversable form.

We climb to the top of a hill and I look up at the sun, seeing that it has already started to drop in the sky. I check my phone.

"Holy shit, Charlie. We've been out for more than an hour."

We scan the horizon. I can no longer see the lake, but I do see the remnants of the fire tower poking up through the trees on the horizon.

"We're about ten kilometres out, maybe more," says Charlie.

I point. "Looks like we've been skirting outside the edge of the old fire burn."

"These paths must be decades old."

"If you can even call them paths."

Tasha points at a deer trail that winds down the hillside. "No!" she yells.

Charlie looks down the track to where she's gesturing. "No what?"

"Man is bad."

"Yeah, yeah, we know. You shouldn't be hanging with us," says Charlie.

She's annoyed. "No." She gestures again. "Man is bad."

I look at the sun and the position of the tower and realize she's pointing north. I point at the trail too. "Man is bad?"

Tasha nods and smiles and I look at Charlie. "I think this trail will take us back to the cabin." But we don't consider this for long because she's sprinted off again, down the other side of the hill. We have to race to catch up.

At the bottom of the hill we come across a muddy, stagnant river and she moves along the bank toward a beaver dam, then steps lightly onto its soft, crackling surface.

"That doesn't look safe," says Charlie.

She's halfway across. We need to follow or she'll leave us behind.

"Just don't fall in," I say.

"Can't be that bad," Charlie says, a slight quiver in his voice.

"Just a cesspool of beaver crap and leeches probably."

Charlie stares down at the dirty water. "Message received."

We clamber over the crisscrossed structure of chewed branches and mud, our legs cracking the mesh several times, and we have to struggle to untangle ourselves.

On the other side, we follow Tasha until the willow and birch trees disappear and an old spruce forest rises above us. The sun is blocked by the crown of the forest and it's no longer easy to tell how late in the day we are. I check the phone. No signal.

Tasha picks up the pace, jogging between the trees, and we follow. We run in silence for what must be another half-hour, three ghosts racing through the woods.

She comes to a halt, ducking behind a tall spruce.

"What?" I ask, catching my breath.

She points again. "Home."

chapter 107

Through the thick forest is a small house built of hewn logs
and mud. Its roof is steeply pitched, a crude little window
sits beneath the peak. It isn't pretty, not something Mom
might call quaint. It's been torn out of the land with blis-
tered hands, scraped arms, and ragged skin through years of
hardship and adaptation.

Tasha walks toward it, but I hold Charlie back.

"What?" he asks.

"We still don't know who she is. We need to wait."

"You really think this is a setup?"

I nod, keeping an eye on Tasha, trying to determine all the
possible ways this could be a trap. I look around for exits,
places that might be safe.

She turns when she realizes we're not with her and waves
us over.

I raise my hand. "Go on, we'll wait here."

She looks confused but continues on to the house.

Charlie moves in a wide arc along the tree line to my left, toward two small buildings perched behind the main house.

"Where are you going?" I whisper loudly.

"Scouting things out," he says, pointing to my right, "you check that way."

I don't like the idea of splitting up, but I move through the trees and try to remain alert to my surroundings. There is very little undergrowth, so there's little likelihood that someone could sneak up without us noticing. I wish we had something to defend ourselves with, and when I spy a thick stick on the ground, I pick it up.

Through the spruce, I see Charlie patrolling the far side, examining the first building. I hope he isn't planning to go inside, but I highly doubt he'd pass up the opportunity.

There's no sign of Tasha at the house. I'm not certain if she's waiting for us inside, but I have no interest in going in to find out. The roof slopes low to the ground on the sides like the witch's house in an old fairy tale. I've seen enough horror movies not to trust a place like this.

Charlie's coming around the back of the smallest of the buildings behind the house. Far behind all the buildings, through the trees, I can just spot a clearing. As I walk toward it, some instinct making me move as quietly as I can, I come across a crudely constructed pair of crosses. Built from driftwood, they've been carved and shaped with care. Scratched into the smooth surfaces are the words MOTHER and FATHER.

Charlie joins me. "The one building looks like some sort of food prep room or smokehouse, and the other is the crapper. I don't know what Tasha eats, but trust me, do not go in there!"

"Didn't Tasha say her mother wouldn't let her leave?" I ask. "But how can that be if she's dead?"

Charlie studies the earth below the crosses. "These graves aren't fresh. The wild grass has grown over them."

"Maybe they died a long time ago?"

He squats and scrutinizes the area. "But look, there's barely any depression in the ground."

"Perhaps she and her sister look after the graves?"

"Or maybe nothing's even buried here."

"You think she's making things up?"

He shrugs.

This guessing game is unnerving, but it's worse because I can tell that Charlie has no clue what to make of any of this either.

We move back to the front of the house where Tasha left us and wait.

"You think she's hiding from us?" Charlie asks.

"Why bring us here then?" I respond.

"Maybe there's an underground lair," he suggests. "Or a tunnel that lets her sneak off into the woods."

My unease escalates and it must show.

"Relax, Shepherd. Unless she's a witch—which I doubt entirely—I'm pretty sure she's still inside."

"Sorry. Just on edge. Something doesn't seem right about this."

"Yeah, I agree, but there's been plenty of time for her to finish us off and she hasn't." He starts toward the house.

"Where are you going?!"

"I think we've waited long enough. Time to move this along."

I tag behind. I've already learned that Charlie and I shouldn't be separated for too long when we do stupid things. The door to the house is made of split wood, lashed together with rope and reinforced with cross pieces. Charlie knocks.

Tasha comes to the entrance immediately and comes outside, closing the door behind her. "Scarlet's sleeping."

Tasha's sister.

"Can't you wake her?" I ask.

"No, Mother says Scarlet should sleep."

Mother? Something's definitely not right.

Charlie seems to have no such concern, though. "Is Mother here?" he asks.

She shakes her head no.

Charlie looks into the sky for the sun. "I think we need to leave soon."

Tasha seems worried. "If I wake Scarlet too early, Mother will get mad."

Charlie ignores her. "You know, if you come with us to see the person who had the blue walls, Tasha, your mother is going to be mad anyway."

Tasha stands there, her eyes questioning, seemingly confused by Charlie's dismissive attitude toward her parent's wishes.

He persists, "If you don't come with us now, then Tony and I need to leave."

She considers this.

Whether she's trustworthy or not, I know it's hard to disobey your parents—especially when people you've been told to avoid are trying to convince you to do it. I've done it more than once since meeting Charlie and it's never gotten easier.

"Okay. I'll wake her," Tasha says quietly.

She retreats back inside but doesn't close the door. For the first time, Charlie and I get a glimpse of her world.

chapter 108

Charlie steps inside first. "Whoa…"

It isn't until I enter that I understand how tiny the house really is. There's a small table on one side, a wood stove in the corner, and a ladder that leads to the floor above. On the other side is a bench and above it, a small shelf of old books, including *To Kill a Mockingbird*, *The Pearl*, *The Old Man and the Sea*, and *1984*. Some of them are tattered and burnt.

Charlie studies the titles. "Some good reading here."

"There's barely any room to move."

"Not all of us get to live in mansions, Shepherd."

I know it's a dig, but I ignore it.

"Hey, Shepherd, look." Charlie has a book in one hand—*Crime and Punishment* by a guy named Dyovsky or something—and a picture in the other. He hands the photo to me. Like some of the books, it seems to have survived a fire. It has a white border like a retro Instagram filter, and shows a young couple in front of a red brick wall with vines trailing all over it.

"You think it's the parents? She sure doesn't look like them."

Charlie shrugs. "If things are the way we think they are, she wouldn't." He picks up another thick book, this one a collection of plays by Shakespeare, and flips through it. "Who do you think Rebecca is?" He shows me the inside cover. The name appears in blue ink over and over, as if a young child had been practising how to print it.

"Another kid?" I ask.

"Three of them?"

"Maybe."

"So where is she?"

Tasha interrupts us as she descends the ladder, holding a tightly swaddled infant in her arms.

Scarlet is a baby.

"Can we help?" I ask.

She looks at us strangely, holding the bundle close. "No."

Charlie shows her the picture. "Are these your parents?"

She gets a distant look. "No. I don't know those people."

"They aren't the ones buried out back?" he asks.

She gives us a quizzical look. "Never go out back."

"Says who?"

"Mother."

Charlie and I glance at each other. The sooner we get out of here, the better.

"Do you need anything else?" I ask.

She looks around the tiny room. "No."

"Then it's time to go."

chapter 109

We follow Tasha, still holding her sister tight, through the spruce forest, and I still can't figure out how she knows where she's going. I can't see the sun, but it's darker now. Night must be coming soon. I could check my phone, but I'd rather not know; by the time we get home, Mom and Dad will be ready to freak on us anyway. And I'm guessing that when they see who we've brought back with us, it'll be even worse.

Charlie falls back beside me. "Man, this is getting messed up."

"Like, who exactly are we bringing back?" I ask.

"Yeah. And if the people in that photo aren't her parents, and the bodies out there aren't them either, then who does that leave us with?"

"I told you before, we have no clue who Tasha really is," I whisper.

"Maybe she's just been out here alone with her sister too long."

"Scarlet? The sister who seems a little too young?"

Charlie shakes his head. "Yeah, I suppose one sort of needs a dad for these things."

"Where's any male, for that matter? Or the mysterious mom? We are so off the rails on this…"

He sighs. "I know. I thought that we'd get answers by coming out here, but—"

"All we have are more questions," I finish.

He walks silently beside me and I can tell he's frustrated.

"I'm used to things falling into place," he says a minute later. "I come up with a plan and things seem to somehow work out. But this time, I feel like we're just drifting along without direction."

I think about how people keep telling me our past luck has been only that—luck. A knot twists in my stomach. "Charlie—"

"No," he cuts me off. "I got us into this mess, Shepherd. I'll see what I can sort out." He scoots ahead and I close in to listen.

"Tasha, who's out here with you?" he asks.

"I told you. Me, my sister, and Mother."

"And where is your mother?"

She nods back the way we came.

Charlie shakes his head. "No, she wasn't. We were there. We saw no one else."

"Sometimes she goes out."

"To do what?"

"Hunt?"

"And what about your father?"

She gives him a questioning gaze.

Charlie tries again. "Do you have a father?"

The question troubles her, like she's trying to piece together a puzzle, until she eventually says, "No. He left."

"Did you know him?"

She shakes her head.

"So he left a long time ago?"

"Yes, before I came."

"Then where did your sister come from?"

"From the earth."

What?

Charlie tries another tactic. "Tasha, babies come from men and women being together. If your father is gone, then how did Scarlet get here?"

"Mother brought her to me."

Maybe she *is* another stolen child. How many children has Tasha's mother taken?

"When?" Charlie asks.

"Long ago—"

"A month? Two months? A year?"

Time doesn't seem to make sense to Tasha and she falls silent. We trod silently along the path, the soft earth cushioning our footfalls in the stillness of the forest, and its then it occurs to me how quiet Scarlet's been.

I walk beside them. "Tasha, can I see your sister?"

"No, she's sleeping."

"I know, but can you show her to me?"

"I don't know…"

But I can be persistent too. "Is she cute? Does she look like you?" I catch Charlie's quizzical look, but I ignore him and focus on Tasha.

"Mother says so."

"Do you think so?"

She smiles coyly.

"I'd love to see how cute she is. We promise to be quiet and not wake her," I add.

Her face softens. "Okay, but only for a moment." She shifts Scarlet in her arms and unwraps the grimy white blanket that covers the baby. I feel the blood drain from my face.

In Tasha's arms is the stuffed corpse of a rabbit.

"This is your sister, Tasha?" I look over at Charlie, who's doing his best not to lose his shit.

A troubled frown crosses her face. "Yes, why? Is she not cute?"

The animal's eyes and mouth have been sewn shut, tufts of grass poke out from loose threads where its body has been stitched together. Its fur is ratty either from age or from being cuddled too much.

"No, she's lovely, Tasha." I swallow hard, trying my best not to upset her while I eyeball Charlie before he says something dumb. "And your Mother brought her to you, you said? From the earth?"

"Yes."

We're way out of our element here. Tasha is a psychologically and emotionally distressed woman we thought we could bring back into the real world. I'm no longer certain that's the right choice. This isn't just some lost kid but someone who's been messed up by someone else, and I'm suddenly really worried that our actions are going to cause even more damage.

Tasha cuddles her rabbit sister close, rocking it a little.

I turn to Charlie and pull him a few feet away. "We can't do this."

"What? Take her back to civilization? It's a little late to change our minds."

"But she's broken. Like, really messed up."

"Yeah, and we can't just abandon her because of it. It isn't her fault. It's her 'mother's.' She stole Tasha from her parents, no matter how messed up *they* were, and did this. We have to see this through." He turns to her. "Tasha, can you tell me where your mother is?"

"I told you. Hunting."

"Where does she hunt? Where does she go?"

"Charlie, what are you doing? We can't go after her! It won't solve anything."

"Shepherd, she can't get away with this. We need to make sure this doesn't happen again." He turns back to Tasha. "When she hunts, where does she go?"

"I don't know—"

"You must have *some* idea."

"You can't—"

"Why not? What does she hunt?"

"She knows—"

"Knows what?" He's in her face and I can see she's ready to run.

"Tasha, what is she hunting?" I ask.

She lifts her finger and points at us. "You."

I take a step back, heartbeat racing. "What do you mean?"

"She's been tracking you. Learning you."

Her words suddenly register.

"You said she knows. What does she know?" My chest is tight, my voice strained.

Tasha's petrified and she clutches the bundled rabbit tightly for security. "She's been watching you."

My mind's racing. "When we came to the woods?"

She nods.

"Every time we've been on the beach?"

She nods.

"When we were lost? You said that was you? What did you mean?"

She wrings the blanket in her hands.

"Which part was you?"

"You were cold…"

"The plastic? That was you?"

She nods.

"And the canoe?"

She nods again.

"But the deer?"

Her eyes narrow, straining from the question, but she shakes her head no.

"That was her?" I ask. "She was there?"

"Always."

She was hunting us, tracking us! "Tasha, did she follow us *everywhere*?"

I stare into her frightened eyes and she doesn't even have to answer.

"You need to take us back to the boat!" I yell, breaking into a sprint. I turn back and Tasha and Charlie haven't moved. "We have to go. *Now!*"

This jolts them and Tasha hurries toward me. I race back to her, urging her to move faster and Charlie rushes to catch up.

"Shepherd, what's going on?"

"She knows where we live, Charlie!"

chapter 110

By the time we get to the hill with the deer trail, my lungs are exploding, but I can't stop. Charlie runs beside me and the two of us urge Tasha on. When we reach the top, I see the distance to the fire tower and my heart drops. I calculate the run back to the boat in my head, knowing it took us at least an hour to get to this point on our way in. Even if we took no breaks and ran all the way, we'd only cut it down by about fifteen or twenty minutes and still have the boat ride back. But it's our best shot.

I drag out my cell phone, but of course I can't find a signal. I jam it back into my pocket and follow the path that leads back toward the lake, Charlie behind me.

Tasha yells, "No, this way!" She's indicating the deer trail she showed us earlier. "Man is bad."

"Tasha… my family." I'm desperate, the most desperate I've ever felt.

"Man is bad," she says with total certainty before dashing down the hill. I follow, not waiting for Charlie. I can only hope that he's behind me.

It's a tough trail, definitely not as well-worn as the one from the beach where we left the canoe. It's hillier, with toppled trees and long trenches, but Tasha navigates us along a path that moves between the obstacles. We have to zig-zag several times but continue to progress forward.

It bothers me that Tasha and her mother have journeyed into our world so much that they have a separate trail. They've known about us for ages, but we've barely been aware of them. The thought brings me back to Tasha's mysterious mother. That young couple looked to be only in their twenties or maybe thirties in the picture, not much older than Tasha is now. They must be sixty or seventy today. Could her mother really be so agile as to track and hunt prey at her age? Sure, living out in the woods seems to have benefited Tasha physically, but the challenges that come with it and the limits of the human body—I just wonder how an older woman could've lasted so long.

And what possessed her to take Tasha—no, Joanna—from her family? Did she think the girl would be better off? Did it start as an act of kindness after she got lost? Or was it something deeper, more maternal? Barry said that the couple had wanted children. If her husband had died before they'd had one of their own, maybe she'd coped by stealing someone else's.

And if she knows we've been making plans to take her child away, what sort of retribution does she intend for us?

chapter 111

When we leave the trees behind, we are on the long dirt road that goes toward Dyson's Point. We race along the rough gravel and by the time we pass the store, the sun has set and the building is dark and closed. We are on our own.

As we approach our cabin, I see a second vehicle in the driveway. There's no way it can be Tasha's "mother's," but I point at it to confirm anyway. She shakes her head and I'm certain she thinks I'm a mental case for even asking if they have a car.

"Shit, what's *she* doing here?" Charlie mumbles and I wonder who he's talking about, but as we get closer, I know exactly who he means.

Face down on the ground, lying in a puddle of her own blood, is Gekas.

I drop to my knees. The upper half of her denim jacket is shredded, and jagged bits of material from her white shirt, matted and red, poke through. Her eyes are closed.

"Detective Gekas?"

"Anthony?" she whispers, and I know it's really bad.

"Right here, Detective." There's a thin, bloody puncture below one shoulder blade, which I'm guessing is a knife wound.

"She's inside…" Gekas turns her head to look for me, but even blinking seems to hurt her. "She came at me from behind…" She's struggles to raise her good arm and grabs my hand. "Call 911. Don't go in there. Promise."

I squeeze her hand. "Promise."

I glance at Charlie. "Wait here with Tasha and Gekas. I'm going to get a signal down by the lake."

"Okay." He stares at the cabin.

I grab him, drawing his attention to me. "Charlie, you need to keep your promise, okay? Keep them safe."

He nods.

I race down the path by the house, keeping low and out of sight. As I rush past the firepit, I consider that Gekas's thinking could be muddled—Tasha's mother could be anywhere—but I don't have time to worry about that now.

I dial the number and by the time I get to the water, the phone is ringing.

"911. What's your emergency?"

"My name is Anthony Shepherd. We're at our cabin at Dyson's Point, near the lakefront at the end of the road. A police officer has been stabbed and there's a woman inside our cabin who may be hurting my family." My stomach tightens at the thought, but I continue, "Can you please send someone as soon as possible? Our cabin is red and there's a sign with our name, 'Shepherd,' at the end of the driveway."

"All right," the dispatcher replies, "please stay on the line while I get more details.

I nod to myself, staring up at the cabin, its tall, bright windows light up the night, but it's no longer a welcoming sight—there's no movement within.

Except Charlie is sneaking around the cabin.

I race back up the hill but can't see him anywhere, so I go back to Gekas, only to find her alone. There's no sign of Tasha.

Dammit, Charlie. Where the hell have you gone?

Gekas is out cold. I kneel and listen; there's a low, soft wheezing, so I know she's alive. But I don't know for how long, and I can only hope the cops and paramedics show up soon.

I briefly wonder where Tasha has gone, but what really worries me is Charlie. It's not that I don't trust him, but he's a wildcard who makes rash decisions that I'm not always sure are the wisest. I don't know what Tasha's mother is like, but I've seen what she's capable of and I'm really worried for my family. It doesn't take me long to break my promise to the detective.

I tell the dispatcher to send help quickly and drop the phone beside Gekas. I run back down to the firepit and pull the axe out of the stump. I'm hoping there's no need to use it, but if I'm going to face off against this woman, I need a weapon.

I move stealthily around the side of the cabin and peer inside the dark window of Mom and Dad's bedroom. The next window over is the bathroom and its light is on, but the window is mostly frosted, except for a tiny crack that I can just peer through. Lying on the floor down the hallway is Ollie. He's on his side, not moving. My stomach clenches and I want to scream, but I hold it in. I force myself to look past him and into the living room, but I can't see anyone else. If it weren't for my pup curled lifelessly in front of me, I'd think no one else was in the cabin—and I'd *really* like to believe it—but I know it's not true.

I push myself to leave and go around the corner, hurrying past the entry. With Gekas lying cut and bleeding, and Ollie wounded or worse, I realize that I don't know what I'm getting into. Better to avoid a direct assault. I need a plan. And where is Charlie?!

I look through the kitchen window. Cowering in the living room beside the fireplace is my family. They're tied together with rope and their feet are bound. Heather is crying, Mom is trying to comfort her, and Dad—shit, Dad has a bloody towel wrapped around his arm. There's no sign of the woman, but I'm guessing by the direction they're looking, she might be by the staircase.

I consider moving along the porch, but the big windows are open. She might see me and my family could be hurt more... it's too great a risk. I could climb the stonework of the entrance to my bedroom but being exposed by the porch light doesn't seem safe either. I move, low and swift, to the oak trees at the back of the property that separate it from the street.

Long ago, Heather and I used to climb them, hanging upside down from the branches and dreaming of sneaking in and out of the upper storey windows like ninjas. The distance was always too great a leap, so we never had the guts to pull it off, but with my family in danger, it's time to take the chance.

Axe held tight in one hand, I shimmy my way to the first bough and pull myself up. From there, I'm able to climb limb to limb until I get to a branch that stretches out to Heather's bedroom window. I scramble along it, holding on for as long as I can, until the branches curve away and I have to balance without support.

The window is still too far away! But, thank God, it *is* open a crack and I'm able to pry it nearly all the way open with the head of the axe. I don't waste time and poke the axe through the screen, tearing it off—I've just got to hope the woman doesn't hear me. I reach out a foot—thank goodness for my growth spurt—and plant it on the window sill, struggling to keep from falling. I push off with the other foot and grab at the sill, but the axe slips out of my hand and tumbles to the ground. There's no time to think—I don't want to follow the axe down—and I reach out again, trying to take hold of the window frame. My whole body swings forward and I hit the house with a muffled thud. Digging my shoes into the wood siding, I pull myself up and climb inside.

chapter 112

I'm soaked in sweat and my arm hurts. I'm lying in the dark beside Heather's bed, hoping that no one heard me climb in. Seconds pass that feel like minutes—I wish I hadn't lost the axe—but no one comes to investigate.

Quieting my breath, I move to the door and pull it open a crack. A woman is talking, but I can't tell if it's Mom or Heather or someone else. Until I move to the staircase, no one will be able to see me from below. My vantage point allows me to see reflections in the front window—I can see the blurry image of my family, not Tasha's "mother"—although she has to be down there somewhere.

Damn! I wish I knew where Charlie went.

My room is across the hall. I rush inside silently, pulling the door nearly shut behind me.

"Charlie," I whisper, hoping for best, but only getting silence in response. I don't dare turn on a light; instead, I pull out my phone, using the glow of the screen to search for a weapon. Unfortunately, I don't even have a jackknife in here and Charlie held onto his backpack full of tricks, so I'm out of luck. All I've got to work with are clothes, dirty towels, and books. If I were Jason Bourne, I could make a weapon out of any of this stuff—but I have none of these skills whatsoever.

Then I remember that I do have a walking stick that Dad gave me on one of our beach hikes years ago. I open the closet door as quietly as I can, reaching to the back to pull it out. It's about five feet long and both ends are angled, shaped by a beaver that chewed through a young sapling. It's got good weight, and although it's a little long for a proper swing, I think it might offer some protection—as long as this woman doesn't have anything worse than a knife.

I have to know more about what I'm dealing with. Leaving the walking stick behind, I go back to my bedroom door and drop to my belly. Using all my concentration on not being seen or heard, I commando crawl to the edge of the balcony that looks over the living room and peer through the railing.

A woman paces at the bottom of the stairs—exactly where I thought she might be—but she's nowhere near the age I expected. She's young, about the age of my sister, Jodi, which makes no sense when I think of Tasha. If either of them is even close to the age they seem to be, this woman would've had to have had her when she was ten years old. Impossible. Whatever's going on, this is definitely not Tasha's real mother.

What worries me more is the knife she's carrying: a curved, thick and stubby hunting knife with a serrated edge along its spine. I've seen what she can do with it—and have no doubt that if I try anything, she'll get to my family before I can stop her.

My family is silent and terrified. Heather glances up—she seems to be the only one who knows I'm here. I deliberately look at the front door and, almost imperceptibly, she shakes her head no. There's no way they can get out. I look meaningfully at the stairs and the woman, but Heather negates that too—she too thinks it's unlikely I can take the woman by surprise. I scan the room, looking for some way to save them, but Heather's watching me and she mouths the one word I don't want from her: "Run." She closes her eyes and turns away, and I know it's because she's fears the worst. I refuse to accept that.

I push backwards into my room, grab the walking stick, and slide into the dark corner beside the dresser.

What the hell am I going to do? Ollie and Gekas are either dead or dying. Mom, Dad, and Heather are being held at knifepoint by a woman Charlie and I brought into their lives, and I'm on my own. I'm sitting in the dark with a damn stick as a weapon, outmatched and scared shitless.

Suddenly, the room slips into total darkness as the door shuts.

"Don't scream, Shepherd," comes a whisper from the shadows.

Charlie's standing behind the door.

"Where did you go?" I whisper back.

"Where'd I go? Where'd *you* go?" Charlie replies.

"I saw you running away!" I growl, "I told you to wait."

"Gear down. Rabbit girl took off into the woods and I tried to catch her because I figured you'd be pissed if I lost her."

"You broke your promise."

"Oh, we're going to start keeping score? *Now?* Okay, well then, you broke your promise to Gekas and came inside." He sighs. "Look, I saw you climb through the window, so I figured I better come in and save your ass."

"I don't know what the hell to do."

"I noticed."

"Charlie... my family."

"We're going to get them out safe."

"I think she may have hurt—"

"Shepherd, get your shit together. Let's deal with the problem. What do we know?"

I know he's trying to focus me, so I do my best to let go of the things we can't control. Coach runs basketball drills like this all the time; it's supposed to help us concentrate during a game even if it seems like we're losing.

"She's got a knife," I whisper.

"Right," he says. "Which means we keep our distance."

"She's also not as old as we thought."

"Yeah, I saw that too. Either our hippy couple got busy long ago or they stole two kids. But it also means we can't rely on her being weak to save our asses."

I think back to the book. "Maybe she's Rebecca."

"And Tasha thinks she's her mother?" He considers it. "Based on everything else we saw in the woods, that makes sense."

"So what do we do?"

"We use our advantages—"

"There's two of us and only one of her."

Charlie nods. "Plus, she doesn't know we're inside already." He scoops up his backpack and goes to the window. "I'll make a distraction to draw her away; you get your family out."

"There's an axe on the ground under Heather's window."

"Thanks."

I skip sharing any sentiments because I know he wouldn't care for them, but I'm as worried for him as I am for my family.

"Charlie—"

"Shepherd, trust me. We'll keep them safe."

chapter 113

Charlie crawls onto the roof above the front door. It's a ten-foot drop, but he doesn't hesitate and jumps down. I wait until I see him wave the all clear and then I step back to the door, swinging it open a crack. The woman's still downstairs, so I move out into the hallway, staying low behind the corner at the top of the stairs, and wait for his signal.

It doesn't take him long. The kitchen window above the sink shatters, and Mom and Heather scream. The woman leaps to her feet, moving from the stairs. He smashes the foyer window next, and the woman crosses to the door and looks out. Until Charlie draws her away, I can't get downstairs to my family. Whatever he's going to do, he better do it soon.

I hear a hiss and the trees by the firepit glow red. There's a hard *thonk* against the front window and I see Charlie's flare roll over the edge of the deck and out of sight.

This definitely gets her attention and she goes to the kitchen door and walks outside, looking back at Mom, Dad, and

Heather, considering whether or not to leave them, before she gives in to her curiosity.

The moment she's off the deck, I rush down the stairs. My parents start to protest, but I hold out a hand to silence them.

The ropes are my first problem, so I run to the kitchen, staying low, to grab a blade from the knife block. I peek around the edge of the island, making sure the woman hasn't come back, before returning to my family.

"Anthony, leave!" Mom whispers, near tears.

"You can ground me later." I grab the first rope and cut away at it. It's rough and the serrated edge of the knife yanks against it.

"Pull it tight," I say, and Mom and Dad tug hard, removing the slack, and I'm able to make progress, the fibres starting to shred.

Now that I'm close, I can see that Dad's cut is deep; he'll need stitches.

He catches my look. "She got me good."

"What happened?"

"She knocked, I answered, and she just attacked."

"Did she say anything?" I'm not ready to admit why she's here.

"She keeps asking, 'Where's Tasha?' over and over."

Mom looks over her shoulder to the window. "She could be a psych patient, but I can't imagine her getting this far from any hospital."

The rope tying them together gives way. I start freeing Mom's hands, but she objects. "No, do Heather's first."

Heather is closest to the front window and helping her leaves me exposed, but I know Mom won't give me any other choice. I crawl around, doing my best to hide behind Heather and Dad.

My sister stares at me and we don't say anything. We both know this is messed up and I'm pretty sure that out of everyone, she's the one who most likely knows that I brought this upon them.

"As soon as I get you free, go straight for the door, okay?"

She nods, but I know she'll ignore my plea, and stay around to help Mom and Dad.

"Heather, this woman isn't good," I tell her. "If I'm worrying about you, then I won't be able to get everyone out safe."

She doesn't like what I'm saying, so I add, "Look, Charlie's out there right now, pissing her off." I force a grin. "If anyone can keep her busy, it's him."

I think she's finally going to listen, when her smile fades and I turn to see the woman standing in the door.

"You!" the woman yells.

chapter 114

I drop the knife next to Heather, hoping I can buy my sister time to cut herself free. I pick up the walking stick and step backwards toward the couch to give myself room, but this unwittingly puts Mom, Dad, and Heather between us and in striking distance.

"You did this!" the woman yells.

If I weren't so focused on the sheer terror of the moment, I'm sure I'd see Mom and Dad trying to figure out what she means by that.

"You came into my forest with your filth and your stink and your machines and ruined it. We didn't need you and we didn't want you."

"You hurt people, Rebecca." It's a guess, but she doesn't argue. I move slowly to the center of the room, pulling her attention away from my family until there's nothing between us except my stick.

"Who did I hurt? That man? That disgusting man with his gun?"

There was that hunter who'd gone missing; I guess he really wasn't abducted by aliens.

"Yes, and Terry, the man with the boat," This is the moment I sense that my family is beginning to understand what I'm talking about. "And the photographer." I'm not certain about this, but it might be my only chance to connect the pieces.

"I tried to warn her, like I warned you—"

"With a slaughtered deer?"

"I only wanted to scare her, but she ran and she fell and died."

I don't know what to believe.

"What about Joanna?"

She flinches at the name. "Who?"

"Joanna Grassing? The girl you kidnapped?"

"I didn't— Tasha is mine."

She has completely reinvented reality. I don't know much I can push. "No, Rebecca, you took her from her mother and her stepfather."

"They were foolish and stupid."

"That wasn't yours to judge."

"She would have died—"

"She wasn't yours."

I can see in her eyes that I've gone too far.

She points the knife at my family. "Give her back to me."

"I can't—"

"Give her—"

"She's gone. She ran away."

She looks deflated by this information but not for long, "You ruined everything, you and that other one."

She rushes me and I take a solid swing at her. The stick connects with her arm, forcing her to drop the knife. The pain is visible on her face, but she bulls through it and before I can pull back and hit her again, she's on me, pushing me backwards.

My head slams into the floor and my teeth crack together—a big white flash bursts in my vision. She fights like an animal, clawing at my face, grabbing my hair, gouging at my eyes. I can't get my arms out for another swing, and she slams my skull into the wood floor again and again.

Everything blurs and then I feel her push off and move away. The knife. She's going to finish me off, but all I can think is that Mom, Dad, and Heather will be next if I don't do something.

I try to pull myself up, but she knocks me back with something hard and she's over me with her arms raised high and everyone is screaming and I know I won't be able to stop her from stabbing me.

But then she's gone. Through the blur, I see her fighting. Is Ollie back protecting the family? As my vision clears, I realize that it's actually Charlie who's come to save my ass.

I roll over and drag myself off the floor. My arms are noodles and my head feels like a swollen beach ball, but I need to do whatever I can to stop this nightmare.

Heather has taken my knife and cut through her ropes and is now working on getting Mom and Dad free. I crawl to Mom to try and lend a hand, but she helps me more by holding me steady until the rest of me catches up.

Charlie fights like a beast. Rebecca goes for his face and eyes, but he pummels her every chance he gets. She can't keep up. She needs distance, but he won't give it, and I think he's got her, until she gets a leg around him and pulls him backwards. She claws at his neck, digging deep gouges into his flesh.

I stumble away from Mom and grab the first thing I find—which happens to be the coffee table. It's light and I swing it at Rebecca's head, but my aim's off and it breaks across her back. Charlie takes advantage and grabs her hair, then clubs her in the ear several times. He's almost got her off him, but she's punching him in the side and it isn't until it's too late that I realize she's got her knife out and it's covered in blood.

People scream and I'm racing for the walking stick. I swing and it crunches into the back of her skull and she tumbles forward. I fall with her from the momentum and land on my knees, then collapse onto my back, and Dad rushes past me, pulling the woman off Charlie. Mom's there and she's already rolling him over and looking at his side and his blood is all over her hands.

My head's ringing, but I hear Mom telling Dad to grab towels and ice and for Heather to call 911. I want to get up and help my friend, but I can't really move. Then I see the woman and she's moving and I know this living hell isn't over yet.

She's on me, the knife flashes and I've got the stick between me and her. Blood pours from her mouth and nose—I've likely broken her skull—but she's putting all her weight behind the knife and my arms are sponges and she's pushing it against my chest.

A gunshot goes off, then another, and another, and the knife drops sideways and the woman falls on top of me.

I lie there, not moving. Mom is dealing with Charlie and Dad rushes somewhere past my head toward the front door, calling out Gekas's name.

She'd slumped at the door, bloody, her service revolver in hand.

Heather kneels beside me, pulling Rebecca away.

"Tony! You okay, little brother?"

"I don't—" I think of the blood on Mom's hands. "I think so. How's Charlie?"

Pain crosses Heather's face, but she doesn't bullshit me. "I don't know."

"Okay... okay..." I repeat, more to myself than anyone in particular.

"I'm going to get you something for your head."

I tell her not to worry about me, but she probably feels as helpless as I do, so I don't argue. She disappears and returns with a bag of frozen peas that she sets on my forehead. It's cold, but it feels good.

I close my eyes.

chapter 115

I pass out until Heather wakes me up. Mom won't let me close my eyes anymore and tells Heather to keep me talking. My mind is pretty foggy and it's hard to think, but I do my best.

"Have you checked on Ollie?" I ask her.

She nods. "Dad looked at him. His breathing is shallow."

"Did she—?" I don't want to imagine Rebecca using her knife on him.

"I don't think so. That foolish dog rushed her after Dad was cut, and she hit Ollie to get him off. He fought her until she knocked him out."

I keep looking over at Charlie to see how he's doing. He doesn't look good. Mom's got a pile of bloody rags beside her and she's wrapped torn bed sheets around him to keep pressure against his wounds. She keeps close to him, though, holding him. His hand looks gray against her red-stained skin.

Dad's sitting beside Gekas and she actually looks better than Charlie. He's got a towel against her back, but he's got her sitting up and leaning forward. She's still holding her revolver, keeping an eye on Rebecca, but I'm pretty sure she's dead.

An ambulance arrives and the EMTs treat Charlie and Gekas, but she tells them to quit worrying about her and help Charlie. When a second ambulance shows up, Gekas doesn't fight off their assistance as hard.

They load me on a stretcher as well because Mom insists I get a full head-to-toe examination, and since they're offering me painkillers for my pounding head, I don't argue.

As they take me outside, the cops arrive. I know there'll be questions and I'll have a lot of explaining to do, which only makes me worry about Charlie more. He'd be stubborn with them and he'd keep me from saying too much.

The thought of him being a smartass makes me smile.

chapter 116

They keep me under observation at the hospital for forty-eight hours. The first night, they wake me several times and ask how I'm doing. My head quits throbbing by the second day, and after an examination and a CT scan, they figure I'm good enough to be on my way.

But I don't leave.

Gekas and Charlie were rushed through emergency and straight into operating rooms. They stitched Gekas back together fairly quickly and filled her with blood and fluids. She's in a cast to restrict movement and they've warned her that she's got a lot of physical rehab ahead of her.

Mom and Dad tell me Ollie was beaten pretty badly, but the vets did X-rays and they couldn't see any serious internal damage. But Rebecca hit him a couple of times in the side of the head and they think he might have some hearing loss, which upsets me. Still, I'm just thankful that he's alive.

Charlie is a different story. They've filled him full of blood and they have to fight to keep it all in. They shoved tubes down his throat and operated on every part of his guts to piece him back together before they even considered closing him up again. When they'd done everything they could, they airlifted him out of Estoria to the nearest city, where they have bigger and better medical instruments. Without even discussing it, Mom, Dad, Heather, and I follow him and book ourselves into a hotel to keep a constant vigil by his bedside.

The doctors and nurses run him through every scanning machine in the building, and test every fluid in him to make sure things aren't worse than they imagine. Their other big problem is keeping him breathing regularly, and they wrestle with this the most. He'll seem fine and then alarms go off and they rush us out and close the door and we sit for hours in the waiting room before we can see him again.

He's unconscious for long periods of time and we sit around his room, reading, playing on our phones, or napping. Flowers begin to arrive from people Charlie knows, like Diane, Laurie, and Ali, as well as a few without any names.

At one point when I look up, I see Mom watching me across the room. She smiles tiredly, then looks at Heather. "Will you let us know if anything changes? Dad and I are going to take Tony down for some food."

Heather nods and it isn't until we're out in the hallway that I realize they're taking me for teatime. I should've figured it was coming, even with Charlie in the hospital. Maybe especially because he's in the hospital.

We go down and get a coffee for Dad and me, while Mom takes a tea, as well as three doughnuts—a cruller, a vanilla, and a maple. As the woman behind the till boxes the pastries up, I can't help but think that no matter how hard these chain restaurants try to be fresh and tasty, they'll never match the excellence that is Cup of Joan's.

The three of us take a seat by a window that looks out on the bustling city. The past few days have nearly made me forget that an entire world still buzzes outside these walls. People are heading to their office jobs, buying iced cappuccinos, and probably worrying about their taxes. The transition from cabin to hospital to hospital has taken me out of the flow of normal daily life.

Mom and Dad stare down at their cups. After taking a couple of sips of tea, Mom looks me in the eyes. "Anthony, what happened?"

It isn't until Mom asks the question that I realize that the events of the past few weeks must have caught them completely off guard. I could give them the bare basics, but they deserve the truth. I start from the day Charlie showed up and don't hold back. I tell them about the shed, skirting around my involvement with Miranda's house, and instead tell them we found out Terry was a dealer through the arcade. I tell them about the burned book, the garbage bags, and the deer. I finish by telling them about our visit with Barry and what we know about Rebecca.

"There was this missing photographer, Rita Dobson," I tell them, hoping they'll have some sympathy. "And we couldn't stop thinking about Joanna. She had a family and a life and she was never given a choice. We felt she deserved that option."

Mom and Dad look at each other and lean backwards in their seats in unison. I think they're equally upset and shocked at everything that Charlie and I went through.

"Anthony, why do you never tell us these things before-hand?" Mom asks and I smile because we both know they'd freak out. "So many things could have happened. You could have been hurt so many times—"

Dad interrupts, "But he wasn't, Keya, if everything he's telling us is the truth." He looks at me, giving me an opportunity to confirm my story and I nod yes.

He continues, "He tried his best to stay safe. Sounds like the shed was Charlie's idea and the canoe was an accident, probably caused by Joanna. He even called Gekas and kept his phone on him."

"No, don't let him off easy," Mom's determined. "He's been stupid. He followed Charlie and made choices that got them into trouble."

I'm not used to the two of them disagreeing in front of me.

"But he did it to try and save two missing women. And to help his friend."

Mom glares at him, but he goes on.

"I'm not saying what he did was smart. Staying at the cabin, reading books, and playing board games is what I'd prefer for him. For both of them. But the two of them found some-thing wrong with this world that no one else noticed or had forgotten, and they did what they believed was right."

Mom looks at Dad, then me, then her cup of tea. She tugs the string that dangles over the edge.

I need to say something. "Mom, I know Charlie can be trouble, that he often does things that cause chaos. I'm not sure why he does it, but I believe he's trying to help."

"But he brought that—no, you *both* brought that woman into our lives! She hurt Charlie and she could have hurt you—" She can't finish without grabbing a napkin to wipe away her tears.

"But she didn't—"

"No! I'm not letting you get out of this. She cut your father, she hurt Ollie, she stabbed Detective Gekas and now that poor boy is upstairs fighting for his life. You got lucky, plain and simple. That's the only reason we're here and not having this conversation after a funeral."

People are staring at us, but I don't look away from her. She's right. I want to tell her I understand, but I don't know how to say it without sounding fake.

She turns to Dad but doesn't say anything, then lowers her head and speaks quietly. "Nevertheless, I *am* proud of you. You fought for what you believed was right and fought to protect your friend." She stares at the bandage on Dad's arm. "But I fear the cost may have been too high this time."

She turns to the window and the city and river it frames, taking a deep breath before looking back to me. "Let's continue this later." She stands and stretches, eyeing the coffee shop's pastry counter. "Charles likes doughnuts, right?" She pulls out a ten-dollar bill. "Why don't you go buy him a half-dozen for when he wakes up."

She hands me the money and when I reach for it, she pulls me close. I tower over her now, but I'm still her boy. She hugs me tightly and I hug her right back.

chapter 117

For the next few days, the four of us stay by Charlie's bed, alternating shifts. I pick 6:00 p.m. to 12:00 a.m., Heather watches him until 6:00 a.m., then Mom waits with him until noon, and after that is Dad. Sometimes we overlap and hang out during each other's times, playing cards or picking things up for each other, but Mom and Dad make sure we stay on schedule and get our rest.

Each member of my family has their own way of spending time with Charlie. Dad brought in Charlie's copy of Hemingway's short stories and reads one or two each time. Mom refreshes the six doughnuts every day, offering the untouched box from the day before to the nurses' station. She also plays full-length recordings of operas quietly by his bed, explaining to him what makes them great while holding his hand. Heather mostly hangs out on her phone, putting in her time without complaint, but she keeps her distance. Yet, one night when I couldn't sleep, I went to the hospital and found her asleep, her head resting by his arm on the edge of his bed.

When Charlie was transported to the city, Mom tracked down Charlie's home number and called, but no one picked up, so she left a message. When nobody arrived the next day, she called again, leaving her number, telling Charlie's mom to call. She never heard from her, but later her phone rang from two unknown numbers and when she answered, there was no one on the other end.

"I can't understand how someone can't be there for their son," Mom says on Wednesday, the fourth day since we arrived in the city. She's watching Dad and me play a game of chess we found in the visitor's lounge. I've insisted that the two of them go out for a nice meal together once Dad's done his shift.

"From what Charlie says, his mom's pretty nonexistent in his life," I say.

"When you bring a child into this world, you'd think you'd be there for them," is Mom's response.

Dad moves his knight. "Sometimes it's harder than that."

"Well, life is hard sometimes—you deal with it," says Mom.

"But what if you can't? What if holding it all together day to day is hard enough? Maybe a son in the hospital is unfathomable."

After I take out his pawn, Dad slides his rook, and I can only assume he's moving in for the kill.

Mom dismisses the possibility. "But you have to *try*."

Dad moves his knight. "And she probably is. You got two phone calls. That may have been a big step for her. Checkmate."

I stare at the board, unable to understand how he's destroyed me so quickly.

Dad looks at his watch. "Looks like we're out of here. Can we bring you anything?"

I shake my head.

"Let us know if things change," says Mom, smoothing the sheet around Charlie's legs.

"I will."

I watch them walk down the hallway, aware that much of their time spent together will be worrying about Charlie. No matter how they feel about what happened, they want him to get better.

I pull out my phone but dump it on the nightstand. No matter how many times I think I'll use it to pass the time, I never seem able to focus. We've set up a television in Charlie's room, so I turn that on with the volume on low to distract me.

Bzzz bzzz.

It takes me a second to realize my phone's ringing.

"Hello?"

"How's he doing?" It's Gekas.

"Okay. He's stabilized, but he still hasn't woken up."

"He will. How are you?"

"Good. And you?"

"Healing. I wanted to let you know that the police, as well as search and rescue, used your information and they've located Joanna. She went back to her home in the woods."

When I don't answer, Gekas continues. "She came out with them willingly, but it's going to be a long transition for her."

"Is she going back to her family?"

"Unfortunately, no. Her parents separated after she disappeared. Her mother passed away a couple of years ago and we haven't found her dad yet."

So the phone number Charlie had for Denise Grassing was only another dead end in the huge rat's nest we dug up.

"So, she's got no one?"

"We're looking for relatives."

I wonder what we've done, what world we've brought Tasha back into. Gekas knows what I'm thinking.

"Anthony, she chose to come on her own. You did the right thing."

"Okay, Detective Gekas."

I must not sound convinced because she adds, "When Rebecca took her, she never had a choice. This time, it was hers alone. It's something she was never before offered. And you gave her that opportunity."

"Do we know who Rebecca is?"

"I shouldn't really—"

I'm sure she's hesitating because it's an ongoing investigation, but I'm hoping she'll have pity on me. "Please, Detective?"

"We feel confident that she's the daughter of the couple you told us about."

"And what happened to them?"

"It's hard to know for sure, but we found marginal notations in one of the books on the shelf—"

"Which book?" I don't know why I ask, but I think it's something Charlie will want to know.

"A collection of essays by Emerson. The entries stop after June 1994—"

"The big fire?"

"We think they likely perished in it. Rebecca's likely been living on her own since then."

"So you think she took Joanna because she was lonely?"

"That's all speculation, Anthony. We have to work with the facts we have and nothing more."

I think how that's the difference between her and Charlie, who chases after every scrap of idea and crazy theory he comes up with.

The thought of him makes me realize what could have happened if Gekas hadn't shown up at the cabin.

"Detective Gekas?"

"Yes, Anthony?"

"Thank you for coming. Thank you for everything. Also, I'm sorry you got stabbed."

She laughs. "Me too. You take care. And tell your friend to wake up soon."

She hangs up and I hold the phone for a while before finally setting it down. Whatever I thought of Gekas back when Sheri first disappeared, I now know she's someone who's looking out for Charlie and me.

I go back to watching TV, switching between basketball and a stupid comedy for about an hour before I finally rise to stretch and go to the washroom.

On my way back, I see a woman standing at Charlie's door. She's thin and over-tanned, wearing a short skirt and a halter top, but when I get closer, she takes off. It's late so I don't call out to her but instead follow her around the corner and see her go into the stairwell. By the time I open the door, she's disappeared and I'm not going to chase around the hospital looking for her.

I walk back to Charlie's room.

Maybe Dad's right and Charlie's mom is dealing with her son's critical condition in the only way she can.

chapter 118

On Thursday, I wake up at 7:00 a.m. in the hotel room. I can't sleep any longer. Heather hasn't returned from her shift yet, and Mom and Dad must have gone over together.

Instead of sitting around by myself, I pull on my shorts and head down to the treadmill for a run. I go for a half an hour at a light pace and eventually quit out of boredom. The hotel pool is next door, so I pull off my shirt and jump in. I do several laps before diving deep to the bottom to sit in the silence until my lungs feel like they're about to explode. When I rise, my heart's beating fast and the humid air feels heavy. I swim some more, doing a front crawl one way and a back crawl the other until I exhaust my arms. I drag myself out of the water, dry off and walk back to the room.

The message light on the phone is flashing. It's Heather: HE'S AWAKE.

I have a quick shower, get dressed, and catch a taxi over to the hospital. When I walk into the room, Mom, Dad, and

Heather are sitting around Charlie, who's munching on one of his doughnuts.

"It's about time you showed up," he says.

"Well, you know, I had to grab a coffee, then there was this cute girl I wanted to talk to—"

"Hey, if it means you get someone's number, then by all means, take your time."

I stand there awkwardly, with Mom, Dad, and Heather looking from Charlie to me, until they take the hint and get up to leave.

Dad pats him on the shoulder. "Good to have you back."

He smiles, scratching his shaggier-than-normal head.

Mom squeezes his hand. "Charles, let the nurses do their job, okay?"

"Will do, Mrs. S."

Heather surprises all of us when she leans down and gives him a hug. "You're still a shithead for what you did."

They file out of the room and it's just the two of us. He looks over at me.

"Shepherd, quit staring at me. You're creeping me out."

"Thank you for saving my ass again."

"Anytime. But if I'd known I'd get stabbed, I might have done things a bit differently."

He reaches over with great effort and suffering to pull out a raspberry-filled bismark from the box before offering me the chocolate dip. I shake my head, smiling.

He takes a big bite, savouring the taste. "Not the best, but still, it's a doughnut, so it can't be too bad."

"I think I saw your mom here the other night," I say, "but she took off before I could talk to her."

"Sounds like her," Charlie shrugs.

"Charlie—"

"Don't worry about it. Besides, I think I'm growing on your family."

"Really? Who says they'd want you?" I joke.

"Who wouldn't?" he bats it right back at me.

I shake my head, reflecting on all we've been through over the past year. "Be warned though, if you try to spend more time around us, Mom's going to sit you down for tea again at some point."

"Cool. I could use a good lecture to keep me in line."

"You really would like that, wouldn't you?"

"What can I say? I'm a glutton for punishment." He shifts and his face crumples in pain. "Well, maybe not totally. Can you call the nurse to give me more drugs?"

I wave someone down from the desk and he comes over with a syringe of something. He screws it into the iv line and slowly pushes the plunger of medication down and into Charlie's system.

After the nurse leaves, Charlie asks, "How's Ollie."

"He'll be okay. Gekas also says hi."

"She survived too?"

I nod. "She says they found Joanna at the cabin and she came back with them. Looks like we were right—"

"I'm sorry, Shepherd. For what I did to your family. For all of it."

"Neither of us could've known."

"But I should have."

"You kept them safe."

"Well, I made a promise." He takes another bite and half chews it before stopping to stare into space. "Whoa, I think the drugs are starting to work."

"Yup." I take the doughnut out of his hand and set it on the side table. "Why don't you lie down and sleep."

"That sounds good, Shepherrrd," he says, rolling the "r" of my name before pointing at me. "Tony Shepherd"—he points to himself—"Charlie Wolfe. The crime-busting duo back at it again." He bursts into giggles, which is a terrifying sight, before falling into a stupor.

"Charlie?"

He doesn't answer.

"Charlie?"

He jolts out of some deep haze and scrutinizes my appearance. I consider his state. This may be the only time I'll catch him with his guard down. "What happened in your past?" I ask gently. "Who did you lose?"

He looks at me and laughs again, smooshing his hand into my face. "Uh-uh, Mr. Shepherd. Nice try." He props himself up, trying to focus. "That is a tale for another time. Now shut up, so I can—" He passes out immediately and I have to catch him before he falls out of bed.

I roll him back onto his pillow, making sure he's safe before leaning back into my own chair. I figure he'll snooze for a while and I decide to put my feet up on the bed.

It isn't long before my eyes are closed too. The way things are when Charlie's around, I figure we can both use the rest.

epilogue

Cousin Rachel watches her son doing laps in the pool from the stands. She looks up every few minutes in case he's looking for her, but she's distracted. On her phone is the most recent edition of the *Estoria Journal*. Turns out the little town got mighty exciting once she left. Thankfully no one's found her handiwork—she's confident they'll never trace it back to her anyway—but the real cause of Terry's death had been uncovered.

According to the newspaper, two women—one of whom had been kidnapped as a child—were found living out in the woods north of the lake, right near where her company used to do their exchanges. Terry must've gotten lost and had a run-in with one of them, and was likely murdered to keep their location a secret. Although Cousin Rachel had suspected foul play, she certainly didn't expect it to have been caused by a feral kidnapper.

What really interests her has nothing to do with Terry or these two women but the attack the woman made on a local family. An off-duty officer, a Detective Gekas, who had been visiting at the time, was seriously injured, as well as an unnamed teenage boy now reported to be in critical condition.

After a bit of online research, Cousin Rachel discovers that this wasn't the first time Detective Gekas had helped the family out, that she'd assisted in a case last year involving a murdered girl connected to the family's son. The son and another boy had apparently later saved a young woman and unmasked the murderer.

It doesn't take Cousin Rachel long to uncover that the friend of the boy is one and the same as the boy in critical condition. It takes only a phone call or two and she has his name: Charles Wolfe.

She doesn't know him, exactly, but she does recognize the last name.

Could it be…?

She looks up. Her son smiling and waving; she smiles and waves back.

A moment later, she looks down at her phone again. Yes, she would need to do more research and see if there was a connection. But if this Charles Wolfe is as curious as he certainly seems to be, she might hear from him at some point anyway.

Unless, of course, he becomes a problem she needs to deal with first.

acknowledgments

Thank you to our first readers, Anna and Kate, and our extreme gratitude to Nathan Mader for helping us out with our draft early on. We have a lot of questions during the writing process, and our thanks go to Angie's students and Constable Blair Randall of the Regina Police Service for helping to answer some of them.

We are indebted to Creative Saskatchewan for their generous assistance in the production of our books, and to Donovan Bergman and the print team at Friesens. We'd also like to recognize our proofreader, Linda Sawatzky, for helping us cross the finish line, and give huge special thanks to Heather Nickel, who works with us to bring our books to life.

Angie would like to thank the Creator for this beautiful, crazy adventure. David would like to thank his wife and kids for their love and support.

Finally, thank you to our friends, family, and readers who have supported us on this journey. Without you, we'd be nothing.

about the authors

DAVID GANE is a writer, teacher, and stay-at-home dad. He writes film scripts and fiction, and has also composed poetry, plays, and academic film reviews. He occasionally teaches screenwriting at the University of Regina.

ANGIE COUNIOS teaches by day, and writes film scripts and fiction the rest of the time. When she's not teaching or writing, she's packing a bag for another adventure, completing a goal list, playing with her camera or practising yoga.

Find them at **www.couniosandgane.com**